The Ambassador

A novel

A captivating piece of historical fiction, a story of leadership in times of crisis, and a painful remainder of the need for Jews to take their fate into their own hands.

Senator Joseph I. Lieberman

No one knew the worlds of ambassadors and the Jewish people better than Yehuda Aver. In *The Ambassador*, Avner and Matt Rees imagine a world in which history had played out very differently, providing us with not only a great and evocative story, but also an urgent reminder that decisive actions by courageous people can, in fact, make a profound difference in our world.

Rabbi Dr. Daniel Gordis

A thrilling tour of what might have been.

Rabbi David Wolpe

If ever one wanted an alternative history it is for the years that consumed European Jewry! More than a novel, *The Ambassador* invites us to consider how the presence of Israel even a decade earlier might have mitigated the outcome of events it could not prevent. I found this valuable to read and important to contemplate.

Professor Ruth Wisse

An informed, intelligent look at a world that never was but might easily have been.

Harry Turtledove

THE
AMBASSADOR

YEHUDA AVNER
AND MATT REES

The Toby Press

The Ambassador

The Toby Press LLC
POB 8531, New Milford, CT 06776–8531, USA
& POB 2455, London W1A 5WY, England
www.tobypress.com

ISBN 978-1-59264-388-2

A CIP catalogue record for this title is
available from the British Library

Printed and bound in the United States

"Where the slain are, there he is."
(Job 39:30)*

* Quoted by Israeli Attorney-General Gideon Hausner in his opening statement at the trial of ss Obersturmbannführer Adolf Eichmann, Jerusalem, 1961

Author's Note 1

"Had partition [under the Peel Commission plan of 1937] been carried out, the history of our people would have been different and six million Jews in Europe would not have been killed—most of them would be in Israel."

David Ben-Gurion, in a letter to Ben Zion Katz,
September 1957

I fought in the war that established Israel. I worked for decades in the highest circles of the Israeli government, with every prime minister up to Rabin's second term, and as Israel's ambassador to Britain and then to Australia. I was proud of my achievements on behalf of Israel, proud to have played my part in ensuring that never again would Jews be victims without a refuge. But one day, in the Mount Herzl Military Cemetery in Jerusalem, it came to me that there was something more I could do.

I sat among the crowd, there to observe Holocaust Martyrs and Heroes Remembrance Day, as then-Prime Minister Shimon Peres addressed us. More precisely, he addressed *them*. The ones taken by Hitler. Apologizing. "We were ten years too late," he said.

And I thought, "What if we hadn't been...?"

This novel is based on the premise that the 1937 British Royal Commission plan to partition Palestine had been put into practice—as it so nearly was. Israel would have come into existence *before* the Holocaust.

Apart from that one change, this novel hews as closely to historical fact as possible. It is a fictional reminder of how the world failed back then. A reminder of what Israel changes for Jews around the world. And a reminder of something that simply must never be forgotten.

I dedicate this book to my Mimi, forever and always.

Yehuda Avner
Jerusalem, February 12, 2015

Author's Note 11

On the morning Yehuda and I decided to write *The Ambassador*, he received the news that he didn't have long to live. I wondered how it would work out. How might the advance of the cancer affect his concentration and his ability to think? I asked him. With the slight Manchester accent that, to any Briton, signifies a person not to be trifled with, he said: "I tell you, Matt, this book is my legacy." He hammered his fist softly on the desk and his features quivered with determination. No, I didn't have to worry about Yehuda's state of mind.

Yehuda Avner's legacy is, of course, so much more than this one book. But I know what he meant. As we plotted and discussed and argued (very gently) and wrote and sang (mostly him) and edited, we found something perhaps unexpected behind our narrative of Nazism, of deportation and death camps, of terror and murder. We found we had constructed a novel filled with life.

After Yehuda was laid to rest yesterday, I stood at his graveside and watched the sun set. Under that sun, men sometimes do terrible things, and that mustn't be forgotten. But they also love. A man may elect which memories and experiences dominate his being—the horrors or the loves. When mortal illness compelled my friend Yehuda to confront this choice, he wrote this book. I think you'll find it clear that he took the path of love to the very end.

Matt Rees
Jerusalem, March 25, 2015

Characters

Dan Lavi, Israeli ambassador to Berlin

Anna Lavi, Dan's wife, a pediatrician

David Ben-Gurion, pre-state Zionist leader, Israeli prime minister

Peter Boustead, British intelligence officer in Palestine and Berlin

Countess Hannah von Bredow, granddaughter of Chancellor Bismarck

Hauptmann Hasso Brückner, von Bredow's nephew, Hitler's Wehrmacht
adjutant

Sepp Draxler, Gestapo officer, raised in Jerusalem's German community

Adolf Eichmann, head of ss Central Office for Jewish Emigration

Wilhelm Gottfried, Israeli embassy official, noted violinist

Reinhard Heydrich, ss head of Nazi security services

Rudolf Höss, ss commandant of Auschwitz

Friedrich Kritzinger, deputy chief of Reich's Chancellery

Arvid Polkes, Berlin Jew, former stage manager of city orchestra

Bertha Polkes, Arvid's wife

Yoni Richter, Mossad agent

Oberleutnant Ansgar Schulze, anti-Nazi Luftwaffe officer

Shmulik Shoham, Mossad station chief in Berlin

Devorah Shoham, Shmulik's wife, Mossad code and signals operator

Aryeh Yardeni, Ambassador Dan Lavi's driver, also a Mossad agent

Prologue

Berlin, 1934

One last concert, then he would leave for Palestine. He passed the main facade of the hall on Bernburger Strasse and entered the Philharmonie by the stage door. "Herr Gottfried," the commissionaire said. It was all he ever said. Not *"Guten Abend"* or "Heil Hitler." But perhaps this time he spoke with a questioning tone.

Wili Gottfried raised his violin case in salute. The instrument was a gift from the Countess, in her family almost since Stradivari constructed it in Cremona in 1719, during his golden period. In Gottfried's hands it was played as never before. *He* was the golden period of this violin's long life. So far.

He found Furtwängler in his dressing room, sitting on a turquoise satin couch in the soft glow of a chandelier. Gottfried set down the violin case. *"Guten Abend, Maestro."*

The great conductor's high, receding forehead gleamed with sweat. The face he showed to Gottfried contorted with mortification. He lifted a sheet of paper and handed it over.

The Reich Music Chamber, a section of the Propaganda Ministry under which the Berlin Philharmonic Orchestra operated, informed him that he was barred from further performances in

Germany as violin soloist, a role he had filled many times over the previous decade. The order was signed by Minister Joseph Goebbels.

Gottfried's scalp prickled under his pomaded hair. His deep eyes of coppery brown teared up. He was about to leave Germany anyway. But he didn't want it to be this way.

"Pull yourself together, Gottfried," the conductor barked. Furtwängler was narrow-shouldered and his chin was weak, but his resolve was superhuman. He lowered his voice to a whisper, as if exchanging confidences. "We live in astonishing times, do we not? I tried to save you. I said to Goebbels you are the best there is. There is a hemorrhage of Jewish musicians from Germany. I told him it has to stop."

"He *likes* to see the blood flowing."

The Maestro leaned his head against the back of the couch and closed his eyes. "He said a Jew is a Jew."

Rage rumbled through Gottfried's soul. "You are the world-acclaimed master of the German orchestral art, the greatest conductor of our age. You have but one choice. You must resign."

"Are you mad?" Furtwängler's face flushed with anger. "Do you forget who you are talking to?

"I am talking to the one conductor in Germany that Hitler himself would never dare cross. Or are you merely an entertainer hired by the Führer for his amusement?"

"No man talks to me like this."

"It would appear that the Nazi superman does."

"I tried to save you, Gottfried. I was sick to the stomach after my meeting with Goebbels. But my responsibilities are different than yours."

"It's the difference in our religions, not our responsibilities, that's at issue here."

"Gottfried, you can take your violin and a suitcase and play as soloist with the orchestras of London, of Paris, of Vienna. You could make your own orchestra in Palestine, for God's sake. I must remain here in Berlin, to protect German music and musicians as best I can. You were simply too prominent to be passed over. I may be able to retain some of my other Jewish musicians, because they're less well-known."

"So the obscure Jews are safe in the second violin section? For how long?"

"You were going to Palestine after this evening anyway."

"I will show those bastards," Gottfried muttered, almost to himself. "Tonight I'll give them a performance they'll never forget."

Furtwängler shook his head. "You still don't understand, Gottfried. It's over. This order applies immediately. Weber will stand in as soloist for tonight's performance."

"Weber? So much for protecting German music. That ham-fisted—" Gottfried halted. "Oh, I get it. He's a Nazi. That's why he's taking over. Damn you, Furtwängler."

He went to the door. In a funereal whisper, he spoke to the conductor, though he didn't turn to face him. "You tried to save me, but you couldn't, because Wilhelm Furtwängler is no longer a free man. He is in the power of Hitler's goons. They can do whatever they like to you."

Furtwängler caught him by the sleeve. "Promise me you will play here in Berlin again. One day. I need to know that you will come back. So that I can go on. In spite of all this—this horror."

The conductor's sudden desperation made Gottfried pause. Furtwängler was a good man, committed to art and the joy it carries. Once he was forced to bend his art to the demands of bad men, evil truly had taken over. "The horror is barely begun, Maestro."

"Then it's still more important for me to hear it from you. Say you will come back."

Gottfried felt a power in himself that usually came only when he held his bow against the strings of his violin.

Furtwängler must have seen it on his face, because he recoiled slightly.

"I will return. I will make them listen to the soul inside me, and it will show them the emptiness of their pitiful, ugly world."

The conductor released his arm. Gottfried walked slowly down the corridor. When he passed the silent commissionaire and exited onto the bustling street, he was no longer in Berlin. He emerged into the desert glare of midday in Palestine. The sidewalk, slippery with ice, seemed to crunch under his feet like the dry dirt of the Judean hills.

But he was not there yet.

He had paid for a reservation on the train from Berlin to Athens, and for a berth on a passenger-cargo ship to Haifa. His one remaining obstacle: the contents of the crate containing his belongings had to be approved by a dozen government departments, and he still lacked one stamp. The Gestapo's form warned that "*No items of particular value may be taken out of Germany. Failure to comply will be met with the severest penalties.*" There followed a long list of the prohibited categories, one of which was "*Musical instruments of antique quality, design, and value.*"

Gottfried assumed that even the former travelling salesmen and beer-hall waiters who now staffed the state security police would have heard of Stradivarius. He could try to sell it. It was worth millions. But he wouldn't be allowed to take the money with him even if he found someone who'd give him a good price. And who was he kidding? He'd rather have surrendered one of his kidneys than abandon the instrument.

He had put off a decision about the violin because he had thought there was one last concert to play. He passed the glowering, dark windows of the Gestapo building on Prinz-Albrecht-Strasse and felt the same energy that had gripped him in the final moments of his encounter with Furtwängler. In an instant he knew what he would do. He hustled home.

Gottfried rushed through his hall and down the kitchen steps into the garden with the Stradivarius in his arms. He hid it in a pile of junk in the shed. Then he climbed up to the attic and took down the violin he had used as a student at the music conservatory years before. He dusted it off, tuned it, and hurried with it to the study, laying it on his desk by the music stand where he always practiced.

The inspector from the Gestapo arrived with the packers the following day at lunchtime. Gottfried's arm shook as he handed over the detailed list of the possessions he wanted to ship. It included his unexceptional violin.

"Show me the violin," the Gestapo man demanded.

Gottfried led him to the study. The man took out a flashlight and inspected the violin's interior. He noted the seal of manufacture on the slip of paper pasted inside the instrument. He wrote down the make and date on the form. "It can go," he said.

The chief packer tied up the violin case with heavy string and wedged it into a tea chest with towels and linens. He marked the chest with red chalk, "*Number 3.*" By late afternoon, everything but the books in the study was packed. The Gestapo officer instructed the removers to cease their work. He checked the French windows that led from the study onto a small balcony to make sure they were locked, pocketed the key, and sealed the study door to ensure there would be no tampering with the items already stowed away. The rest could wait until the morning.

As soon as darkness came, Gottfried went to the garden shed and retrieved his Stradivarius. He brought it inside the house, opened the small window in the toilet, and wormed his way through it out onto the terrace. He found himself before the French windows of the study. Gottfried took a spare key from his pocket and entered.

The air was rank with the sweat of the packers and the metallic scent of the Gestapo man's cigarettes. Gottfried laid the Stradivarius on the floor and took a pair of pliers from his pocket. Carefully he extracted the nails from the lid of tea chest number 3. His hands trembled as though he were an ill-worked puppet. He took out the towels and the linens, and removed the cheap violin, replacing it with the Stradivarius. He set to work trying to duplicate the knots tied around the violin case, cinching them over and cursing as they fell away, loose and clumsy. He worried that he simply wouldn't get it done. He had to have the Stradivarius. It was all he could take with him of the Countess.

Gottfried reached for the technique that brought him calm before his concerts. He hummed Mozart's Violin Concerto No. 5 in A Major, and it was as though the bright, sweet adagio refrain with which the soloist enters went straight to his furthermost nerve endings. Within a few minutes the Stradivarius was bound just as the other violin had been. Gottfried repacked the remaining contents of the crate and hammered down the nails to the beat of the Mozart concerto.

He left as he had entered. He took his student violin to the basement and watched it burn in the furnace of the central heating system.

Next morning, the movers finished packing swiftly. The Gestapo man sealed the crates, and a horse cart rattled them away to the railway sheds.

That evening, Gottfried arrived at the Anhalter Station, Berlin's gateway to the south. He stumbled through crowds that headed for trains to Dresden and Munich. He tried to soothe himself with the Mozart concerto again, but found he could no longer summon the tune to his lips. He knew the scores of hundreds of violin pieces—concertos and sonatas, waltzes and minuets—but all fell silent, subdued by the discordant babble of a metropolis that refused to bid him farewell.

At the sixth and final platform, the train for Athens awaited him. From the Greek capital, he would board a ferry to Haifa. To Palestine. He struggled along to his carriage, mouth dry, ticket fluttering in his hand.

He found his seat. It was occupied. He fought for the breath to speak, to correct the error of the man sitting there. Then he saw that it was the Gestapo officer.

"*Guten Abend*, Herr Gottfried." The man stood and leered. "Come with me, please."

They knew. Gottfried was sure of it. They had found the Stradivarius, had seen through his deception. He would never reach Palestine. It was the Prinz-Albrecht-Strasse torture chambers for him, then Dachau.

He trailed the Gestapo man across the concourse into the freight annex. Three warehouse hands waited impatiently by Gottfried's crates.

"I cannot let it go, Herr Gottfried," the Gestapo officer said.

Gottfried stared at the man. His jaw shook. He couldn't speak.

Perhaps if he confessed, the Nazi would shoot him and all this suffering would simply be over.

"You have failed to pay certain charges due to the Reich, Herr Gottfried." The Gestapo man rubbed his hands together and opened his palms.

Gottfried shook his head. "I…I don't—"

"He wants his bribe," the youngest of the warehouse hands called out.

The others smiled.

"Come on, pay him," the young man said. "We were supposed to knock off shift ten minutes ago."

Gottfried pulled out his wallet. He fumbled for his last twenty-five reichsmarks, about enough for a good bottle of wine.

The Gestapo man sneered and twitched his fingers. He wanted more.

Gottfried stammered, "I have no other money. It's all been—"

"All been what?" The Gestapo man was close. Cigarette breath and a bratwurst belch hit Gottfried's face.

He would've said *stolen*, because the process of emigration for a Jew after only one year of Hitler's rule was simple theft. Taxes and levies and duties. Whatever they were called, they were no different from the greedy hand the Gestapo man extended now.

"Open that box." The officer pointed at the young warehouse worker and then at one of Gottfried's crates. "Number 3." Gottfried felt his lungs seizing up, his heart thundering.

"What for? It's been checked, *Kumpan*." The worker grinned insolently.

Kumpan was what communists called their buddies. The Gestapo sent communists to concentration camps.

"Take his overcoat or something if he doesn't have any cash. You don't need to be shy about it. He's only a Yid."

"*Open it.*"

The worker shrugged and set to work on the seals of the crate with a crowbar. "I'm supposed to meet a girl, you know. You're going to let a few marks come between a man and some nice ass?"

"Shut your face."

The worker mumbled something just as the lid of the crate lifted. The other men laughed loudly. They fell silent as the Gestapo officer stalked toward them.

"What did you say?" he growled.

"You wanted it open. It's open."

"Repeat what you said." He poked the worker with his finger, then gave him a harder shove with his clenched fist.

The young man wasn't going to back down now. One of the other workers reached to restrain him, but he shrugged free. "I said, that thing below your hat is proof that not everything with two cheeks is a face."

The Gestapo inspector laughed. He stepped back from the worker, shaking his head, acknowledging the low wit of the remark.

The young man grinned at his comrades, relaxed. He had put one over on the secret policeman.

In a flash the officer seized the crowbar from the worker's hand. He swung it hard into the man's jaw, then into the back of his skull with vicious, frenzied blows. The man dropped to his knees. The Gestapo officer hammered the end of the bar down on the crown of his wavering head. The man's skull crunched like an egg under a spoon. A spray of gore squirted across Gottfried's pine crate.

Panting, the Gestapo man snarled at the other workers. "Shut this crate, you pair of shits." He tossed the bloodied crowbar inside, where the unseen Stradivarius lay.

Gottfried reached for the wall for support, quivering and faint. The Gestapo man grabbed the thin wad of reichsmarks from him. "Go on, fuck off. Before I decide it was you who killed this shitty Commie."

Gottfried rushed back to the train. His stomach churned and his guts felt like they were in flames. He threw himself into the bathroom, dropped his pants, and sat on the toilet just before he truly lost control of himself. As the train jerked into motion, he drained his bowels, weeping and shuddering. After some time, his stomach settled. He cleaned himself up and went to his seat.

The ticket-collector entered before they were out of the Berlin suburbs. He took Gottfried's ticket and frowned.

My God, what now? Gottfried thought.

"Are you hurt, *Mein Herr*?" the conductor asked.

Gottfried shook his head.

The railway man gestured to his face. "You're bleeding."

Gottfried snatched his handkerchief and rubbed at his face. The linen came away smeared with the blood of the man the Gestapo officer had murdered.

Part 1

The time cannot be far distant when Palestine will again be able to accept its sons who have been lost to it for over a thousand years. Our good wishes together with our official good will go with them.

Das Schwarze Korps, ss newspaper, May 15, 1935

A Templer-owned hotel, home of the German consulate in Jerusalem, 1933

Chapter 1

Palestine, 1937

Dan Lavi watched his wife from the kitchen. Curled up in a deep armchair, her big almond eyes shut, she was lost in the music from the phonograph. He felt a surge of love in his chest that seemed truly physical to him, like a warm wave rushing into Tel Aviv beach. Anna moved her hand gently, conducting, as the soloist went into a striking cadenza.

Dan ran the hot water over the dinner dishes in the sink. "That violinist is amazing. Even with my tin ear I can hear it. Who is it?"

"Wilhelm Gottfried. With the Berlin Philharmonic. Mendelssohn's concerto."

"You don't say? I'm supposed to be going to a concert by him this week. Gottfried's playing with a new orchestra that's been formed here in Jerusalem."

"*You're* going? What about me? I adore Gottfried."

"You're always too busy to join me on these official engagements. I didn't think you'd want to come."

"Can I help it if little children get sick and need their pediatrician? But you're right. I don't have time."

Dan watched as his wife reached for *The Palestine Post*. He had more reasons than he could list for loving her. She was intelligent and beautiful, calm and good. She was a healer of children. She made *him* a whole person, by bridging his contending identities. Growing up, Dan had never been able to reconcile his desire for the cosmopolitan world his family left when they emigrated from Berlin and his love of the dusty, vibrant, holy city to which they had moved. Anna experienced no such contradiction. Though deeply cultured, she loved nothing more than the sun and the sand of the Judean Hills, and she was naturally gifted with the candor he and other Zionists worked to cultivate. He recalled his first glimpse of the woman who would become his wife, in the Widener Library at Harvard, her thumb and finger pinching her chin thoughtfully over a Hebrew textbook. He remembered the note he had written her in that language, slipping it across the oak desk: *Are you interested in a Hebrew tutor?* And the words she scribbled on the paper before pushing it back toward him: *Only if he will go Dutch for dinner.*

"We *could* both go and hear Gottfried play, if you like. I think Shmulik and Devorah might join us. You and Devorah really did get along like a burning barn."

"A house on fire," she corrected.

Even after six years spent studying in Boston, Dan was still more comfortable speaking German and Hebrew. He liked to hear his American wife's laid-back accent, though, and consequently spoke English to her all the time. "A house on fire," Dan repeated. "Yes, you got on like a house on fire, for the ten minutes Shmulik spared to attend the reception. If you think you've been busy, imagine what it's been like for him. Every time there's a terror attack the Old Man wants to know why Shmulik didn't see it coming."

"That's your fault. The more Jews you bring over from Germany, the angrier it makes the Arabs."

"You can't please everyone. Not the Old Man, that's for sure."

"You're the *only* one capable of pleasing David Ben-Gurion. No one else could do what you do in Berlin."

Dan let the hot water rush over his hands in the sink. *Berlin.* He shut his eyes. It felt as though the lives of Germany's Jews were sweeping through his hands, spilling down the drain where they were forever beyond his grasp. He went on regular trips to the German capital as head of the Palestine Emigration Office, a body recognized since 1933 by the Nazis as part of the deal with Hitler's underlings known as the Transfer Agreement. The Nazis allowed departing Jews to keep most of their property, as long as they left for Palestine. If they went elsewhere, they were robbed of almost everything. Hitler wanted the Jews out of Europe, where he intended to create his Aryan empire.

Ben-Gurion caught hell for signing a deal with the Nazis, and Dan was accustomed to being called ugly names by Zionist leaders for his role in facilitating these emigrations. But the Jews he brought to Palestine were no longer beaten up by Brownshirts or kicked out of their jobs because of their race, the way their brethren who remained in Germany were. That was what kept him going.

He turned off the water and came into the living room. "Dishes all done." He wedged himself next to Anna and kissed her silky black hair.

"There's no room, you oaf," she laughed.

"I know." Dan rubbed the back of her neck. "But I hardly see you these days. I didn't want to be all the way over there."

"In Berlin?"

He pointed across the room. "On the couch."

She giggled. They kissed.

"How many was it this time?" she said.

"Two thousand. It took a lot of arranging." He frowned and looked down.

She touched his chin. "I'm sorry. I shouldn't talk about your work when we were just going to—"

"It's only that it's never going to be enough. Never enough."

The telephone rang. It was Shmulik Shoham. "Dan. Is this a bad time?"

"It was a good time until you called," said Dan. "Go away."

"Okay, okay. The Old Man wants you over at his house right now. You won't believe the developments. Absolutely mind-blowing."

"Can't it wait till morning?"

"See you over there. Bye."

Anna stretched out on the armchair and picked up a paperback. "I don't need you. I have other men in my life. Hercule Poirot will keep me company."

"I'll see you in thirty years, when I'm retired." With a last, lingering stroke of her hair, Dan set out into the cool Jerusalem night.

Within five minutes he was at Ben-Gurion's home. The Old Man's wife opened the door, wiping her hands on her flowered apron. Paula Ben-Gurion was a daunting woman, with a petulant chin and suspicious eyes. She was as short and powerful as her husband. Her intimidation was employed to protect him.

"Tea?" she asked. It was somewhere between a question and a command.

Dan stepped inside. "Coffee. Thank you."

"He's in the study with Shoham." She shuffled off to the kitchen.

Chapter 2

The room was very warm. Ben-Gurion was examining a piece of board with strips of paper pasted onto it. Sitting at his desk, he wore his usual shapeless woolen dressing gown and a thick red scarf. Shmulik stood stiffly by his side—too controlled, Dan thought, as though he concealed an enormous restlessness.

"Sit down." Ben-Gurion's chill made his voice raspy.

Dan removed a heap of books from the simple chair by the desk and placed them among others on the floor. The study was crammed with volumes stacked in corners and jammed onto shelves. Paula waddled in and placed a glass of hot tea with honey and lemon in front of her husband. She brought coffee for the others. "He's still fighting off a cold," she cautioned. "Don't keep him long."

"You think that's up to me?" Dan smiled.

In his early fifties, Ben-Gurion was thick-set, squat, and heavy-jowled. His small, shrewd eyes, beetling eyebrows, and bristly white hair gave him a pugnacious look, and indeed he was argumentative and cantankerous in the extreme. He was also not given to formality. He had yet to look at Dan. He slipped a cube of sugar into his mouth and took a noisy slurp of tea, his eyes still fixed on the page before him. "How did you say this turned up? Where exactly did you find it?"

Shmulik reached his fingertips into his light brown beard, as though the paper had emerged from within it. "In Professor Warrendale's room at the King David Hotel."

Ben-Gurion glanced up at him.

"In the wastepaper basket." Shmulik gave the Old Man a raffish shrug. "We have people on the hotel staff. They have access to the rooms of the members of the Royal Commission."

"When did they find this?"

"A couple of nights ago. After a preparatory meeting for today's council."

Ben-Gurion's voice rose, staccato and hoarse. "What kind of nonsense is this? Who gave them permission to pry in the bedrooms of high-ranking British officials? On whose authority was this done?"

Shmulik lost his smug grin and delivered an uncomfortable underling's cough. "On my authority," he said.

That was a pretty good act, Dan thought. *You might actually think Shmulik was a little uncomfortable.* He shook his head in admiration. Shmulik winked at him.

"I took every precaution," Shmulik said. "Our people were out of the rooms long before the meeting ended. The British all went straight to dinner afterward, but I had our people leave even before that to avoid discovery."

Ben-Gurion pointed at the paper on his desk. "And how do you know for sure this belongs to Warrendale?"

"It's his handwriting."

The Old Man sniffed and sipped his tea. Dan noticed that Ben-Gurion didn't bother to ask how Shmulik recognized the handwriting. His outrage had really been about authority, not security.

"Dan, what do we know of this Warrendale?" Ben-Gurion asked. "I don't mean his official biography. I've seen that. I mean what do we *really* know about him?"

One of the few British officials who can look at a Jew or an Indian and see a human being, Dan thought. "I used to attend his lectures on government and colonial history. He was a visiting fellow at Harvard when I was doing my doctorate. He is, by far, the best brain on the Royal Commission."

"But is he just an academic or is he also political? Are his feet on the ground? Does he live in the real world?"

"He's a highly respected consultant to Whitehall. On matters to do with the workings of government, the structure of states, what creates a nation."

"What's that supposed to mean—'what creates a nation'?"

You mean, what does Warrendale think it means? Dan thought. He knew exactly what Ben-Gurion would have meant by it. "It means, what are the minimal affinities necessary to enable diverse groups to come together to form a nation. Is there a coherent principle that explains how groups make the choice between union and separation?"

The Old Man, thoroughly fed up with his cold, griped, "I wish you'd speak simple Hebrew. We're not at Harvard, we're in my study."

Dan looked about him at the bare walls and Spartan furniture, at the shelves of books in Russian, Polish, and Yiddish. *No, we're certainly not at Harvard*, he mused. When he had been there, the fact that Harvard was not Jerusalem had been part of its appeal. In Boston he had found himself in a cultural center, away from the boorishness affected by many of the refugees from European gentility he knew at home, in Palestine.

He forced his mind back to the present. To Ben-Gurion. "I'll give you an example. Last year, when there were those terrible riots in northern India between the Hindus and the Muslims, the British India Office asked Warrendale for his long-term assessment. His conclusion was that, given the contrasting and conflicting interests between the two groups, the only chance of peace was separation. He advocated partition."

Ben-Gurion raised his head, as though finally Dan had said something interesting. "Partition?"

"Into two separate states. Northern India to the Muslims, the rest to the Hindus. Whitehall kept it all very hush-hush, but in one of his lectures Warrendale gave us a hint that let us know where they stood. He suggested that, while it may take some time to create the right circumstances for partition in India, most of Britain's top echelons agree with him. So I can tell you now that whatever Warrendale has to say about us here in Palestine, Downing Street will listen, even if they don't like what they hear."

Dan pointed at the page lying in front of Ben-Gurion, the strips of ripped up paper pasted together on the cardboard. "I don't know what Shmulik's jigsaw puzzle says, but if Warrendale wrote it, we should take it seriously."

Ben-Gurion glared at the page between his fingertips. Dan moved around the desk. Shmulik stepped aside to let him get closer.

It was a roughly sketched, pencil-drawn map of Palestine, shaded in different colors and crisscrossed with demarcation lines. One delineated the coastal plain and much of the northern territory. It was crayoned in green. Another patch, including all of the Negev and most of the mountainous territory west of the River Jordan, was colored blue. A corridor stretching from the sea to and around Jerusalem was crayoned red. Annotations filled the margins, written in tight, illegible scribbles and then crossed out, as if the author had experienced a hasty change of mind. The Royal Commission was supposed to figure out how Britain should unload the territory over which it had ruled for sixteen years at the behest of the League of Nations. Ever since the commissioners had set foot in the country, there had been rumors as to what solution they might eventually come up with—anything from autonomy to Swiss-style cantons. This rough map, evidently, was connected with one of those proposals.

"How are we supposed to make head or tail of this?" Ben-Gurion asked Shmulik. "You said it was absolutely urgent I see this tonight. Do we have transcripts? Any transmissions explaining exactly what it is?"

"That's the problem," said the Old Man's intelligence chief. "There was a major hitch with the bugging system in the conference room. When the upholstery was cleaned the day before—"

"I thought it was supposed to be more reliable than that." Ben-Gurion was really in a bad mood now.

"The system is checked weekly. We've already fixed it. But between that and the static—"

Ben-Gurion jabbed at the paper. "So you've nothing to tell me beyond this scribble that one of the commissioners threw away? Why did you get me out of bed?"

Dan stepped back. This was Shmulik's party.

Shmulik took a long breath. *What a showman*, Dan thought. *He got the Old Man into a lather, and now he's bringing out his big trick.* Shmulik removed a few typewritten pages from the pocket of his jacket, unfolded them, and smoothed them out in front of Ben-Gurion. "Despite the unsatisfactory condition of the recordings, one of our monitoring agents managed to transcribe this. It's Warrendale speaking in closed session this morning. Prepare yourself for a surprise."

Ben-Gurion studied the pages. Revelation stole across his face and his fingers trembled slightly. He whispered, "He's proposing a Jewish state."

Dan was back at his shoulder now. He tried to see the document, but Ben-Gurion's hair obscured his view.

"He wants to partition Palestine into separate Arab and Jewish states." Ben-Gurion slapped his hands flat on the desk.

"May I see?" said Dan.

The chairman of the Jewish Agency—who was at that very moment no doubt having visions of himself as prime minister — handed him the pages. "Read it out loud. I want to make sure I've understood every word."

Dan read: "*...so I shall ask you, Professor Warrendale, since you are the main author of this proposal, to sum up for us the sense of the discussion of these last few days.*"

"That's Lord Peel asking Warrendale to speak," interrupted Shmulik.

Peel, the chairman of the Commission, the man whose name the report would bear.

"*I believe I am expressing the view of this Commission—*"

"This is Warrendale now," Shmulik said.

"*—when I say that all of us—or I should qualify that, Mister Chairman, by saying, most of us—are of the feeling that British rule over Palestine has become untenable, indeed unworkable. We must get out. So what comes in our place? National assimilation between Arabs and Jews has been ruled out. The Jewish national home to which His Majesty's Government has been committed as of 1917 cannot cease to be national. In these circumstances, to maintain that Palestinian nationality has any meaning within a Jewish national home is a mischievous pretense. The answer to whether Arab or Jew will govern all of Palestine must surely be: neither of them. But while neither race can justly rule all Palestine, we see no reason why each should not rule part of it. There is little value in maintaining the political unity of Palestine at the cost of perpetual hatred, strife, and bloodshed.*"

"Slower. Read slower," Ben-Gurion ordered.

Dan realized that his excitement made him rush. His mouth was dry. He tried to let his adrenaline settle down. Then he read on.

"*An irrepressible conflict has arisen within the narrow confines of this one small land. Arabs and Jews differ in religion and language. Their cultural and social life, their ways of thought and conduct, are as incompatible as their national aspirations. There is no common ground between them. Therefore, they have to separate. It is, I believe, the consensus of our group, by and large, that partition seems to offer at least a chance of ultimate peace. I think I speak for most of us when I say that I can see no such prospect in any other plan. Therefore, in the spirit of our deliberations over these last few days, I propose in the name of the Commission a scheme for partition. As you can see in this most preliminary of maps I have sketched, the Jewish state will encompass the region of Palestine with heavy Jewish settlement, meaning much of Galilee, the northern valleys of Jezreel and Hula, and the coastal plain stretching from Tel Aviv to Haifa. This area, as you see, I have marked in green.*"

"Wait," wheezed Ben-Gurion. "What was that again? Are you sure of what you're saying? Galilee, Tel Aviv, Haifa? That's it? Let me see again." He grabbed the page.

Dan trembled. He was a student of history, but now he was part of it. He had held it in his hand, had spoken it into the ear of a statesman—a man who was about to lead the Jewish people in their own land for the first time in two thousand years. He wanted to rush home, to tell Anna.

Ben-Gurion pored over the page.

"Warrendale must have had a large scale map drawn from the sketch," said Shmulik. "It must be on display and he's pointing at it as he speaks."

His eyes still focused on the map, Ben-Gurion thrust the transcript back at Dan. "Go on. Go on reading. *Slowly.*"

"*Much of the rest of Palestine will constitute the independent Arab nation,*" Dan read, "*and that, as you see, I've marked in blue. Great Britain will retain control of several sensitive areas, notably Jerusalem and Bethlehem, due to their universal religious significance. This area I've marked in red.*"

"They're taking away Jerusalem. They're not giving us Jerusalem. Is there anything else?"

Dan scanned the rest of the page. "An initial intelligence assessment. It says partition is likely to split the Arabs, with the Grand Mufti leading the campaign against, beginning with political assassinations of his opponents."

"And the Jews?"

"The proposal is thought likely to split Jewry, with a majority against and very few in favor. American Jews will certainly be opposed. 'The Jews are likely to leave no political stone unturned to undermine the report, but are unlikely to use force.' That's a direct quote."

Rising stiffly to his feet, Ben-Gurion leaned on his desk. "It's not that simple. *Eretz Yisrael* is not ours to tinker with. It belongs to the Jewish people. It is not only the possession of we who live here. It is the historical heritage of Jews everywhere." It seemed to Dan that the Old Man's words cut through the quiet night air like a steel blade.

Shmulik sifted through a wad of notes and said, "There's something more. Here's a snippet our stenographer managed to decipher yesterday. We think it's Peel speaking."

Ben-Gurion glared at him. "They're dismembering *Eretz Yisrael* and you say there is more? What more can there be?"

Shmulik read, "*With the level of Arab violence being what it is, we should endorse London's attitude of radically reducing further Jewish immigration until a possible partition plan has been considered, so as not to provoke new Arab attacks. If the partition plan is not accepted, no more than five thousand Jews should be allowed to enter the country annually for the next five years, when the matter will be reviewed.*"

The chairman of the Jewish Agency blew out a long breath tainted with fever and frustration. "If we don't surrender to our own self-truncation they will strangle us by choking immigration." He turned on Dan. "*Nu?* Come on, let it out. You have something to say?"

Dan had been working for Ben-Gurion only a year, but the Old Man's antennae were already attuned to his young assistant's thoughts. He did, indeed, have something to say. He had been dazzled by the magical words "Jewish state" used in a high-level proposal by a British government commission.

When he answered, the intoxication was evident in his voice. "Forget the details for a moment. What's important here is that for the first time in two thousand years, a world power, the ruler of Palestine, is talking about Jewish sovereignty—not a colony, not something vague like a national home, but a sovereign nation, a state."

"What they're offering is not a country," Ben-Gurion said. "It's Lilliput. It's a weak little pocket-sized state. Tel Aviv, Haifa, the Galilee. Where are we going to put people without the Negev? It's a ghetto they're giving us, an invitation to a pogrom. The Arabs could sweep down on us, wipe us off the map. We'll have to turn ourselves into an armed camp under perpetual siege. Britain's obligation is to help build and protect a Jewish national home in the *whole* of Palestine, and I shall hold them to that."

"If there is a war following partition, which seems more than likely, then the final borders of the Jewish state will be settled in that conflict. That's not a disaster. Unless we lose."

There was a long, brittle silence which was broken when Ben-Gurion mumbled, "Who could live in such an environment? A Jewish state must be a magnet to *attract* Jews. Who'll want to live in a ghetto?"

"People with no choice," Dan said. "Which, eventually, is just about any Jew."

Ben-Gurion seemed to hear something harder in Dan's voice. "The Germans?"

"The Germans. You made a deal with the Nazis in 1933. To let any Jew who wanted to come to Palestine leave Germany without forfeiting their possessions. It isn't getting any pleasanter over there. I don't know where it's going to end, but it isn't going to end well. If we don't accept partition, the British will clamp down on immigration, and then where will our people go when they need a refuge from that madman in Germany?"

With a cold, pinched expression on his face, Ben-Gurion spoke in the hushed tones reserved for moments of dread. "The disaster of German Jewry is not limited to Germany alone. Nazism places the entire Jewish people in danger. Hitler's regime cannot long survive without a war for *lebensraum* in Poland, Czechoslovakia, and Soviet Russia. Not to mention a war of revenge against France and Great Britain. So you're right, Dan. We have to get the Jews out. But we have to have room for them. There are nine million Jews in Europe. I can't put them all in this cubbyhole the British Commission is talking about."

"I agree that Hitler intends to refight the Great War," Dan said. "He talks about it all the time. Zionist policy should be directed toward pressuring the commissioners to improve their proposal, to expand the area of authority of the Jewish state."

"You're a practical man, Dan. I like that." Ben-Gurion smiled, but his eyes held a challenge. "Are you also enough of a dreamer?"

"At this time of night, I like to dream."

"Good. Because the alternative is purest nightmare."

Chapter 3

The amphitheater was a gentle, terraced incline overlooking the Judean Desert. As the sun descended it turned the hills purple, far across the Jordan Valley. In biblical times, this slope had been a refuge for rebels and zealots. Now it was to host something as close to a formal event as could be countenanced by the open-shirted Zionists who mingled there, waiting for the orchestra to play the music of a continent they had left behind. They found flat places in the dust and kicked aside rocks to set up their folding chairs.

The one terrace that had been thoroughly swept clean and furnished with upholstered chairs was roped off for dignitaries. General Sir Arthur Grenfell Wauchope, the British High Commissioner to Palestine, took his place behind the rope. A tall, gaunt patrician in his mid-sixties, Wauchope wore an elaborately stitched, gold-braided uniform. His campaign medals, earned as a young officer fighting the Boers and as commander of a highland battalion in Flanders and Mesopotamia during the Great War, sparkled in the indigo light of the declining sun. Beneath them hung the massive pendant crosses of the Order of the Bath and the Order of St. Michael and St. George. The High Commissioner fluttered his ostrich-feathered cocked hat to whisk away the flies. At his side his political officer, Peter Boustead, whispered advice to his superior on the guests whose presence he ought to note. Boustead had met them all and, through his network of agents, knew details of their characters which he would never have dreamed of sharing with the General. Unless he had to.

The High Commissioner needed no murmured suggestion to greet Ben-Gurion, who arrived with Dan Lavi at his side just as the conductor wound through the musicians to his podium. He reached down for the little Polish Jew's hand. "My dear Ben-Gurion, this damned outfit I'm wearing—it's too hot. My social secretary told me today's affair was to be some sort of a ceremonial inauguration requiring full regalia. The man's an idiot."

"Not such an idiot." Ben-Gurion's voice seemed unnaturally high-pitched against the mellow drawl of the Englishman. "It is the first performance by the Israel Philharmonic Orchestra in Jerusalem, the capital of our future state."

"A bit presumptuous, what?"

Ben-Gurion leered. "Whatever maps your Royal Commission may draw do not represent our final borders. Jerusalem shall ultimately be ours."

Boustead stifled a laugh, but Wauchope flinched. Dan saw that Ben-Gurion enjoyed the High Commissioner's discomfort. He was using his knowledge of the supposedly secret deliberations of the Royal Commission like a boxer's jab, the mild blow a signal of the big hook that was coming soon.

"I meant the name of the orchestra, man. There *is* no Israel yet," the High Commissioner said.

"There has always been an Israel." Ben-Gurion turned toward the stage. "Since before you British were painting yourselves blue for war and conducting human sacrifices in sacred glades."

Wauchope appeared ready to assert that no ancestor of his had painted himself any color at all. Then Ben-Gurion gave him a sly, sideways smile and the High Commissioner laughed and flapped his hat at the flies.

The conductor raised his arms and all was silent for an instant, except for the calls of the birds wheeling on the desert thermals. He led his musicians into a desultory rendering of "God Save the King." The High Commissioner executed a whirling salute, his face reverent.

Dan glanced at the stenciled program. The conductor was listed as "*Wilhelm Gottfried, formerly of the Berlin Philharmonic Orchestra.*" This was the man whose astonishing violin he had heard on Anna's phonograph. Last year, in Tel Aviv, the great Italian maestro Arturo Toscanini had conducted the inaugural concert of the orchestra, officially called the Palestine Orchestra, but Gottfried was surely the most prominent virtuoso to have taken up permanent residence in the country. With the British anthem out of the way, Gottfried moved on to "*Hatikva.*" Ben-Gurion whined out its soulful stanzas in a toneless drone.

A bullish man with close-cropped blond hair and ruddy skin marched up to the VIP section. He wore a khaki shirt that bore the insignia of the British police force, and a black tie. *At least he removed his damned swastika armband when he joined the force,* Dan thought. The man shifted his weight impatiently, arguing with a British soldier who refused to let him enter. Dan shut him out, singing the last lines of the anthem with his eyes closed, imagining the day when the Jews would indeed "*be a free people in our land, the land of Zion and Jerusalem.*"

"You must let me pass," the blond man yelled, his German accent harsh in the quiet that followed the music.

The High Commissioner looked along the line of chairs with a genteel contempt imparted by generations of breeding. "Dear Lord, it's our very own bloody Nazi."

Boustead spoke for the first time since Ben-Gurion's arrival. His voice was a smooth baritone. "Draxler is rather useful to us as police liaison with the German Colony, sir."

"Useful to us? Useful to *you*, you mean, Boustead."

"Quite so, sir. But I trust I'm useful to you in my turn." Boustead gestured to the soldier to allow the blond man to come forward.

"Herr Draxler, I see that some urgency has you in its grip," the High Commissioner said.

The blond man wiped at the sweat on his upper lip. "This performance by Gottfried is a cause for considerable dismay among the German Templer community in Jerusalem."

The small community of German Templers in Jerusalem descended from Messianic Christian forebears who had set up a colony during the 1870s. They were subject to the same political struggles as their compatriots in Europe. Draxler was a member of the local branch of National Socialists, despite having lived his entire life in Palestine, among Jews and Arabs. Dan wondered how deep his ideological commitment truly was.

"A musician is cause for dismay?"

"Gottfried is not just any musician. He is perhaps the most prominent violinist in Europe."

"Indeed? Never heard of him. My taste runs more to light operetta. In any case, he's not in Europe now, is he?"

"He was expelled from the Reich. Some among the German community believe it's an insult to the Führer that he should be allowed such prominence here in Palestine."

"Well, that's overdoing it a bit."

"People will register your presence here as approval of this insult to the Führer."

"My good man—"

Ben-Gurion may have been half the German's size, but that didn't stop him from interjecting. He waved his hand dismissively. "Save your protests for your Nazi friends in the German Colony, Draxler. We are here to sample some of the culture of Europe, the continent your Führer has embarked upon destroying."

Boustead rested a calming hand on the German's sleeve. "You've made your point, Sergeant Draxler. I appreciate your keeping us informed. Why don't you enjoy the performance with us? I believe the program is made up of a good deal of German music."

Draxler scowled and wavered a moment, then took a seat beside Boustead.

The conductor waited for the audience to settle. The musicians quickly leafed through their scores, prepared their instruments, and awaited their cue.

Wilhelm Gottfried turned away from them and addressed the crowd. "Ladies and gentlemen, I escaped Germany with only one possession of any value. I smuggled it past the Gestapo agents who would have confiscated it. I did so because it is beyond all value to me." He picked up a violin case that rested by the side of the podium. Gently he eased out his instrument, cradled it under his chin, and played a solo piece, Bach's chaconne from Partita Number 2, with incomparable virtuosity. Then, with Paganini's Caprice Number 1 he grew wild, his bow ricocheting across all four strings, his fingers speeding along the neck of the instrument in descending scales.

The ovation that followed Gottfried's final notes was thunderous, echoing across the mountains and into the desert. Dan imagined startled Bedouin out there, with their herds of goats. It did not end until Gottfried, caressing his violin as though it were a cherished child, led the orchestra into their program of Mozart and Beethoven.

Draxler's face was marked with hatred so intense Dan thought it could leave a bruise.

At the end of the performance stewards moved among the terraces, inviting guests to the marquee for refreshments. Once inside, Ben-Gurion scooped up a fistful of almonds and joined in an argumentative discussion with his Jewish Agency associates. The High Commissioner dispensed "How do you dos" to acknowledge church leaders and university professors and white-tied orchestra members who chatted with him in atrocious English.

Dan found Gottfried in a corner of the marquee. He seemed spent, soaked in sweat. His thick hair was wild and his eyes were distant. Dan shook his hand. He felt a vibration in his palm as though the music still played there, and realized it was the musician's elevated pulse.

"Who was that German?" Gottfried murmured. "The one who wore the British police uniform. Sitting near the High Commissioner."

Dan was impressed to find Gottfried so attuned to his surroundings. Draxler did look entirely German, even in a British police uniform, but still, the conductor had noticed it all the way from his podium. Perhaps he had heard him demand entry to the VIP section. "Draxler's from the German community. He reports on their activities to Boustead, the High Commissioner's political chief. He's also a member of our local Nazi Party."

Gottfried flinched. "A Nazi Party? Even here?"

"Even here. Visit the German Colony in the south of the city and you will see the swastika flags flying brightly."

"It can't be."

"Don't worry, Herr Gottfried. They have no real power."

"That's what we said in Germany six years ago."

"Draxler is soon leaving us, in any case. He's immigrating to Germany to be part of the Führer's great new Reich." Dan put a reassuring hand on Gottfried's trembling shoulder. "But tell me, why did you have to smuggle your violin out of Germany?"

"It's a Stradivarius." Gottfried lowered his hand to the violin case leaning against his leg. "Not just any Stradivarius either. It's from the great master's golden period."

"It must be worth a great deal."

"It was a gift. I could never have afforded it."

"From a lover of music?"

Gottfried lifted the violin case and clutched it to his chest, a small, private smile on his face. "Yes, that's right. A lover of music."

"Did you arrive in Palestine recently?"

"I've been working on a kibbutz in the Galilee for some years. When I heard about this new orchestra, I decided I'd had enough of goats and chickens."

"You took the baton tonight, but you were not a conductor at the Berlin Philharmonic. Am I correct?"

Dan's musical ignorance drew Gottfried out of his creative exhaustion. "Of course not. That is the domain of Maestro Furtwängler. He *is* the Berlin Philharmonic."

"And he continues to conduct for the Nazis."

Gottfried sighed. "You're German, aren't you?"

Dan inclined his head to one side. "I was born in Berlin. My family came here when I was only seven years old. I don't know that I could still be considered German, given what's happening there."

"Perhaps you're not German, after all. If you were, you'd understand that the real Germany is a culture before it is a country. The culture of Goethe and Beethoven. Of Schiller and Bach. I will return there. I will play this very violin there once again. It is a promise I made before I left."

"You won't deny us the continued pleasure of your music here, I hope. My wife would love to hear you play. She's quite an aficionado."

Gottfried sneered and threw out a dismissive hand at the crowd of professors and functionaries gathered around the tall figure of the High Commissioner. "Look at these provincials. In Berlin I knew everyone. Counts and countesses. The great musicians and writers. The leaders of industry. I knew all the best people."

The man's snobbishness repelled Dan. "But not all the *right* people."

Gottfried deflated. His mockery and vanity left him. He rubbed his hand on the violin case. "I think I'd very much like to meet your wife."

Chapter 4

As the months passed, Dan Lavi could barely believe that the dream of statehood that had entered his head during the late-night session at Ben-Gurion's home didn't die. The Old Man took it up and defended partition at the World Zionist Congress in Zürich, despite severe criticism from American Jewish leaders who believed he should hold out for the whole Land of Israel. Then, in March 1938, Neville Chamberlain convened his cabinet for a meeting that lasted well into the night. The British prime minister was tired of the terrorism and murder being perpetrated across Palestine against British troops and civilians. He was occupied, too, by the mass unemployment and extreme poverty in the northeast of England. He saw the drawn faces of protesting hunger marchers every day on his way to Parliament, and considered their plight a more pressing concern than the resolution of the dispute over the Holy Land. The final report of the Peel Commission recommended partition, as Shmulik had foreseen. Accordingly, Chamberlain set out to persuade his cabinet colleagues to dump the problem of Palestine.

"Most of us concur that our Mandate in Palestine has become untenable," he told his ministers. "There is a simultaneous Arab and

Jewish assault on British forces. Both communities have resolved to rid themselves of our presence and then settle accounts between themselves. There is no British military solution to the turmoil, and with each passing month, our capacity to contain the violence deteriorates. The course we are on means constant strife. It means loss of British lives. It surely means war between Arab and Jew. It must not mean war for Britain."

"Am I to understand that you're inclined to accept the partition of Palestine, Prime Minister?" the foreign secretary, Lord Halifax, broke in. "Need I remind you that British interests are overwhelmingly shaped by developments in Europe, and everything must necessarily be measured by that yardstick? There are clear signs that the Arabs are turning to our rivals in Europe—not least to Germany—for support against us. Partition will not only earn us the hostility of all the Arabs, both inside and outside Palestine, but it will lead to an increasingly close association between the Arabs and our European rivals. The consequences may be far-reaching, and extremely perilous to ourselves, in terms of our oil supplies, our lines of communication, and, above all, the protection of the Suez Canal."

Foreign affairs were not Chamberlain's preferred topic. He had been a successful mayor of Birmingham and he ran Britain as though it were a grand municipality. He had no stomach for a foreign war. But war, if it could not be successfully avoided, would be what he was remembered for—not the Factories Act or the Housing Act, or anything else he had done to improve the conditions of the underprivileged. He cleared his throat and resumed. "I thank His Lordship the Foreign Secretary for articulating his misgivings. I must clarify that His Majesty's Government has no power under the terms of the Mandate to award the country to the Arabs or to the Jews, or even to partition it between them. We must, therefore, take such steps as are necessary and appropriate, having regard to our existing treaty obligations under the Covenant of the League and other international instruments, to submit the Palestine question to the judgment of the League of Nations. We do so in the earnest hope that the League will recommend an appropriate solution which will secure an effective measure of consent on the part of all the communities in Palestine."

The cabinet ministers avoided the prime minister's nervous glance. They were drawn from all three major political parties, the economic emergencies of the Thirties having forced politicians to put aside their differences. Each of them thought now of how a coalition designed to fight against the Depression might easily be converted to face the even more dire situation of war, should it occur. Hitler's troops had moved into Austria only a few days earlier, annexing the country to the great acclaim of its masses. The *Anschluss* made Chamberlain very uneasy. He knew Hitler wasn't finished with his expansions. If Palestine was a foreign policy problem of which he could wash his hands, then now was the time to do so.

"We shall inform the League of our intention to terminate our responsibility as the Mandatory Power for Palestine as soon as is feasibly possible," he said. "All British personnel, civilian and military, will withdraw."

Malcolm McDonald, the secretary of state for the colonies, spoke up in his precise Highlands accent. "We shall be squandering a British asset, Prime Minister. When war comes—" He raised his hand to silence the protests around the table, then adjusted his round glasses and continued. "When war comes, we shall have given the Jews an important card to play against us. They shall sit close to the Suez Canal, more or less right on our most vital access route to India."

Chamberlain twitched the smallest of smiles under his graying mustache. "If the League decides in favor of partition, in all probability there will be a war between the Jews and the Arabs. There is every likelihood the Arabs will win, in which case, with our influence in Transjordan, we shall have a friendly state in Palestine. And if the Jews *are* able to hold their own, the policies of Herr Hitler will inevitably push a Jewish state into our arms and thus, again, we shall be the beneficiaries."

He looked about the table with satisfaction. Perhaps Birmingham hadn't been such a bad training ground for international affairs. "I think that has settled the matter. Now, let's turn to these hunger marchers."

Chapter 5

In Geneva, the League of Nations debated the partition of Palestine for three days. While the world deliberated on whether there would be a Jewish state, the Jewish leaders engaged in a battle over whether to accept one, should it be offered. Dan, who had accompanied Ben-Gurion to Geneva, found it unconscionable that some of his people's leaders could be against partition when the Jews in Germany were suffering such persecution. The Old Man faced constant anger from those who believed the Zionist Movement should refuse any deal that gave the Jews less than the entirety of the Land of Israel. These were the same people who had opposed Ben-Gurion's transfer agreement with the Nazis in 1933, even though it had allowed Dan to bring new emigrants to Palestine.

Rabbi Stephen Wise, a leader of the American Reform Movement, had been pushing for a boycott of Nazi Germany for years, and continued to decry the ongoing dealings with Berlin. He buttonholed Ben-Gurion in the lobby of their hotel as Dan accompanied his boss to the Palais des Nations for the final vote on statehood.

"I can only express revulsion at your attitude," the rabbi said. "Fifty thousand people—*fifty thousand*—packed Madison Square

Garden at a rally in support of a total boycott of German goods not long ago. Macy's, Gimbal's, Sears & Roebuck, Woolworths, and a good many other major American stores have removed German goods from their shelves and ended all commercial transactions with Germany. How can our people in Palestine, to whom we all turn for moral leadership, do anything less? Dealings with the Nazis of any sort are abhorrent, but your signed agreement is despicable. Now you would do a similar deal with the entire world, in which you will agree to sign away our Jewish birthright in favor of a mini-state just so you can have control over it."

Ben-Gurion rubbed his belly as though Wise's attack disturbed his digestion. "The calamity that has befallen the Jews of Germany casts a shadow over all else. Trading with Hitler is acutely distasteful, but if that's what is necessary to save Jews and bring them to Palestine, I will deal with the Nazis—even if it brings benefit to them. It is a true Zionist answer to Nazism."

To Dan's eye, Wise looked remarkably like the White Anglo-Saxon Protestants who ran Harvard. The rabbi was tall, with a thin mustache and a long, aristocratic face set in a combative frown even when he wasn't angry. But now he was angry. "You're dealing with the devil."

"How else are we going to save Jews? How do you get an agreement unless the other side—in this case, the Nazis—sees something to its advantage in it?"

"It pains me to say this, but your whole attitude is dishonorable. You are behaving like a Levantine merchant at the expense of the honor of the Jewish people."

Dan caught his breath. "Levantine" was, after all, a euphemism for the grasping, untrustworthy Jew of anti-Semitic prejudice. But the Old Man was a master of the unfair rhetorical advantage, easily able to shame a critic for his anger and shut him down.

"Rabbi Wise, we are old colleagues, so I shall ignore your impetuous comments. Just let me say that the difference between us is that I have to deal with harsh Jewish realities, not virtuous American liberalities. While you American Zionists are mounting your boycott campaigns, we Jews in Palestine are struggling to provide a safe haven for German Jewish refugees—refugees to whom your president is denying entry to the United States. We have to find a practical Zionist response. Speeches in Madison Square Garden do nothing."

The rabbi took a step back, as though Ben-Gurion had jabbed his chin. He turned and went quickly from the hotel.

Ben-Gurion twitched his head to the side. "You think I made a mistake, Dan?"

"He's quite an influential man."

"American Jews will support us once we have a state. So will Rabbi Wise."

"If we lose the vote today, there'll be nothing for them to support."

"If we lose today, there'll be nowhere for Germany's Jews to go. That's what I care about. Come on." They walked to the Palais, where Ben-Gurion tapped every last influential contact he could find outside the hall.

At the end of another day of arduous debate, amid a hush blotted by nervous coughs, the representative of each state responded to the question of partition in Palestine with "Yes," "No," or "Abstention." When the last country's vote was heard, the Assembly Hall erupted. The Resolution was accepted. Palestine was divided. The Jews had a state.

Ben-Gurion fought his way out of the chamber through a scrum of exhilarated well-wishers, shepherded by Dan Lavi. Neither spoke as they crossed the Avenue de la Paix to their hotel. Ben-Gurion stomped along with his eyes to the ground, as though he were making his way through a repulsive slum in the dead of night, but Dan took in everything around him with the kind of joy that comes to a man who has just seen the luminous face of his child for the first time. The Alps shone in the spring sunshine and the breeze off Lake Geneva seemed to carry him with it like a dancing partner.

The phone rang as they entered their suite. Dan ran to pick it up. Through earsplitting static as raucous as the atmosphere in the Assembly Hall had been, the international exchange connected him to Jerusalem.

"Can you hear me?" Shmulik shouted. "Is the Old Man with you?"

"Yes. I'll give you to him now. Isn't it a miracle, Shmulik? A state for us. For the Jews."

"We'll need another miracle to keep it. Give me the Old Man *now*."

Ben-Gurion grabbed the phone, growling impatiently. He listened as his intelligence adviser spoke. Finally he demanded to know, "What's that din I hear in the background? Celebrations? Are they meshuga?"

He hammered the phone down.

Dan caught the heaviness in his boss's demeanor. The struggle wasn't finished. It was barely beginning.

"Shmulik reports that the Arab armies are already on the move." Ben-Gurion slumped into a wing chair, but was uncomfortable in its stiff leather and upright back. He stood and punched a hand down on the side of the chair. "We have the independence we wanted. Now we are to have our war to keep it."

Chapter 6

Dan drafted the Jewish state's Declaration of Independence on the plane back to Tel Aviv. He gave it to a committee of union leaders and politicians to haggle over the final text, and went to Jerusalem. He didn't have much time to celebrate with Anna. Ben-Gurion was to read the Declaration in public the next day. After that, Dan expected to join the new Israel Defense Forces, fighting the Arab armies to secure the Jewish state's borders.

The disputes over the wording of the Declaration went on until the last minute, but at 4 p.m. the following day, Dan entered the Tel Aviv Museum with Ben-Gurion for the ceremony. Anna and Wilhelm Gottfried were with them. In the hall, the man who would soon be prime minister of the Jewish state stood beneath a portrait of Theodor Herzl, the journalist who had been an early proponent of Zionism. Voice of Israel broadcast the event over the radio.

The first thing listeners heard was the impatient banging of a gavel. The Old Man called the hall to order. "I shall now read the scroll of the Establishment of the State," Ben-Gurion declared.

It took sixteen minutes to read the Declaration, and every moment was a transport of joy for Dan. From amid the bureaucratese and clumsy ideological phrases inserted by the committee, he recognized his words. When Ben-Gurion laid down the scroll, he called upon Rabbi Yehuda Leib Fishman to recite *Shehecheyanu*, blessing the new state.

"Blessed are you," the rabbi sang, "Lord our God, King of the universe, who has granted us life, sustained us, and enabled us to reach this occasion."

The leaders of the Zionist movement mounted the stage to put their names to the Declaration of Independence. When the last signature had been affixed to the scroll, Dan nudged Gottfried and sent him to the front of the hall with his violin. The great musician walked slowly, as if in a trance. His jaw trembled with emotion as he raised his bow. He played the piece that, in that moment, became the national anthem of a state, "*Hatikva*," the song of longing suddenly fulfilled. Jews had their own land.

Ben-Gurion's jarring, nasal tones rang out over the final, perfect note from the Stradivarius. "The State of Israel is established. This meeting is adjourned."

Dan pushed through the crowd to his boss. He wanted to say goodbye before he left to join the fighting. War was clearly on Ben-Gurion's mind. His eyes were downcast and his face was grim. Dan wondered what it would take for the Old Man to smile. If not the foundation of a Jewish state after decades of his commitment to Zionism, then what?

Ben-Gurion gripped Dan's forearms and stared at him, his eyes hard and probing.

"I cannot even begin to express how proud I am to have been with you during this historic time, Prime Minister," Dan said.

Ben-Gurion regarded him tenderly for an instant, then tilted his head disdainfully, as though he had heard something that meant little to him. "You'd better get used to *not* being with me."

"Well, I hope to be back from the army before too long. Back with you in your office."

"You're no longer needed as my assistant. But you're not going to war."

Dan started to protest, but fell silent when Ben-Gurion did, briefly, smile. "I need you to be my ambassador," he explained.

"To where?" Dan couldn't stand to be away from Jerusalem. Especially during a war. He wondered if he was to be sent to Washington or London.

"Not to where. To whom." Ben-Gurion reached up and put his hand on Dan's shoulder. "To Hitler."

Chapter 7

T he Chancellery corridor stretched so far its polished marble floor seemed to narrow toward the seventeen-foot-high double doors, like a rail track approaching some dark gateway. Dan Lavi trod carefully on the shiny surface, his neck stiff in a starched collar and white bow tie. He mirrored every move of the Wehrmacht adjutant who accompanied him, keeping to the careful choreography of diplomatic protocol. When he went to see Ben-Gurion, he wore neither hat, gloves, nor tie. In Israel, the rejection of formal protocol was prized as an assertion of the Jewish state's independence and unique character. But here, rules were sacrosanct. So Dan carried his hat in his left hand, as Hauptmann Brückner did, and suffered the constriction of the white vest and tailcoat. He would give these people no additional reason to despise him. His mission was more important than his comfort.

"Our embassy is in the house next door to your aunt's home, I believe," he said to the adjutant.

The ornate house on Monbijoustrasse had belonged to a Jewish banker named Loeb. It had been taken over by the Reich's foreign ministry when Loeb fled to the United States. The banker had quietly agreed to fund the establishment of an Israeli embassy, as an act of Zionism and a finger in the eye of those who had robbed him, so the ministry had been persuaded to give it over to the meager group of diplomats Dan had been allowed to bring with him as his staff. Soon after their arrival in Berlin, Dan had received a visit from his immediate neighbor, Countess Hannah von Bredow, a granddaughter of Chancellor Bismarck. She told Dan that her nephew, Captain Hasso Brückner, was an adjutant to Hitler, his liaison to the Wehrmacht. "But don't hold that against him," she had said. "He's a darling boy, really. He can't help being taken in by that mad Austrian corporal. *Everyone* is, just now. It can't last."

Walking down the Chancellery corridor, Dan wasn't so sure of the Countess's assessment. Brückner's stern jaw and stiff march matched the sinister stance of the ss honor guard and the intimidating architecture of the Chancellery.

"You're very lucky to have found such a suitable location," he said. His voice was crisp and tense. He made no comment about his aunt. It occurred to Dan that these Nazis were more on edge about today's occasion than he was.

You're on a diplomatic mission, Dan told himself. *Try to build a relationship here. With the darling boy.* "I gather from your aunt that you are the great-grandson of Count von Bismarck. What do you think the chancellor would've thought of—"

"Your embassy will soon be extremely busy." Brückner snarled in a low murmur, as though the words forced their way, overriding his adherence to the silence and formality of the ceremony. "With Jews wanting to get out."

"We certainly look forward to facilitating their emigration."

Brückner snorted. "As rats *immigrate* to a garbage can."

Chapter 8

The ss honor guard's drum roll sounded through the Chancellery. Reinhard Heydrich watched Hitler's posture stiffen. He knew the signs of rage in the Führer. It grew, like his speeches, low key at the opening but building to a hysteria that electrified his voice and limbs. If Heydrich had been given to outward reaction, he would have sighed at the prospect of the lengthy harangue he saw was coming.

"An honor guard for this swine," Hitler snapped.

"Protocol compels us, my Führer," Heydrich said. "Though it's hard to use the term 'honor' in connection to the subhuman in whose presence the drums are being sounded."

Hitler stumped to his desk. "If it wasn't you who asked this of me, Heydrich. If it wasn't you."

Heydrich understood why Hitler showed him such favor. When the Führer looked within himself, he saw what Heydrich saw when he stood before a mirror. Dark hair and medium stature notwithstanding, Hitler believed himself to be an Aryan hero just like his elegant, fair-haired security chief, who stood three inches over six feet. "'The Blond Beast," some called Heydrich. To others he was "The Hangman." But not to Hitler. To him, Heydrich was the man who got things done, the bureaucrat who knew how to break the rules, a man of insatiable ambition, profound intelligence, and superhuman ruthlessness. He had been appointed the head of the Gestapo when it became a national force. He had drawn up the list of Brownshirt leaders to be wiped out on the Night of Long Knives. He fomented the demonstrations that became the pretext for the Nazis to move into Austria, and implemented the decrees whereby enemies of the Reich disappeared "under cover of night and fog." Most of all, he was the man Hitler would've liked to have been.

"The drums are not an honor, for him. More like the accompaniment of a criminal's final walk to the gallows," Hitler said. "The swine does not know it yet, but that trek is under way for his entire verminous people."

Heydrich suspected Hitler wanted to do more than expel the Jews from Europe—he believed the Führer's ultimate plan was their total extermination. The Jews were being allowed to flee to the Holy Land because there were more pressing issues to deal with. When he first came to power, Hitler focused on ridding the Reich of communists and liberals. With the help of Heydrich and his network of concentration camps, that issue was now settled. Next, Hitler would need land, whether at the cost of war or not. But Heydrich guessed that very soon he would be called upon to formulate a plan for the Jews.

Hitler spread his fingers over the sword inlaid in the surface of his desk. The blade was partially withdrawn from the scabbard. It was intended to make those who entered his enormous office wonder when he would swing it at their necks. He never sat at the desk—it was five yards long and made him look small. Instead he stood behind it, while those facing him squirmed in their chairs. A bowl of *Lutschbonbons* lay halfway along the sword. Hitler took one of the fruit drops, then snatched his hand behind his back, rubbing his thumb over the raised Swastika molded into the candy. Heydrich was accustomed to such nervous motions, when Hitler's grandiosity was suddenly undercut by an uncharacteristic gesture of insecurity. The Führer was intimidated by him. Hitler was lazy and Heydrich was a workaholic. Hitler had no time for the systems and policies and networks that Heydrich employed to control and ensnare people. Hitler needed sugar just as he required the adulation of other people. Heydrich prized the bitterness with which people feared him.

"We are in a life-or-death struggle," Hitler said.

"Yes, my Führer, it is so."

Hitler's eyes took on a strange, fanatical gleam, looking inward to where the world's future lay. He spoke quietly, as though the words came to him in a vision. "This is a day for which my greatness has prepared me. A weaker leader, one who had not set great objectives for the German people and the German Reich as I have done, would reject the idea of accepting this criminal Jew in the State Chancellery as an obscenity."

The drums halted. Hitler glanced at the double doors of his office, three times the height of the ss men stationed at each side of them.

Heydrich knew the protocol. It was timed to the minute, down to the last beat, as if by the metronome in his study where he practiced on his violin each night. The Jew would be passing through the cavernous corridor now. The architect had made the floor of polished marble, so that visitors had to concentrate just to stay on their feet. *Though not the Jew*, Heydrich thought. *He will be accustomed to slipperiness.*

"In 1933, I ventured an accord with the Zionist cabal in Palestine. Those Jews who emigrated from Germany would be allowed to take their property with them if they left for Palestine." Warmed up, Hitler's voice was powerful, his *r*'s rolling like the percussion of a machine gun. "Those who departed for other countries would have to pay the Reich Flight Tax and lose at least half of their wealth."

"About fifty thousand Jews have left the Reich for Palestine since your accord, my Führer."

Hitler hesitated. Statistics were not his field. They threw him off. Heydrich blinked slowly, a silent signal for the Führer to go on.

In his mind, Hitler entered a battle with the Jews. He firmed his lips. He was on the field, on the attack, resolute. "By removing the Jews, I eliminate the possibility of some sort of revolutionary core or nucleus being created in Germany. If our opponents were victorious, the German people would be eradicated. The Bolsheviks would slaughter millions and millions and millions of our intellectuals. Anyone not murdered by a shot in the neck would be deported. Children would be taken away and eliminated. And this entire bestial plan has been organized by the Jews. Don't expect anything from me other than the ruthless upholding of the national interest in such a way as to obtain the greatest effect and benefit for the German nation."

"You may count on me, my Führer."

"The arrival of this criminal Jew here today represents an opportunity for us to cleanse the Reich more fully." Hitler struck his fist into his hand. "Until now, under the British Mandatory authority, immigration to Palestine would sometimes go up, sometimes down. When it went up, the Arabs would complain, so the British would cut the number of Jews they let in. They wanted to protect their oil interests in the Arab region. In response, the Jewish cabals in London and New York would issue their orders, and their henchmen on Downing Street would increase the quotas to allow more Jews to immigrate. Because policy is dictated to men like that asshole Chamberlain by Jews. He is in the pocket of the Jews."

Each time he said the word "Jew," Hitler's voice rasped with derision.

The Führer slapped his thigh. "The emigration was not fast enough for me. I cannot allow the National Socialist project to be dependent on the political balancing act of weak-willed shills for the Jews of London. I am not interested in politics. I am interested in destiny. So now, thanks to the pathetic League of Nations, Palestine and its British regime is no more. Now there is Israel." He stamped his foot and barked a sarcastic laugh. "I knew that there was always the possibility that the Jews would win a state for themselves. Such is the extent of their malign influence. I thought it would take longer— another ten years at least, but then the British came along with their Peel Commission and recommended a Jewish state, and here it is. So, the German people shall have their reckoning with the Jews earlier than anyone expected. That is a good thing."

An adjutant opened the big doors. He started to cross the floor, but Hitler waved him back. He knew it was time. The Jew would be approaching the reception hall. Hitler walked to the door, stopping by the huge globe that stood taller than a man. The architect of the Chancellery had built it for Hitler so that he could ponder the range of his future power. He spun the giant sphere and thumped his fist down on the eastern edge of the Mediterranean.

"This criminal Jew may call his patch of desert a state if he wishes, though I think he will hardly dare to once he has observed the functioning of the German Reich. He may even call it a place of refuge. I will call it what it is—a dumping ground for Polish peasants and Ukrainian Reds. Let us hope they will now be joined by the parasitic bankers and shopkeepers from within our midst."

"The security service is implementing your policy to the letter, my Führer." Heydrich had worked hard in committee rooms and cabinet chambers to ensure that the SS was responsible for the Jewish issue, over all other government ministries. It wasn't only a security question, or a matter of politics. The very blood of the German people depended on the implementation of the Führer's ideas. And the blood of the Germans ran with absolute purity in the veins of the SS.

"I want to be rid of the Jews and their degenerate practices. This criminal wants Jews. So let him take them." Hitler folded his arms, slowly, a grand gesture of finality. "While he still can."

Chapter 9

Mythic portrayals of Nordic heroes and classical archetypes glowered from between the pillars of blood-red marble on the walls of the reception room. Dan waited in the center of the floor, beside Brückner. The massive doors in the far wall swung back, the motionless ss guards at each side like hinges, screwed into place by their steel helmets. Dan glimpsed Hitler's private office beyond the doors. Two figures emerged. Heydrich, tall and blond, wearing the black uniform of the ss, his face expressionless. And the hunched figure of Adolf Hitler, hands clasping and unclasping, clasping and unclasping with each step across the marble toward Dan. He came to a halt a few yards away, staring down at Dan's shoes. The air was still and, once the adjutant had clicked his heels, all was quiet. Dan felt the invisible presence of hundreds of thousands whose lives depended on him, and on the conduct of his office. They crowded round him for a glimpse of the man who would decide their fate.

Hitler widened his eyes and linked his hands in front of his gray double-breasted jacket. He seemed to expand out of himself, like a silent-movie vampire, a nightmare dragon floating on the air in a child's story.

The adjutant snapped out his arm in salute. "My Führer, the ambassador respectfully requests that he may present to you his credentials."

Dan noted the omission. The name of his country. Were he the ambassador of the United States, the young officer would have announced "the ambassador of the United States." Or of Belgium or Mongolia, Iceland or Peru. But he had not given the name of the new state that had sent Dan to be its first emissary to the capital of the German Reich. The corner of Dan's mouth rose very slightly, lifted by the brazenness of independence, the insolence toward old masters, that his country cultivated.

Hitler brought his chin up as though at some effrontery. *Did he read my thoughts?* Dan wondered. He reminded himself that his job was to manage Hitler, not defy him. He made his face as neutral as he could, but he doubted that would be enough. His every sinew was an affront to Nazi ideology. Even in formal morning dress, anyone on a Berlin street could have picked him out as a Jew. His hair was combed back and pomaded, yet uncontrollable curls still rose like a glimmering halo over the crown of his head. Even if the Mediterranean sun hadn't deepened his skin to the tobacco tone of an Arab goatherd, it would have been several shades darker than that of Hitler's beloved Aryans.

Adjutant Brückner cleared his throat and tilted his head, indicating to Dan that he should take the next step.

Dan addressed Hitler in the perfect German that was his mother tongue, the language of his parents and grandparents. The language in which his father wrote and published countless papers as a professor of ancient history at Humboldt University, before he left Berlin for Palestine. But Dan's ancestors had never spoken German in quite this way. They had employed it to make themselves acceptable to the Germans around them, to disguise and deny their true selves. Dan used the language now to say exactly who he was, and the very words seemed to glow in his mouth, illuminating the image and soul of his people for the Germans forced to listen to him. "Allow me to present the letters of credence by which Prime Minister David Ben-Gurion has appointed me to be Ambassador Extraordinary and Plenipotentiary of—"

Brückner coughed loudly. Hitler glared at his shiny boots. Heydrich licked his lips.

"—of the State of Israel to the German Reich."

Dan held out a slim envelope. His arm quivered. He relaxed his muscles and his hand steadied.

With a swift motion, Hitler grabbed the envelope and flicked it toward Heydrich. His mustache twitched. Dan thought it was thicker, bushier than it seemed in the newsreels.

The words of the Old Man echoed in Dan's mind in Ben-Gurion's nasal Polish accent, orders delivered in between reports from Shmulik on the first maneuvers of the war of independence. *"You will dine with the Devil, Dan. You will do everything the Devil requires. Whatever it takes, you will maintain the transfer of Jews from Germany to Israel."* Then Ben-Gurion had moved closer to Dan, speaking quietly and with concern, as a father to a son. *"Remember not to fear him. After all, he thinks it is* you *who is the Devil."*

Hitler spun around and headed back to his personal office. Heydrich went with him. Dan understood what the presence of the tall blond security chief meant. Any other ambassador would have been greeted by Hitler and the foreign minister, Joachim von Ribbentrop, but the Jews were the business of the ss, the shock troops of the Nazi future.

The door slammed. Dan's scalp prickled and his tongue stuck to the roof of his mouth. Hitler was worse than he had expected, more than just a political leader with a vicious hatred for Jews—those were common enough all over Europe. Dan couldn't determine just how bad this man was, but he felt it in his stomach. He sensed that the imperiled souls crowding the reception hall experienced the same disturbance in their guts. The invisible desperation of all those Jews needled him, buffeted him like a panicked animal herded through the gates of an abattoir. For an instant, Dan felt fear.

The diplomatic protocol said there had to be a handshake. But Hitler wouldn't touch a Jew, and neither would a senior ss man. It fell to the adjutant to reach out his arm. He did so with his lips twisted, as though they were clamped down on the curses he wished to spill over the Israeli ambassador.

Dan filled himself with the single-mindedness he had so often observed in Ben-Gurion in the two years since he had completed his studies at Harvard and returned to Palestine to work with the Old Man. The longer he held on to this hand, the less likely it would be to strike out his people. He folded his fingers around Brückner's tentative grip. His ears filled with noise, the hammering of his heart. He pressed the handshake. Was that the man's erratic pulse under his fingers? So Nazis were afraid of him. *Perhaps I am the Devil, after all.*

The doors opened and the ss guards stamped their jackboots.

Hauptmann Brückner let go of Dan's hand. "It's time for the official photo."

They made the long walk to the steps of the Chancellery accompanied by the ominous drum-roll of the ss honor guard. "I'll hand you over here," Brückner said.

Three burly men in long leather coats stepped forward. Their leader looked out from under the brim of his fedora with piercing, insolent eyes. Dan recognized the former intelligence advisor to the British police, the man who had kept watch over the Germans of Jerusalem for its colonial rulers.

"Draxler?" Dan said.

"This is your protection detail," Brückner said. "From the Gestapo. Apparently Kriminalinspektor Draxler speaks Hebrew."

"Move it." Draxler spat at Dan's feet. "*Herr Ambassador.*"

Chapter 10

The lines for visas at the Israeli Embassy on Monbijoustrasse were, as Brückner had predicted, overwhelming. The skeleton staff Ben-Gurion allowed Dan to bring with him barely coped, particularly as most of the supposed diplomats weren't there to be diplomats at all. They worked in the basement, under the authority of Shmulik, who headed operations for the Mossad, Israel's new intelligence service. Shmulik's wife, Devorah, passed her days down there poring over code books. Yossi Richter, nominally a consul in the visa department, was Shmulik's right-hand man. And Aryeh Yardeni, Dan's driver, was usually out on some errand for the Mossad station chief. The only diplomat fully available to Dan was Wili Gottfried, who had agreed to serve as first secretary.

It was the communications network in the basement that brought news of an assassination attempt. A Jewish teenager, a refugee who had fled Germany, appeared at the German mission in Paris. Demanding to see a consul, he was shown into the office of a young Nazi diplomat, whom he proceeded to shoot.

"Dead?" Dan asked, when Shmulik entered his office.

"He's been arrested."

"Not the Jew. I mean the German who was shot, Shmulik. I'm worried about the repercussions."

Shmulik grinned darkly. "He'll be dead soon enough. Even if this Grynzspan fellow's shot only grazed him, the German diplomat will die. Goebbels will see to it. It's too good an opportunity for the Nazis to miss."

Two days later, at eight in the evening, the mortally wounded German died. By midnight, the Israeli Embassy in Berlin was crowded with fearful Jews. The Brownshirts were out on the streets with sledge-hammers and axes, smashing Jewish stores, ransacking homes and burning synagogues. Dan took call after call from Jewish communities around Germany, reporting terrifying stories of beatings and murders.

Torches held by a crowd of Brownshirts on the sidewalk lit the windows of the embassy. Dan watched them, waiting for them to enter. How much respect would the Nazi regime show for diplomatic protocol when the streets were noisy with lynch mobs and the night sky was bright with the fire of burning synagogues?

Shmulik came to his side.

"Will they come in?" Dan asked.

The Mossad man didn't answer. He pressed a pistol into Dan's fist and closed his hand around it. "How many dead?"

"Ninety-one. At least. And that's only the official reports so far."

"Devorah is coming up with a more accurate figure by going through the calls we've made all around Germany."

Dan shook his head. "Ninety-one Jews."

"Ninety-one future Israelis. And thousands more are being rounded up. They're taking them to the concentration camps." Shmulik stared out the window at the mob of Brownshirts. "I'm not burning the code books yet. But be ready."

Across the street, the rococo pediments of the Monbijou Palace flickered in the glow cast by flames from Oranienburger Strasse. The Jewish center of Berlin was burning. A Mercedes pulled up outside the palace railings and a man in a fedora stepped out. It was Draxler.

The Gestapo agent hustled across the street, shoving through the crowd of Brownshirts. Something in his movements suggested extreme agitation. Dan knew he wouldn't be opposed to the night's anti-Semitic depredations. So what was it that disturbed him? He went to the door of the embassy as Draxler hammered on it. The refugees in the hallway whimpered. Dan held the pistol behind his back and nodded for Richter to draw back the bolt.

"Where is your wife?" Draxler demanded.

The hidden pistol trembled in Dan's grip. "What do you want with her?"

Draxler frowned at the quivering wretches around the staircase as though it had barely occurred to him that a massive pogrom was underway. He drew closer to Dan, but didn't cross the threshold of the embassy. "My daughter is sick. She can't breathe. Fever very high."

"So you came to us?"

"Our usual doctor can't come."

"Why not?"

"He's a Jew. By the time I got to his house it was burning. I don't know where he is. I remembered your wife had a reputation as a very good pediatrician back in Jerusalem."

"You perpetrate this evil, but you won't live with the consequences? Your Jewish doctor is, perhaps, dead. So your daughter suffers. Draw your own conclusions, Kriminalinspektor."

Draxler wasn't accustomed to asking twice. For a moment, the struggle against the urge to beg wrote itself across his face. Then he made himself calculating. "Let's talk about consequences, shall we? Those boys in the brown shirts outside—they're my boys, and they're eager to have their fun. Your embassy is filled with Yids. I'm in charge of protecting you, but I only have a small Gestapo detail. I don't know that they could hold back a determined gang." He leered. "On the other hand, if you do as I ask, I'm sure I can get the Brownshirts to protect you from the things that are going on everywhere else in Berlin tonight."

Dan could still hear the frantic voices of the Jewish leaders who had phoned him from around Germany to catalog the depredations being carried out against their people that night, and his disgust burst out of him with a shout. "Get out of here. Do you hear me? This instant."

Draxler squared his shoulders and opened his mouth to respond. Anna pushed through the refugees to him.

"Stop this argument." She wore her coat and carried her medical bag.

Dan stepped toward her.

She saw the gun behind his back and gave him a harsh look. "Dan, don't say anything," she said. "I have a duty to any sick person."

"But Anna—"

"Let's go, Herr Draxler."

"At least let me go with you, Anna."

His wife put her hand on his neck and spoke softly. "You have work to do here, darling. These people need your help. Get them out of this country. That's *your* job. Now, let me do mine."

The Gestapo man glared at Dan, then turned and led Anna through the crowd of Brownshirts to his car.

As the Mercedes pulled away, Dan shivered. His wife was riding in a car that so often took people where they didn't want to go.

Chapter 11

The days after the pogrom that became known as Kristallnacht were chaotic for the embassy staff. The Gestapo had picked up more than thirty thousand Jews and sent them to concentration camps. It seemed as though the rest of the country's half a million Jews were at the consular entrance on the side of the Israeli Embassy, clamoring for help in emigrating.

After a long day processing visa applications, Dan slouched over his desk in the dim light of evening and read the reports from Jerusalem. The War of Independence had been won and, as Ben-Gurion had predicted, the new state's borders extended beyond the boundaries the Peel Commission had recommended. By pushing back the invading Egyptian army, Israeli troops had added the Negev Desert to the plains around Tel Aviv and the hills near Haifa. In the north, where it sent the Syrians and the Iraqis running, the entire Galilee was under Israel's control. Most astonishing of all was the victory against the Transjordanian Arab Legion. Israeli troops beat them back enough to secure a corridor of land to Jerusalem and to retain about half of the holy city, although the ancient quarters were lost. But war had a price, and not only in lives. Ben-Gurion struggled to control food and resources. There were bread riots spreading across the new country, and the prime minister's opponents, who had pulled behind him through the exigencies of war, now sniped about rising prices, unemployment, and the lack of housing for new immigrants. For his dealings with Nazi Germany, they gave him hell.

Dan would've liked to send back good news to lighten his boss's load, but the report he was preparing as the embassy shut its doors for the day was far from pleasant reading. Kristallnacht, the "night of shattered glass," had witnessed the complete demolition of one hundred synagogues, while several hundred others were burned out. Eight thousand Jewish businesses had been destroyed. According to Shmulik's informants, the thirty thousand Jews who had been taken to concentration camps were being tortured and starved. Now Göring, Hitler's economic chief, had ordered the Jews to pay for the damage perpetrated against them. The Nazis fined the Jewish community one billion reichsmarks.

Dan wrote up the last details and slumped back. He was about to take his report down to Devorah in the coding room, for transmission, when Anna entered the room.

"You look like you could do with some cheering up." She smiled and came around the desk.

His kiss was lackluster and distracted. He lifted the report. "I'm sorry. It's just such awful news. Everywhere. Everything."

"Things can only get better, then."

"You're so optimistic about the world. It's hard to believe you're Jewish."

"It's the part of me that's American. Come on, let's go." She stood up.

He realized she had her coat folded across her arm. "Go? Where?"

"You forgot our neighbor's soiree?"

Dan rubbed his face. "I can't. Not tonight, so soon after such awful things have happened."

"Ambassador Lavi, there are few enough Germans prepared to even acknowledge your existence. The least you can do is to be gracious to the one gentile Berliner who appears to be thrilled at your presence." Anna spun Dan's chair and lifted him up by the lapel of his jacket. "Besides, Wili is going to play."

"Of course. Now I remember." She was right that he ought to go. A major factor in the choice of Gottfried as first secretary at the new embassy had been his connections in Berlin society from the days before the Nazis, when he had been a popular guest in the salons of nobles, diplomats, and industrialists. "Well, I suppose we must make an appearance. Let me take this report downstairs first." He hauled himself out of his chair and went to the steps.

Shmulik's domain in the embassy basement was dark and shadowy and full of complicated machinery. His wife Devorah hunched over a set of code books by the embassy's transmitter. Richter and Yardeni worked the phones, calling their contacts across Germany to arrange for transports out of the country. Dan ran his hand along the bare brick. On the other side of the wall was the Countess's basement, a proximity that annoyed Shmulik, who considered it a security risk. Somehow, Dan found it comforting. He laid his report in front of Devorah.

"Sorry it's so long. I'm afraid you'll be working late to send that," he said. "It really should go out tonight."

"Never mind. It's not like I have the prospect of a quiet night with my husband to look forward to." She glanced at Dan's careful script.

"Where is Shmulik?"

"Out."

Dan gave her an amused, questioning look. "Out where?"

"Looking for communists and liberals who aren't yet dead. He figures they might be able to help him."

"Help him do what?"

She opened a new code book. "Do I look like the Mossad station chief to you? Ask him yourself."

Dan went back upstairs. Anna waited in the hall. Wili Gottfried was beside her, wearing a tuxedo. He held his violin case across his chest protectively, just as he had done at the Mount Scopus concert for the British High Commissioner. His face was as white as his tie. Anna stroked his arm.

"Is my cultural attaché ready to bring some civilization to these Aryan heathens?" Dan slapped his hand down on Gottfried's shoulder.

Gottfried opened his mouth to speak, but he only nodded and turned to the door.

Chapter 12

Wearing a simple black dress, Countess von Bredow spun through her salon from one friend to another. Excitement radiated from her sapphire blue eyes. She took the elbow of a straight-laced general whose pants bore the red side-stripe of the Wehrmacht High Command, and her touch seemed to shoot energy into him. He started to talk expansively of the weekend he had recently spent at the Führer's Bavarian retreat near Berchtesgaden. "Everyone jockeys for the chance to be at Hitler's side when he takes his walk," he said, "and the rest stump along behind, feeling miserable and outmaneuvered."

Dan Lavi watched his hostess from the doorway. The sixty-year-old Countess seemed to have forsaken fashion entirely. She wore no jewelry, and her hair was cropped short and untended. She paid no attention to her posture, which was unstudied and loose, and she was so thin that her collar bone stood out like a coat hanger through a laundered shirt. When she had first stopped in at the embassy next door, Dan had thought she was another of the refugees recently discharged from the concentration camps seeking transport to Israel. The comparison no longer seemed apt. The desperation of the Jews who came to his embassy pushed them almost to madness. The people here were perhaps the only Germans left with a commitment to sanity.

A Luftwaffe officer broke into the Wehrmacht man's reminiscences of Berchtesgaden. "You should visit Göring's castle some time," he said. "It's even worse there. The fat oaf dresses like a medieval knight, in a leather doublet and leather boots halfway up his thighs. Then he roasts a pig on a spit right in front of you."

"He eats the entire pig himself, I assume?" The Countess slapped her spare stomach.

The group laughed at her reference to Göring's girth.

"Hitler's oafish deputy pays for all his extravagances through theft. No doubt he'll pocket the money he and his kind are forcing the Jews to pay after Kristallnacht." The Luftwaffe officer was somber, staring into his champagne flute. The group grew silent. It appeared that the horrors of the previous days weighed on them.

"How much longer must we suffer these bastards?" the Wehrmacht general said. "After all, fifty-percent percent of Germans didn't vote for them."

The Luftwaffe man gave a harsh, cynical laugh. "How long? Until the *next* election, of course. About the time pigs learn to whistle."

The Countess grabbed for the hand of a morose man with a high forehead and a spray of curly hair above each ear. "Maestro Furtwängler, you are a musical genius. Please teach the pigs how to whistle, so that we may be rid of the Nazis."

Amid the laughter that brought relief to the others in the room, the famous conductor sneered. "The pigs are already singing the 'Horst Wessel Song.'"

The General and the Luftwaffe officer sang the opening lines of the Nazi march, grunting like swine. "*Hitler's banners fly above the streets, the time of bondage will last but a little while now.*"

"Amen to that." Gottfried stepped forward and held out his arms.

The Countess noticed the Israelis in the doorway. She rushed over and embraced Gottfried, then turned to Dan. He took her hand and kissed it. She laughed at his formality and turned her face up for a kiss. She hugged Anna, and then returned to Gottfried, bubbling with enthusiastic comments on their clothing and their looks and her happiness that they had come.

Anna nudged Dan, and whispered, "I think it was more than just Zionism that made our friend Gottfried so eager to secure a place on your staff."

Dan watched the smile on Gottfried's face as the Countess whispered to him. It showed the unfeigned joy of a deep emotional connection. He realized that he himself had felt very little happiness thus far in Berlin. He faced weighty responsibilities, but life should not be totally reduced to that. He reached out to smooth his wife's hair, pulling her close and kissing the crown of her head.

Furtwängler walked over and reached out his hand to Gottfried. Dan noticed that it quivered. Gottfried gripped it immediately.

"It's good to have you back." Furtwängler spoke nervously. It was four years since he had allowed the Nazis to prevent Gottfried's performance under his baton at the Berlin Philharmonic. No doubt he was unsure that all was forgiven.

Gottfried kept hold of the maestro's hand, triumph glowed on his face. "It was you who asked me to return. Don't you remember? The night before I left Germany. Now I represent a new country, but an old people. With every performance I give, I will remind the Germans that their prized culture is at its best when mixed with the genius of other races."

He touched the conductor's shoulder reassuringly. "Don't be embarrassed, Maestro. If my own country were in the role of oppressor, I might also be tempted to make excuses for it."

"Excuses?" The conductor bridled. "Do you know the sacrifices I have made—"

The Countess laid her hand on Furtwängler's chest. "We are all friends here, with a common love for music, Maestro. Let's not march to the same tune of hate as the whistling pigs."

Laughter defused the tension. The "Horst Wessel" oinking started up once more. Everyone was eager to seize on their common dislike of the regime. The differences between them were minor compared to their shared horror at the brutality on the streets.

The Luftwaffe officer came over to Dan, clicked his heels, and extended his hand. His hair was blond, cut in a boyish mop, and his cheeks were flushed with wine. "Oberleutnant Ansgar Schulze, of the Luftwaffe Staff Command."

Dan took the man's hand and Schulze drew him close, giving him a meaningful look. "You may be yourself tonight, Herr Ambassador. You are among friends."

Schulze turned to Anna, bowed, and kissed her hand. "Frau Lavi, the Countess tells me you risked the streets on Kristallnacht to treat the child of your Gestapo guard?"

"The little girl had a viral meningitis. She'll be fine."

"Well, if you ever need to work as a veterinarian, you'll have some experience behind you. The child could not have been human, considering who her father is."

Anna wasn't drawn by the Luftwaffe man's evident contempt for the Gestapo.

Gottfried was eager to play, but the Countess insisted he wait for her last guests. When they arrived, Dan immediately recognized the former political advisor to the British High-Commissioner in Palestine. Beside him stood a man in an old-fashioned collar whose features displayed considerable nervousness.

The Countess called Dan over. "I believe you are acquainted with Herr Boustead," she said. "And this is Herr Kritzinger, the deputy chief of the Chancellery."

Peter Boustead seemed thinner in his dark suit than he had been when last Dan saw him. His face displayed a resolve that hadn't been evident in Jerusalem. Perhaps in Palestine the man had been conflicted about his role and here, in Berlin, he no longer was.

"Your Excellency." Boustead shook Dan's hand. The Countess winked at them, then walked away with Kritzinger.

"I didn't know you were in Berlin."

"This isn't my first time in Germany. My father served on the Military Inter-Allied Commission of Control after the Great War, and he was based in Berlin. My mother and I lived here with him for a couple of years. He administered the place. Then he handed it over to the Germans."

"Perhaps you should've kept it."

"We couldn't have done worse than the swine who rule here of late, eh?" He lowered his voice. "I've been in touch with your friend Shmulik Shoham."

So Boustead was now in British intelligence. The lineup at the Countess's soiree was now clear to Dan. No wonder Kritzinger, the Chancellery official, looked nervous. If Hitler found out where he had been this evening it wouldn't reflect well upon him. A gathering of opponents. German officers critical of the Nazi leadership. A Countess making disrespectful remarks about Göring's weight. A British intelligence official.

And the Israeli ambassador.

He wondered if it was risky for him to be here. The Nazis certainly wanted to unload the German Jews onto Israel, but there were probably some Germans who'd like nothing more than to discredit the Israeli ambassador and send him packing, back to the Middle East. The soiree might be most dangerous for Gottfried, as a lower-ranked diplomat than Dan. An ambassador should be at least somewhat untouchable.

"Of course, your Mister Shoham is much more clandestine than I am," Boustead continued. Like all British officials, he acted the harmless dimwit very well. "Political officer at His Majesty's Embassy here, that's me. Not even departmental chief. A bit of a demotion, really. Like all other things about Palestine, my government sought to sweep me under the carpet."

Dan had great regard for Boustead's intellect. It was clear that Berlin would be the center of European events in the coming years. If Boustead had been swept away, he had ended up not beneath the carpet, but at the head of the table. "I can't imagine your chiefs in Whitehall have anything but the greatest faith in you."

Boustead shrugged. "Far from it, old man. You, on the other hand, have gone up in the world."

"Only because the world is on the way down."

Gottfried tuned his violin and the room hushed. The virtuoso performed the same pieces Dan remembered from the concert at Mount Scopus. This time the music was still more soulful, as though the longing Dan heard in the first performance had been sated. Happiness had taken its place. Anna squeezed his hand. She felt it too. Dan watched Gottfried play, eyes closed, fleshy cheek spilling onto the violin's tail piece, sweat in his hair and brows.

When the music was over, Gottfried collapsed into an old Louis Quatorze sofa. Dan brought him some champagne and sat beside him.

The violinist downed the champagne quickly. His jaw shivered and his eyes were red.

"Are you sick?" Dan asked.

Gottfried caught his heavy upper lip in his teeth and shook his head. "Thank you, Dan. For bringing me back here."

Dan almost replied that Gottfried and his music were a great asset to the embassy, but he held back. He wasn't talking to his cultural attaché now. This man had been hounded from the work he loved with the Berlin Philharmonic, chased from the heart of the culture that had nurtured his talent. And now he had returned.

Gottfried's eyes were misty, his voice choked. "This is all because of you, Dan."

"Not because of me. It's because of Israel. Because we have a state."

Gottfried gazed at the Countess with love. She was by the window, speaking quietly with Anna. The women's faces were hidden, but the stillness of their bodies suggested a serious conversation.

"I will never see Israel again," Gottfried said.

Perhaps he *was* ill. Dan grabbed his hand. "Of course you will. We've dreamed of that land for two thousand years, Wili. Now it's ours. We must all glory in that."

"My dreams have been different than yours." Gottfried watched the Germans drink their champagne. "My Countess and her friends believe everything will be fine again here, in the end. They detest the Nazis. Some in this room are communists, some are just snobs who think Hitler lacks breeding. I know all of them from way back." He drew himself up. "None of them will survive, Dan. Unless *you* help them."

"Gottfried, my mission is to get Jews out, not Prussian aristocrats."

"Our country needs people like these."

"Our country? Are you talking about Israel? Or Germany?"

"Israel, of course. These people would bring it culture and refinement."

"Our country needs Jews. That's all. Refined or doltish, it doesn't matter. Germany has smart Germans and dumb Germans and hateful Germans and loving Germans. We need Jews in each of those categories too." Dan swept his hand around the room. "If the people in this room decide to play along with the regime, they can maintain their privileged positions. That's not an option for Germany's Jews."

"Their privilege doesn't matter to these people. Their country is going to hell. Sooner or later they will try to do something about that, and we should help them. *That's* how to save Jews, Dan." Gottfried stood abruptly. "Not by shipping them off to the desert with all those ignorant Russian peasants and Arabs."

He marched over the Turkish silk rug to the Countess in the window. He laid his hand on her back. She slipped her arm around his waist. Together, they looked onto the dark street. Dan wondered if they were watching the Gestapo detail in the Mercedes outside the embassy.

Anna sat down beside him. Her eyes fell on Gottfried and the Countess.

"Would you do that for me?" she said. "Come back to a place where you might be in danger? Just to be alongside me?"

"I brought you to Berlin. *Into* danger."

She smiled. "Does that mean you love me more, or less?"

He tried to think of a funny remark to divert her. But a witticism would have deflected *his* emotions, rather than hers. Her face was lit by the flickering gas light. "I'll die before I let anything happen to you," he said.

Chapter 13

When they returned to the embassy, they found Richter on guard duty, a Schmeisser submachine gun on the desk beside him. The Gestapo was supposed to keep intruders away, but Shmulik refused to leave embassy security in the hands of the very people who might one day want him dead. He and his Mossad underlings alternated keeping watch until all the staff was accounted for and locked down. Dan heard the light pop of pistol fire filter through the soundproofing and into the lobby. He sent Anna up to bed and said goodnight to Gottfried. He went down into the basement. He waited for a pause in the firing and opened the door of the shooting range.

Shmulik pushed a round into the magazine of a Luger P08 and slotted it into the pistol's wooden grip. Dan shut the door. As it clicked behind him, Shmulik turned to the gallery. He lifted the German pistol in both hands and fired. Inside the room the shots boomed loudly. The last cartridge ejected, tinkling onto the concrete floor. Shmulik put the pistol down, marched to the target, and ripped it away.

Dan touched the pistol on the table. "Why aren't you using your Colt?"

"The Luger's more common here."

"Meaning you can dispose of it more easily after you do something you don't want traced?"

"*Nothing* I do should be traced." Shmulik slapped his target onto the table beside the pistol. It was a newspaper photo of the British prime minister waving a piece of paper. In September, Chamberlain had let Hitler occupy the Sudetenland region of Czechoslovakia in return for what he called "peace in our time." With astonishing accuracy, Shmulik had put all seven of his bullets into the document in Chamberlain's hand.

"Did you run out of photos of Hitler?" Dan asked.

"When I shoot at Hitler, it'll be the real thing." Shmulik stripped the Luger. He smelled of cigarette smoke and beer.

"Devorah told me you were out meeting sources."

"You sound suspicious. Why else would I be out? Do you think I have a girlfriend?"

"Only if she's a communist."

"I have my job to do. It's best that you don't know what I'm doing."

"I don't want to know the details, but I do want to be sure that your actions accord with policy. With the wishes of the Old Man."

Shmulik snorted an angry breath. Dan wondered how much he had drunk. "If the Old Man was here, he'd *change* the policy. Are you going to just sit around, handing out visas and working with the Nazis, until they come to take *you* away?"

"My job is to help people emigrate. We need new settlers in Israel, and German Jews are outcasts."

"So the Jews go to their land of milk and honey, while the Nazis get a Jew-free Reich, and everyone's happy? But where will it stop, Dan? Do you ever wonder that? We sit here in our lovely embassy, representing our country, believing that gives us some protection. What good is diplomatic protocol when Hitler recognizes no power other than his own?" Shmulik brandished the photo of Chamberlain before Dan. "Diplomacy didn't help the Czechs at the Munich Conference. It won't help them in a few months, when Hitler goes back to claim the rest of Czechoslovakia—"

Dan started to speak, but Shmulik held out his hand to silence him. "Don't argue with me. You know that Hitler will do it. Diplomacy won't help Poland, either, when the bastard decides it's time to seize the *Lebensraum* he's always wanted in the east. So what makes you think he'll respect the office of His Excellency Dan Lavi?"

"I have no expectations of Hitler." Dan hammered his hand down on the table. The pistol jumped. "I *do* expect you to understand that any action you take against the regime could destroy our mission. The Nazis could shut down Jewish emigration."

Shmulik didn't back down. "Get it into your over-educated head, Harvard boy. The Germans don't want the Jews. They want the Jews to leave. The only way they'll shut down emigration is if they decide to kill us all."

"That's ridiculous."

"It's not ridiculous, it's inhuman. Perhaps you haven't noticed, but inhumanity is a characteristic highly prized by the Nazis."

"They're not going to kill two hundred thousand people. That *is* ridiculous."

"On Kristallnacht they killed one hundred Jews. Wouldn't it have been better if I killed one German Führer to save even that many lives?"

"Is that your plan?"

Shmulik waved his hand dismissively. "I'm in touch with a few members of the piffling German resistance movement. I can hardly call it a movement, it barely even exists these days. Let's say it's comprised of the handful of leftists who haven't yet been executed at Buchenwald and Dachau."

"If you aren't careful, that's where you'll end up."

"One of my contacts escaped from there. He tells me that it says *"Jedem das Seine"* above the gate. How would you translate that?"

"Everyone gets what he deserves."

"Right. Well, if I ever go through that gate, I'll be in full agreement with the motto."

Dan touched his hand to his brow. "Shmulik, let's stop fighting each other. I'm begging you not to do anything too risky. That's all."

"Like putting my trust in the Nazi regime?"

Dan grabbed Shmulik's shoulders to shake him, then realized the man was close to tears. His anger drained away. He pulled the Mossad man close, and embraced him.

When they separated, Shmulik grimaced. "I'm sorry, Dan. When you move in my circles, you start to believe that all morality is gone from Germany. Then you wonder if it ever existed anywhere. If *we* are even moral."

"It's too late at night for philosophy. You'll have nightmares."

"Sleep is my only escape from this nightmare."

Wearily, Dan left the gallery and went upstairs. From the door of his suite, he heard Shmulik shooting again.

Chapter 14

Anna combed out her hair as Dan undressed. The lamp on her vanity was the only light in the bedroom. It shimmered on her silk negligee. She watched him in the mirror. "You've had a fight with Shmulik."

He dropped his shirt onto a chair and sat on the bed in his underwear. "It's only natural that there's a debate between us. The same thing happens back in Israel when the Old Man's attacked by the rightists from Herut and Hatzohar. We're all on the same side in the end."

"My mother seems to think we'd be safer leaving it all behind. Not just Berlin, but Israel too. She wrote me again, asking me to persuade you to go to Boston. She never understood why I wanted to go to Palestine. Berlin is *completely* beyond her capacity to grasp."

"She always was a sensible woman. You'd have to be a lunatic to take in what's happening here and stay sane." His body felt slack, his muscles deteriorating with the long hours at his desk. He wished he could go out and walk, could keep walking until he was in the desert around Jerusalem. Under a full moon, the landscape there was barren and pale, like the surface of the moon. Here, there were reminders on every corner of the horrors facing his people. An ugly remark from a Brownshirt. A row of Swastika banners on the avenue. A burned-out shop painted with a Star of David and a caricature of a big-nosed Jew. There was nowhere to go for respite.

Except to this room, and this woman.

"I was too hard on him," he said.

She crawled across the bed and hugged herself to his back. He tried to relax into her, but his mind wouldn't stop racing. From Shmulik, to Hitler, to Gottfried and the Countess, to the refugees who came to him every day, each one convinced that their story was more dreadful than anything he could have heard anywhere else—and they were right, at least until the next one arrived to weep at his desk.

His head nodded and he dropped briefly into sleep, into other people's nightmares, making them his own. He was marching through the Chancellery to present his credentials to Hitler, the dead bodies of Shmulik's family walking beside him, joining him from the pogrom that had killed them in Kiev twenty years before. And this time, Hitler grinned and shook Dan's hand, brushed his face with his mustache in a delicate kiss, and whispered Gottfried's name in his ear. Shmulik was there, covered in his mother's blood, raising a pistol to kill the Führer, but Dan leapt at him and took the bullet in his own chest. He shuddered.

"Sweetheart," Anna said.

The concern in her voice made Dan realize that he was crying. "I'm sorry. I've been working too hard."

She rubbed his neck and shoulders. He lay back on the bed. As soon as she kissed him, he was asleep.

Chapter 15

Berlin, August 1939

Dan waved as the train pulled out of the Anhalter Station. The engine's smoke shrouded the children who leaned from the windows, calling to their parents on the platform. A consignment of Jewish youngsters, sent to the new Israeli state ahead of their parents, who had to wait until they could find more money or plead for the official Gestapo documents that would allow them to follow. The couples huddled in the steam and the flow of passing commuters, watching their little ones disappear.

Who's really disappearing, though? Dan wondered. There was a whole life ahead for those children in Israel while everything closed in on their parents. The mothers and fathers huddled around him. He had been in this exact spot so many times in the year since he became ambassador to Berlin. He knew the rush of emotion, the excuses for letting the children go without them, the pleas for help in their own emigration. Always, he let them talk it out and promised to do what he could.

But now he heard a new strain of desperation in the voices around him. The year had been worse than ever for the Jews of Hitler's Reich. They were leaving as fast as they could. Many cultured German

Jews couldn't picture themselves in the heat and dust of Israel. But the US had imposed a strict quota on Jewish immigration, as had thirty-one other countries at a conference in the French town of Evian. These countries claimed to want farmers and workers, not doctors and middle-class businessmen—by which they meant German Jews. Even those who did find a country to welcome them faced difficulties getting out of Germany. The Reich Flight Tax had been increased to ludicrous proportions, so that any Jew leaving for anywhere but Israel would have to abandon two-thirds or more of their capital. Anything they did manage to take with them could be stripped at random by Gestapo officers before they were allowed to leave Germany. There could be no complaints, or the Gestapo would withdraw the "certificate of harm-lessness" which Jews had to present at the border.

Draxler and his two Gestapo henchmen watched Dan from a café on the edge of the concourse. They followed him everywhere these days, "for his protection." Since Kristallnacht, Draxler had spoken to him no more than was absolutely necessary. Clearly, he hadn't forgiven him for trying to stop Anna from treating his little girl's illness.

Draxler sipped coffee from a small glass. The whipped cream on top adhered to his upper lip. He licked it away and stared insolently at the ambassador.

Most of the Jewish parents wandered away across the grand concourse of the station, hugging each other. Eventually Dan was alone with one last couple, their heads lowered, their clothes worn through. When the woman raised her face, he saw a resemblance immediately. The almond-shaped eyes, the olive skin, the low hairline. It was as though Anna stood before him—or, an Anna who had been forced to bear some suffering almost beyond her capacity. The woman opened her mouth to speak, but she could only sob.

The man spoke up. "My wife is a relative of the Frau Ambassador's family."

"I'm delighted to meet you. Herr...?"

"Polkes. Arvid Polkes."

He was massive in the shoulders and chest. His clothes suggested they had been cut for an equally commodious belly.

The fat was gone as surely as his children, no doubt thanks to the rationing of butter to one-fifth of a pound per week and the cutbacks in other fineries. He lifted a big hand toward the woman beside him. "Bertha's mother is the first cousin of the Herr Ambassador's father-in-law."

Dan gestured toward the café. "Will you be my guests, please?"

They shambled at his side into the café, awkward and nervous. Cafés elsewhere in Berlin had tacked up signs that read *Jews not wanted*. In the stations, the signs weren't displayed, for the sake of Germany's reputation with international travelers. The fact that one table was occupied by Draxler and his thugs wasn't considered detrimental to that reputation. Dan sat a few tables away from his bodyguards, and ordered coffee and strudel for himself and his guests. The waiter glanced at Draxler, as if checking that he might serve these Jews. Draxler shrugged and lit a cigarette. The waiter went to prepare the order.

"Why haven't you been to visit us at the embassy?" Dan said. "Anna would love to meet you."

The couple shared a glance of embarrassment. When Bertha spoke, her voice had the same low timbre as Anna. "We were ashamed, Herr Ambassador. Look at us."

"Please, call me Dan. And when it comes to shame, it isn't the Jews who should be experiencing it here in Berlin these days. Your children left on the train just now?"

"All four of them. Between six and ten years old. A boy and three girls." The woman's pride beamed through her pain. "They'll be in Israel within a month. By the end of September."

"Waiting for you."

The bereft parents didn't return Dan's encouraging smile. If they hadn't left yet, it wouldn't get any easier.

The waiter brought the coffees and strudel. The Polkes pair ate quickly. They were hungry, but evidently too nervous to take pleasure in the food.

Arvid wiped his mouth with a napkin. "Herr Ambassador—Dan—may we ask for your assistance?"

"Of course."

"You see, we moved to Palestine in 1934. Things were already uncomfortable for Jews in Germany." Arvid squirmed in his chair. "It didn't work out. We decided that Palestine was not—not a good place for our children."

"Don't be embarrassed. I'm not offended. The life there is a big change from Germany."

"Also, my experience as a stage manager at the Berlin Philharmonie—well, it seemed I would have to take a job with a lower status if we moved there."

The Philharmonie's stage manager was required to heft scenery and instruments, to load trucks and even drive them. No doubt that helped explain Polkes's powerful physique. Dan didn't blame him for deciding against performing the same kind of physical labor on a kibbutz in Palestine. Germany was full of people who hadn't imagined life would get so bad. "So now Israel is the only country that'll take you, but you can't go because the Nazis won't allow Jews a visa to leave once they've gone and come back."

"Exactly."

"I will do what I can."

"Thank you." Polkes reached for his wife's hand.

"Perhaps you're acquainted with my first secretary at the embassy. He's responsible for consular and cultural affairs. You may know him from his days as a soloist with the Philharmonic. Wilhelm Gottfried?"

Joy transported Polkes. His face lit up as though he had been suddenly illuminated by a spotlight on the concert stage. It wasn't only status that kept him at the orchestra, Dan realized.

"He plays like no one else," Polkes murmured.

A deep voice called out from the entrance to the station. The three turned to see a young man sprinting in panic across the concourse, a half dozen Brownshirts running after him.

The Polkes woman gasped. "That's Haskel." She started to her feet but her husband pulled her back down into her chair. She reached for Dan. "His father's the cantor at our *shul*. You have to help him."

The youth headed for the platforms. The ticket collectors braced to tackle him, so he dodged toward the café. The Brownshirts followed.

Dan got to his feet.

He felt a hand on his chest, shoving him into his seat. Draxler leered at him. "Eat your strudel, Herr Ambassador."

The Brownshirts caught the fleeing youth and wrestled him to the ground. Commuters halted, offering encouragement to the Nazis as the kicking started. Draxler sauntered toward the Brownshirts and muttered some words. One of them glanced at Dan and sneered. The others lifted their victim to drag him away, but this man drew a truncheon from his pocket and, without taking his eyes off Dan, hammered it repeatedly into the back of the boy's head. A shocked silence came over the concourse as with each blow, he drove more life from the prone youth.

"They'll kill him," Bertha gasped.

"They *have* killed him." Her husband whispered, taking her hand.

Draxler snapped his fingers and the Brownshirts hauled the body away. A smear of blood marked the polished floor. The killer sauntered toward Dan and spat at the entrance to the café.

Bertha sobbed. Dan stared at the trail of blood. It seemed to him like the shoot of a tree that would split into hundreds, millions of branches, and whoever it touched would die with the same brutality as had this terrified Jewish boy. At first the commuters stepped around it, but within a matter of minutes, newcomers hurried right through it. By that contact they were all marked for death, Dan thought. All of them guilty, and doomed.

Draxler returned. He stubbed out his cigarette in the ashtray on Dan's table and breathed smoke over the Polkes couple. "You two, show me your papers."

"Why didn't you let me help that boy?" Dan said.

"I'm your bodyguard, Herr Ambassador. Those Brownshirts would've thumped you to death, too. Even if you do carry an illegal weapon."

Dan felt the weight of his Mauser inside his jacket. He hadn't known that Draxler was aware of it. He also hadn't thought of using it against the Brownshirts. It would've been suicide, yet still his passivity shamed him. "You could've let him get on the train and go. Why not let him just leave the country?"

The train the boy had tried to reach pulled out. Draxler squinted toward the platform and read the departure board. "That train's going east. To Poland. That's definitely the wrong way for a Yid to run."

"What on earth do you mean?"

"Did you ever hear the joke about the man who sees a bunch of people running? They're shouting that a lion has escaped from the zoo. 'Which way did it go?' the man asks. Someone shouts back, 'You don't think we're chasing it, do you?'" He held his hand toward Arvid and Bertha Polkes. "I'm waiting. Come on, papers."

"There's no need for that. They're my guests."

Draxler leaned over the table and brought his face close to Dan. "And you're *my* guest. But my hospitality is wearing thin."

"That's not very Middle Eastern of you. For someone who grew up in Jerusalem."

"I'm not a Bedouin and I'm not a Yid. I'm a German. No matter where I was born." He took the papers from Arvid's hand. He read them over. "Polkes. I'll remember that."

Draxler took the last scrap of strudel from Bertha's plate. He ate it and licked his fingers, staring at the woman's body. "Tasty," he said. He turned to Dan. "She looks like your wife. Any relation?"

"None. My wife's family is all in America. Safe from you." Dan felt the cowardice of his lie. He avoided Bertha Polkes's eyes.

"No one's safe from me." Draxler lit another smoke, his eyes still on Bertha. "Very tasty, yeah."

Chapter 16

The bell of the embassy roused Dan from his bed a little after 5 a.m. He pulled on his dressing gown and padded to the lobby. Shmulik came up from the basement, fully clothed and half-awake. He held his Luger at his side and opened the door.

Draxler stood on the step like a man arriving at a party, full of energy and bonhomie. "Good morning, Herr Ambassador and Herr Shoham. What a wonderful morning it is."

Dan found he couldn't answer. Something in the Gestapo man's vivacity was too exultant. It could only mean something dreadful had happened. He wondered where the Polkes couple was.

"What do you want?" Shmulik said.

"A half hour ago, responding to provocative actions on the border by Polish troops, German air forces bombed Poland. Our navy started a bombardment of Danzig. Our troops are crossing the border." Draxler's festive energy disappeared. "Now we shall set about killing you Jews in earnest."

Shmulik laughed. Draxler stared at him, offended, deflated.

"No more Mister Nice Guy, huh?" Shmulik said. "Get lost, Draxler."

"If you had any sense, it'd be you who would get lost." Draxler went down the steps to the street. His underlings lounged against the hood of their Mercedes. "You don't have long."

Shmulik slammed the door. "There are three-and-a-half million Jews in Poland."

"Our embassy in Warsaw will be busy," Dan said.

Shmulik stared at him with pity, almost contempt. "What is wrong with you? You're so determined to maintain your dealings with these Nazis, you can't see that they're not bureaucrats. They're murderous bastards."

There was a heavy rap on the door. Shmulik reached for his gun once more. Dan pulled back the bolts.

Countess von Bredow hurried into the lobby. She was wrapped in a man's overcoat, holding it closed around her neck. Her feet were bare. "Where is he?"

Gottfried. It was his overcoat, too. "He's upstairs, I expect. Asleep."

The Countess ran for the stairs. She called breathlessly to Dan. "You have to get him out of here. It has started. Surely you see that?"

"What has started, Countess? The war?"

"The end. The end has started. The end of everything. In war, people stop seeing the enemy as human. They have to, so that they can do terrible things to them without going insane. Germans have already been trained to see Jews as inhuman. The war will only give that cruelty the perfect outlet."

"We are diplomats. Wili has diplomatic protection." Even as he spoke, Dan felt disdain for his weak reply. But how could he resolve this insane situation? It wasn't that he was feeble. If he didn't have a reasonable answer it was because events were being shaped by a man whose mind had no connection to reason.

The Countess hugged the coat tighter to her. "My grand-father, the Chancellor Bismarck, said, 'Moral courage is a rare virtue in Germany. But it deserts a German completely the moment he puts on a uniform.' Now there is war and everyone will put on a uniform."

"You think they'll come for Wili."

"They will come for all of you Jews." She ran up the stairs, the coat flapping against her thin, bare legs. "But Wili is the one I love."

Chapter 17

I was called "Führer weather" when the sun shone with unexpected brightness on the days Germans had some new military adventure to celebrate. The Führer sent cloudless skies into Poland along with his troops, and in Berlin it seemed the blue expanse would stretch on all the way across Europe for the advancing Wehrmacht. But the exultation that had filled the streets when Hitler took Austria and Czechoslovakia was absent this time. Dan strode along Oranienburger Strasse, under the plane trees and the vivid red Swastika banners, and though he greatly feared what was to come, he was no more grim or silent than the Germans passing him. The British government seemed to have finally run out of patience with Hitler's expansion, and French politicians, too, had found enough backbone to force a mobilization, though their military was more worried about domestic communists than foreign Nazis.

Dan turned onto Monbijoustrasse. He pushed his steps harder. He had to be home by a quarter past the hour for Chamberlain's statement. Today was the deadline for Hitler to respond to the British prime minister's ultimatum. Quit Poland, or face war with Britain.

Hitler thought Chamberlain was bluffing. "I saw my enemies at Munich," he had said. He meant Chamberlain, and Daladier of France, trying to persuade him not to go to war and handing him a big tract of Czechoslovakia in return. "They were little worms."

Worms eat corpses, Dan thought. *They will be fat soon.*

He jogged up the embassy steps. The staff gathered around the illegal long-range radio in his office. Shmulik glared like a resentful schoolboy. Richter and Yardeni, who understood no English, watched Anna's reactions. They read the gravity of Chamberlain's statement in her stricken face, the hands she clutched involuntarily at her throat.

"This morning the British ambassador in Berlin handed the German government a final note stating that, unless we heard from them by eleven o'clock that they were prepared at once to withdraw their troops from Poland, a state of war would exist between us."

Dan heard the sense of betrayal in Chamberlain's voice. The prime minister had dealt with Hitler as though the man weren't a maniac with a fetishistic delight in death and suicide and murder. Now he saw his mistake and understood that he and his people were being forced into direct combat with the Führer's evil.

"I have to tell you now that no such undertaking has been received, and that consequently, this country is at war with Germany."

Shmulik let out a breath of relief. Anna covered her eyes.

"You can imagine what a bitter blow this is to me that all my long struggle to win peace has failed."

Dan took in the prime minister's words, but his mind turned eastward, as if he were rumbling across Poland on one of the Wehrmacht's horse carts, watching the battle unfold, Panzers crushing machines and men, the Poles fighting harder than anyone credited. The civilians running. Not fast enough. Now there would be no pretending by the Nazis, no concern for the world's opinion. If Dan could not secure their emigration, Jews anywhere under Hitler's control would be persecuted. To what extent, he shuddered to imagine.

"His action shows convincingly that there is no chance of expecting that this man will ever give up his practice of using force to gain his will," Chamberlain said. "He can only be stopped by force."

Shmulik turned off the radio and clapped his hands. "Thank God."

It was Sunday lunchtime, but the embassy was open for business, as it had been almost around the clock since Friday, when the Germans invaded Poland. The applicants for emigration crowding the hall had hovered in the doorway of Dan's office to listen to the broadcast. They babbled to each other about the meaning of the British entry into the war. Would it make life harder for Germany's Jews? Was their emigration to go ahead?

"What now?" Dan asked.

"I expect Hitler's saying the very same thing." Shmulik grinned. "The bastard didn't expect a war. He thought the British and French would cave again."

"Will they invade Germany? Or go to fight in Poland?" Anna whispered.

"I wouldn't count on them doing anything for a while. They haven't been preparing for war the way Hitler has." Shmulik slapped his hand on Richter's shoulder. "Anyway, we'll have plenty of work to do."

"We all do." Dan cut him off. He disliked Shmulik's satisfaction at the onset of war. He knew what was behind it. Shmulik wanted someone to fight against the Germans as tiny Israel could never do. But Shmulik, for all his swagger and self-assurance, didn't know what Dan knew. He hadn't met Hitler. Once more Dan felt the souls who had crowded around him when he entered the Reich Chancellor's office, the desperate, doomed spirits of Jews whose lives depended on the whims of an ugly man who understood only hatred and force.

"Our task has not changed," he said. "Jews aren't safe here. We need to get them to Israel. Let's get at it."

The staff sloped away, reluctant to leave the radio though it was silent, held there by history and perhaps by fear of the future. Dan settled behind his desk and beckoned to the family waiting at his door.

An hour later Richter came to call him to the entrance of the embassy. He found Draxler there.

"Apparently the Führer doesn't have enough Jews to deal with." Draxler lit a cigarette. "He wants you to bring him another one."

"I'm pleased that he has seen the error of his ways."

"It's good that you have a sense of humor. You're not going to have anything to laugh at soon enough. In the meantime, go down to the basement, where your friend Shmulik keeps his transmitters." Draxler leered, enjoying the surprise that Dan failed to disguise. "Send a message to your Prime Minister Ben-Gurion."

If the Germans wanted to communicate with the embassy, they should have sent someone from the foreign ministry, but there was no Israel desk there. There was only one reason that Israel had been allowed to set up a mission in Berlin—to evacuate Jews—and that was a matter for the ss and the Gestapo. So Draxler's job was more than simply protecting the embassy. In his gritty, uncouth voice, he brought the messages that should have been delivered by a cultured undersecretary at the foreign ministry.

"A message for the prime minister that says what?" Dan asked.

"That the Führer summons him to the Reich's Chancellery. Tomorrow at eleven."

Now Dan had his face under control, but his stomach turned, and a harsh rush of bile spread across his tongue. "What's it about?"

"Maybe the Führer wants a Hebrew lesson. How the hell would I know? Just tell him to get himself over here. Fast."

Chapter 18

Ben-Gurion touched down at Berlin's Tempelhof Airport after a long flight via Cyprus and Trieste. The "Führer weather" continued, but the Israeli prime minister shivered. He was accustomed to desert warmth. That, along with the war and an imminent meeting with a man who promised further persecution of his people, had put the Old Man in a foul mood. The drive through streets decked with Swastika flags and the long walk across the marble floors of the Chancellery only made him more irascible. By the time the adjutant, Brückner, showed them into Hitler's office, Dan feared Ben-Gurion might simply declare war and have done with it.

Hitler was at his long map table, silhouetted against the sunlight through the tall windows. He had gathered a small audience for the show Dan knew was coming. Reichsführer-ss Heinrich Himmler bobbed back and forth at Hitler's side, expressing his agreement with the Führer's opinions on the maps. Beside them, Reinhard Heydrich observed his ss commander's sycophancy with polite attention. A cluster of Wehrmacht chiefs fawned around Hitler no less abjectly than Himmler.

"My Führer," Brückner said. "The Prime Minister and his Ambassador. At your command."

He still won't say the name of our country, Dan thought. *But we're important enough for Hitler to take time from his campaign in Poland to summon us.* He knew that it was Israel's position on the maps laid across the gigantic table that had brought them here. The locale of the new state was filled with historical and spiritual meaning for Jews and Christians, but for the Nazis it represented only a matter of strategy.

Ben-Gurion crossed the carpet, scoffing at the swastikas woven into the design. Dan took in the massive furniture and the décor designed to awe. Hitler's office was even more imposing than the adjoining reception room where he had presented his ambassadorial credentials. A tapestry on the wall showed the Germanic tribes massacring the Roman legions in the Teutoburg Forest two thousand years before. The desk in the corner was the size of a limousine. Its front was inlaid with images of Mars, the god of war.

Hitler drew himself up and stared into the light that spilled through the nets over the tall windows. He did not look at the Israelis. His voice was deep, cast low for deliberate effect, but strangely hollow. "You know why the Third Reich recognized your so-called state?"

"Out of the charity of your soft heart?"

The officials around the map table quivered with rage at such sarcasm from the upstart Israeli.

Hitler turned and stared at Ben-Gurion.

Dan wondered if Ben-Gurion could compass the emotions that had to be flooding through him under the scrutiny of those eyes and the megalomaniacal consciousness that lay behind them. He shook his head. Unlike Hitler, the Old Man could soften his heart. Because he had one. Because he was capable of the human attachment that eluded the Führer. But Dan knew that Ben-Gurion could also make himself unyielding and fearless. He sensed that in him now.

"We share certain short-term interests," Hitler intoned. "Nothing more than that."

"Agreed."

"National Socialist logic dictates that Jews are a distinct race. They live apart from other races, according to their own laws. Reich policy is for the German people also to live apart from other races, so that we may be masters over them, as befits the qualities of the Aryan. Thus Jews must be expelled from the Reich. No other country is prepared to take them, so the Jews must go to your new midget state."

Ben-Gurion's shrug was as insolent and dismissive as a teenager caught with a cigarette. "Israel is small, but democratic. That's better than a big dictatorship."

Hitler raised his voice. "We have entered a new phase of the war."

"You have. I haven't."

Hitler's face took on the wide-eyed outrage and incomprehension of a man who expects the road to be clear and comes face to face with a lengthy traffic jam. Clearly he was unaccustomed to anything that resembled dissent.

"Your aim," Ben-Gurion continued, "is to keep America out of the war. To annihilate France. To reach an accommodation with Britain."

Hitler glanced at his generals. These were his stated war aims. But his face was confident and superior with the knowledge of other, secret plans the Israeli couldn't possibly know.

Ben-Gurion sharpened his tone. "And to divide Poland with Stalin."

The Old Man had decided to give up one of his secrets.

Hitler clasped his hands in front of his groin and stared down. No doubt he wondered how the prime minister of a piffling little Middle Eastern country knew about a confidential detail of the secret treaty he had made with the Soviet Union only a month earlier.

Shmulik wasn't the only Mossad agent who'd been busy.

"I've always said the Jews are the most stupid devils that exist." Hitler glowered at Ben-Gurion. Himmler nodded sagely. "They have no true musicians or thinkers, no art, nothing, absolutely nothing. They are liars, forgers, deceivers. They have only got anywhere through the simple-mindedness of those around them."

"Evidently we have a lot in common with you Nazis."

Hitler trembled with rage. "If the Jew were not washed by the Aryan, he would be unable to see for filth. We can live without the Jews, but they can't live without us."

Ben-Gurion swiveled his squat hips as though loosening his back. He made no comment. Perhaps because there was something in Hitler's comments that was true—the Jews of Germany, and now of Poland, couldn't live without Nazi cooperation.

"I want you to hear this directly from me." Hitler delivered each word with crushing force. "If you join with France and Britain, there will be no more emigration for the Jews of Germany. I will not send Jewish manpower to you that might be used against me. I shall have to find some other solution for Germany's Jews, one with greater finality." Dan sensed a sudden tremor among the souls of the silent Jews who, once again, walked beside him.

Hitler swept his hand toward the map table. "In addition, I will invade your country, and the fate of Palestine's Jews will be the same as the Jews of Poland."

"You want the Jews out of Europe. So send them to us. Fine. But you have no strategic interest in the land of Israel."

"From your territory, my forces could threaten the Suez Canal, the British Empire's lifeline to its Indian colony. Now that I have washed your eyes of their filth, I expect you to see your situation with clarity. I am giving you an order, an ultimatum." Hitler brought his hands to his belt. He rolled his arms, as he always did when he turned up the volume. "If you support Poland and its allies, Britain and France, I will make your subhuman people hostage to your actions."

In all his years of negotiating with union leaders and kibbutz representatives back in Israel, Dan had never seen Ben-Gurion simply accept or reject an ultimatum. Even now he played for time. "International justice demands that the peoples of occupied countries be treated with humanity. We should very much like the Jews of Poland and Germany to become citizens of Israel. But until they do, they are not our responsibility. The world looks to you to protect them."

Hitler threw back his head, an overdramatic gesture of contempt.

The Old Man's voice rose. "But don't overlook this—throughout history, those who killed us were in their turn killed. Those who sought to destroy us were in their turn destroyed. That's not an ultimatum. It's a fact. When the thousand years of your Reich have passed, there will still be Jews. We will not be destroyed."

For the briefest of moments it seemed that Hitler might be forced to consider some new factor. Then he waved a dismissive hand and bent over the map table again.

The Old Man had one last thing to say. "We have a Yiddish phrase, '*A shlekhter sholem iz beser vi a guter krig.*' A bad peace is better than a good war. Whether you think your war is good or bad, your people will soon long for a bad peace."

Hitler showed no sign of having heard.

Brückner approached the Israelis and gestured toward the door. As they passed the ss men, the bodyguards stamped their feet and shouldered arms. Ben-Gurion snorted dismissively as he shambled by them.

Chapter 19

The British had bought their embassy on Wilhelmstrasse from a Hohenzollern prince, who in turn had purchased it from a bankrupt Jewish industrialist named Strousberg in the mid-nineteenth century. As he passed under its neo-classical facade and followed the guard's directions to the gardens, Dan wondered who would become its next owner. He found Peter Boustead and his staff constructing a bonfire of files and papers on the lawn.

"The difference between the Germans and the British," Boustead said, "is that they burn books and we burn memos."

"While we Jews just burn."

Boustead brushed a hand across his hair. It was grayer than when Dan had seen him last, only a week earlier. "Light her up, Dickie."

A pale young diplomat in shirtsleeves and suspenders struck a match and lit the bonfire. Boustead stepped away from the heat. "Even if it rained, this stuff would burn. Dry as dust, you know." He looked up into the blue sky and tugged at his collar. "Führer weather. As with everything else about the rotten sod, it makes you uncomfortable. Come with me, Herr Ambassador."

He led Dan into the great hall of the embassy. Big enough to hold six hundred guests at grand balls given in better times, the Baroque room was now piled with the luggage of the departing British diplomats. "It's like Victoria Station after the arrival of a boat train. Probably would've been moving out of the embassy to a new location soon enough anyway. This place is no longer suitable. They've built up the bloody Hotel Adlon to five stories above us. Leaves no light in the garden and the cooking fumes from the damned hotel kitchens make all our offices smell like the inside of a Brownshirt's boots."

Boustead headed for a corner away from the windows and leaned his tall frame into an alcove. Dan realized that the diplomat wanted to pass on some confidence, so he sidled into the space between the elaborate moldings.

"Your Shmulik gave me a fill-in on Herr Hitler's ultimatum to Israel, after your prime minister left Berlin yesterday," Boustead whispered.

For once Shmulik had acted at Dan's request. The British had to be made aware of the pressure Germany was putting on Israel. He wanted London to understand why Ben-Gurion, of all leaders, would be silent about the onset of the war.

"We must secure as many Jewish lives as we can," Dan said. "That has to guide our policy. Germany's Jews are at even greater risk now that war is under way, and the war also brings Poland's Jews into danger. Not to mention those in Czechoslovakia and Austria."

"Quite. Of course I passed that along to London. I have our response to give to you now."

Dan waited. If Boustead had good news, he would've spilled it a lot quicker than this. His hesitation was unnerving.

"Mister Chamberlain has an ultimatum for you, too," Boustead said.

"Your prime minister appeased Hitler for years," Dan snapped, "but for us he has no patience?"

"I rather think his patience is all used up. No fault of yours, I'm afraid. But there it is." Boustead watched the porters lift a leather chest and heft it to the door. "Israel must join the Allied cause at the earliest opportunity."

"But that means abandoning the Jews of the Nazi-occupied countries. We need German cooperation to get them out."

Boustead frowned hard. "Should Israel fail to join the Allied cause, Britain will—at the earliest opportunity—reoccupy Palestine. That is, Israel."

"You'd invade us?"

"Have to protect the Suez Canal, you see. If Hitler were to get to Palestine—to Israel—before us, it would be a perfect jumping off point for an invasion of Sinai. We don't have a major force in Egypt to defend the canal. We'd have to divert troops there from India— troops that are currently designated to move into Iraq and Persia to protect our oil interests. No manpower, you see."

"I can guarantee Israel's support in a covert sense. But we must maintain the appearance of neutrality."

"Problem is, dear chap, that Prime Minister Chamberlain isn't a foreign policy man. And now that he's been drawn into the war, he's being forced to take a firmer line all over the place. He's already named Mister Churchill to the cabinet and, as you know, Winnie was someone who opposed any accommodation *whatsoever* with Herr Hitler."

The porters returned. They picked up a tea chest and shuffled across the floor.

"Mister Churchill won't allow action against Israel," Dan said. "He is a longtime supporter of the Zionist cause."

"Up to a point, old chap."

Dan had known enough Englishmen in Palestine to understand that "up to a point" was their polite way of saying you had the wrong end of the stick entirely. "So now we have two ultimatums."

"I think my old Latin master would insist that you actually have two *ultimata*. But I see that you've got the message."

One of the porters stumbled and the tea chest hit the floor with a thud and the sound of shattering china. The porter scratched his head.

Boustead looked sadly at the tea chest. "There'll be trouble when the ambassador hears about that," he muttered.

Chapter 20

The roundups came a few days after Hitler delivered his ultimatum to Ben-Gurion, in one of the poor neighborhoods of Berlin
where Jews forced out of their original homes by joblessness and
persecution now clustered. The ss followed Gestapo agents into the
tenements and dragged away any Jew who had previously emigrated
and subsequently returned to the Reich. Such people were automati-
cally designated as aliens, even if they had come back to Germany
years earlier, like the Polkes family.

Frantic phone calls alerted embassy staff to the situation. Dan
saw the roundups for what they were—an indication of what was in
store for Germany's Jews if Israel didn't obey the Führer's command
to remain neutral. He and Shmulik hurried out of the embassy and
headed for Friedrichshain, but they were too late. They found weeping
women and stunned men gathered in the courtyards of the apartment
building where Arvid and Bertha Polkes lived, but no sign of Anna's
cousin and her husband. A dozen other Jewish families had been
taken from the same street. Dan gathered their names and promised
he would inquire with the ss.

Shmulik drove him to the Central Office for Jewish Emigration, but the guard on duty told him Eichmann wasn't there. And all the while Draxler tailed them, leering at the suffering of this detested people. Smirking whenever he caught the ambassador's eye.

Outside Eichmann's office, Dan slipped back into the passenger seat of the car and Shmulik turned the ignition. Behind them, Draxler's Mercedes purred into life again. They rolled along Kurfürstenstrasse and turned north for the embassy.

"The Old Man doesn't know what to do." Shmulik's words were tinged with something close to disgust. *He* knew what to do.

The ultimatums from the Germans and the British. The *ultimata*, Dan corrected himself. "He'll figure it out."

He watched the quiet streets as night closed over Berlin. The war in Poland was going well, according to German reports, but the people of the capital weren't celebrating. They knew this was different from the easy victories in Czechoslovakia and Austria. In a sense, Dan thought, the Berliners faced their own ultimatum from the madman who led them, just as Israel did. They must triumph, or he would consign them to the flames.

Shmulik shook his head. "In the old days he would've known what to do right away. But now he's a prime minister. It slows you down, that kind of responsibility."

"You'd rather we didn't have our state?"

"I'd like him to delegate a certain amount of authority."

"To whom?"

"In this case, to me."

"Because you know how to handle Hitler's ultimatum *and* the British ultimatum?"

Shmulik changed gears angrily. The BMW jumped and Dan rocked forward in his seat.

"Advise me then, Shmulik," he said.

"You're making fun of me. I'm serious."

"So am I. Here are the options. Tell me which you'd pick. We do as Hitler demands, and we can keep bringing Jews out of Germany. And out of Poland, Austria, Czechoslovakia. Or we do what the British want and in return, they won't invade Israel. But Hitler will still hold in his power the lives of millions of Jews and we'll have no chance of getting them out and giving them refuge in Israel."

Shmulik took the car over the Landwehr Canal, a sneer on his face.

"Come on, smart guy, if you've got it figured out, let's hear it." Dan spat his frustration out along with his words.

"I'd order the killing of Hitler." Shmulik's voice was firm and low. "That's what I'd do if I were Ben-Gurion."

"Just like that. Wave a magic wand and Hitler's dead. Problem solved."

"Not a magic wand. Me."

"You're going to kill the Führer?"

"First of all, don't call him that. He's *their* Führer. He's not *the* Führer. And yes, I'll kill him."

"*If* Ben-Gurion asks you to do it, you'll kill him. That's what you mean, right?"

Shmulik stared at the dark road ahead. The Gauleiter of Berlin, Joseph Goebbels, had instituted a blackout to protect Berlin in the utterly unlikely case that France and Britain should send bombers. The Allies had yet to order a single soldier into Polish or German territory.

"Shmulik, what are you planning?"

The Mossad man sighed. "I'm planning on a long bath. I feel like I'm covered in shit every time I go out in this damned city."

They pulled across Unter den Linden. The Nazis had replaced the linden trees on the central pedestrian walk of Berlin's grandest boulevard with arcades of white columns, each topped with a gold eagle. Swastika banners ran three floors high from each building all the way to the Brandenburg Gate. Dan put a sympathetic hand on Shmulik's shoulder.

They crossed the Spree and pulled up at the embassy in silence. Draxler glided to a halt behind them. He jumped out of his Mercedes and leaned over the hood to light a smoke. "Good evening, gentlemen. At least your prime minister managed to escape in time. Maybe you should've run away with him."

Dan felt Shmulik's rage at the insolent Gestapo man. He took his elbow and pulled him into the embassy. Once inside, Shmulik headed for the basement.

So, Shmulik fantasized that a single bullet might solve his problems. *Then it falls to me*, Dan thought, *to think things through responsibly*. Until Ben-Gurion decided what to do, Dan had to maintain the balance here in Germany. He was responsible for saving the lives of millions of people. For every trapped Jew who yearned to reach the one country where he was truly welcome and would be given refuge. They all looked to Dan Lavi now. In the coming months he would either fail them or save them.

Dan had no idea how he would do it, but he would not disappoint the spirits he felt hovering in the cold air of the embassy lobby. He shivered as he shut the door. Behind him, Draxler's cigarette glowed in the blacked-out street.

Gottfried came into the lobby. "Any luck?"

"No. Eichmann wasn't there. Where's Anna?" Dan headed for the stairs to his living suite.

"She's not up there. She's in the basement."

Dan frowned and changed direction. Gottfried hurried back into his office.

Dan squeezed past Devorah's code desk. Shmulik was dictating a message for his wife to send to Tel Aviv.

"She's in there." Devorah jerked her thumb at the door of the shooting range.

Dan went into the gallery and saw Anna. She hugged a small woman in a worn overcoat. A hefty man unpacked a suitcase on a camp bed in the corner. Anna turned to her husband. Her mascara had run with tears.

Arvid Polkes turned and dropped a pile of underwear on the camp bed. His wife Bertha came hesitantly toward Dan.

"Please," she said. "We have nowhere else to go."

Part II

State boundaries are made by man, and are changed by man.

Adolf Hitler, *Mein Kampf*

Villa Marlier, site of the Wannsee Conference, 1942

Chapter 21

Berlin, July 1941

Hitler clapped his hands onto Heydrich's upper arms and clasped them. As with all his gestures, it was awkward, like an estranged father struggling to bond with the children who loved and feared him. He stared closely into Heydrich's eyes. The Obergruppenführer saw that Hitler was trying to transmit some of his power, the mysterious genius that was beyond even himself to describe. He wanted Heydrich to possess just a little of it, for what he required him to do.

Heydrich knew his own strengths and he needed no others, but it was smart to please the Führer, so he made his eyes glow with a new fervor. He prepared himself to be told of a new mission, evidently one of great significance. The room was empty of generals and adjutants and Chancellery officials. He was alone with the Führer but for his commander, the Reichsführer-ss Heinrich Himmler, at the map table.

"They didn't think it could be done," Hitler said, fluttering his hand at the corridor as he moved toward Himmler. "The chiefs of the general staff. The field marshalls. The military college people." Tiny flags dotted the map on the table, representing the current deployment of troops on the Russian campaign. Hitler drove his fist onto the table, grinding the cities of the Ukraine and Belorussia beneath his knuckles. "But even so it's not quick enough."

"My Führer." Himmler drew up his weak chin.

Heydrich knew that the gesture was meant to convey to Hitler the man's pride in German achievements. But Himmler was always an open book to him, despite his show of inscrutability. He was nervous. Like Heydrich, he saw that Hitler meant to divulge something big, something that only the SS could handle. "Our troops are moving at a rate no other soldiery could match. Your campaign is masterstroke upon masterstroke."

People said that Himmler's brain was named Heydrich. At times like these, Heydrich felt a little insulted by that. The Russian campaign was going well enough, but Heydrich knew of the intelligence reports suggesting the Soviets had far greater forces at their disposal than anticipated. The Panzers would have to slow down soon for lack of fuel, too.

Hitler folded his arms and nodded in acknowledgement of Himmler's sycophancy, but his voice betrayed impatience. "The campaign progresses well. That's true. But I need a faster solution to the Jewish problem."

"As our men advance, my Führer, detachments of SS are exterminating Jewish saboteurs who have sneaked behind the lines." Himmler gestured with his small, pale hands toward Heydrich.

The *Einsatzgruppen* task forces Heydrich had sent in at the rear of the advancing army found every Jew guilty of sabotage. Entire villages, executed.

"That's not enough." Hitler spread his arms and leaned over the map. Siberia taunted him with its vastness. He poked a finger at the expanse of the taiga. "I wanted the Jews to go there. One of the reasons we undertook this campaign was to conquer land where we could dispose of the Jews. To send them to Siberia and leave them to fend for themselves, or starve. But certainly for them to be cleared out of Europe and the territory of the Reich once and for all."

Heydrich clicked his heels. "The Central Office for Jewish Emigration continues to work full speed with the Israeli embassy, my

Führer. The Israelis have an endless appetite for emigrants. They also continue to maintain a neutral position in the war, thanks to your brilliance in dictating an ultimatum to Ben-Gurion."

"Quite so."

"As the Reichsführer-ss points out—" Heydrich bowed to Himmler "—our task forces in the east are disposing of Jews in considerable numbers. Those who are not killed are fleeing from fear of capture."

"But there is something more that we must discuss." Hitler drew a long breath, his eyes lowered to the map. The ss men waited. It was coming, the confidence he wished to share, the mission he had for them, emerging from their leader's vision of the future by which the world would be forever remade.

"Emigration is not a plan that can fulfill the destiny of the German people. Even were you to take every Jew from Europe and send him to the Middle East, our task would not be complete. To cleanse Europe of Jews is merely the first task before us. Once the war is won, we must dispose of the Slavs, the Poles, all non-Germanic peoples. So now we ship a few million Jews to the Middle East. But where are we to send thirty million Slavs?"

Heydrich saw it now. The Jewish question was an audition for the ss. They must prove themselves with the Jews, to win the responsibility of carrying out the Führer's ultimate aim of clearing *all* alien peoples from German living space.

"The criminal Jewish race remains within the territory of the Reich. Emigration is merely a stop-gap solution. It is clear to me, despite the success of our campaign in the east, that we will not have Siberia for another year, and even when it is in our possession it cannot represent a final solution. Meanwhile these Jews consume more than their fair share of food and resources. We cannot afford to delay a truly final solution of the Jewish question."

"We can increase the pace of emigration to Israel," Himmler offered.

Heydrich heard the fear in Himmler's voice. The man was weak. He hadn't opened his mind to the tremendous purity and insight of the Führer's words. Perhaps he couldn't. More than ever, Heydrich felt that fate had marked him out to be the Führer's successor. The one man hard and strong enough to lead his race to the fulfillment of their destiny.

Hitler shook his head at Himmler's comment, stroking his chin like a philosopher in deep thought. "There must be an ultimate reckoning, gentlemen." He spoke quietly, glaring at the map as though hoping the ferocity of his vision might burn away entire cities. "There must be physical extermination."

Himmler's knee jerked back and forth with nervous excitement. Heydrich closed his eyes briefly, savoring the moment, like a wine waiter approving a fine choice of Riesling. When he opened them again, Hitler's glare was focused on him. It was like a blessing from a father to his heir, he thought.

"It shall be done, my Führer," he said.

Chapter 22

Berlin, September 1941

T he dark windows and stone columns of Kurfürstenstrasse 116 were brushed with industrial grime. The facade looked like the face of a psychopath, a thin smile disguising the ugliness within. Dan Lavi crossed the street to the former Jewish charitable commission that now housed the Reich's Central Office for Jewish Emigration. It seemed to him that he trod on invisible bodies, some lifeless, others still crying out to him. He passed the black-coated guards from the ss *Leibstandarte Adolf Hitler* standing at attention in the doorway, wondering that they didn't stab at him with the bayonets on their rifles. Surely they were trained to sniff out the genetic enemies of the Aryan race.

The Hauptscharführer at the reception desk recognized him. Dan had made at least one visit to this office every week since its chief had transferred from Vienna in late 1939, charged with repeating in Berlin the success he had had in facilitating the emigration of Jews from the old imperial capital. Still he waited, making Dan tell him the purpose of his visit to Office IV-B4.

"A personal meeting with Sturmbannführer Eichmann," Dan said.

"Go up." The Hauptscharführer shot out his arm and barked, "Heil Hitler."

Dan headed for the stairs.

Adolf Eichmann greeted Dan with a conceited smirk and a raised eyebrow, like a matinee idol in a publicity shot. He flicked a riding crop at his boots and lowered them from his desk, but remained seated. Though Dan was not particularly tall, he was clearly tall enough to make the Sturmbannführer self-conscious about his own lack of height.

Eichmann gestured to the gramophone on the filing cabinet. The record revolving on the spring-drive played the delicate chaconne by Bach that Dan had heard performed by Gottfried. "Do you know this one?"

Dan remained standing. "I do."

"The recording was a gift to me from the Obergruppenführer. From his personal collection. He plays it almost as well as this. Almost. He's a very talented violinist."

The Obergruppenführer. The General. Reinhard Heydrich, tall and blond and head of the Security Service, of the Gestapo and the Kriminalpolizei. He played the violin? *Well, of course he would, wouldn't he*, Dan thought. Heydrich fenced with great poise too. He was as accomplished and intelligent as Hitler was pedestrian and banal. Dan wasn't sure if that made him worse or just—different—in his evil. He forced an ingratiating smile and a comment to flatter the ego of the man across the desk. "I'm sure he couldn't outplay you."

"I'm a very good violinist. But be assured the Obergruppenführer outplays everyone," Eichmann replied. "Is this not fine German music?"

"Fine."

Eichmann sighed. "You're all business, as usual. You're too much of a German, Herr Ambassador. We Austrians know how to enjoy life's finer pleasures, even when under great stress. When I was in Palestine I found the people there less given to hurry than you. I wonder if you ever really lived over there."

Dan had heard this kind of thing before. Eichmann liked to talk about Austria because he had grown up in Linz, the same town as Hitler, and attended the same high school some years after its most famous student. He had also spent a couple of weeks in 1937 masquerading as a journalist in Palestine, until the British discovered his SS affiliation and deported him. He considered himself an expert on Jews and Jewish life and often displayed to Dan how little knowledge it took to be considered a specialist by the Nazis. Really what Eichmann knew was how many Jews there were, and how many ships or trains it would take to move them out of the Reich.

And, of course, his personal experience in Palestine had made him familiar with deportation.

"We Israelis like to think of ourselves as New Jews, Herr Sturmbannführer," Dan said. "Whatever you thought of us during your Palestine sojourn, you would find us a different people now."

"I doubt it. Some characteristics never change. You're just too close to the subject to see it clearly, as I do. Well, I shall accommodate your preference for haste. We have much to do."

Dan took a thick file from his briefcase. He laid it on Eichmann's desk and turned it toward him. "The applications and our approvals."

"Very good." Eichmann surveyed the six inches of paper stacked in the file, each page representing a German Jew requesting permission to leave the Reich for Israel. He ran his finger down the statistics on the weekly summary page at the top. He lifted his gaze and nodded toward a memorandum in his tray. "Take a look at that, while I read over these figures."

Dan picked up the sheet of paper. The memo came from SS Sturmbannführer Rolf-Heinz Höppner, head of the Security Service in Posen, the Polish town from which much of western Poland was administered by the Germans. He read with such horror that the paper seemed to burn his fingers.

There is a danger this winter that the Jews can no longer all be fed. It is to be seriously considered whether the most humane solution might not be to finish off those Jews not capable of labor by some sort of fast-working preparation.

Eichmann plucked the memo from Dan's shaking hand. "You see the kind of thinking I face, Herr Ambassador. If it were not for me, men like Höppner would resort to their 'fast-working preparations,' whatever they might be."

"He can't mean…. What does he mean?"

"Don't worry about it. He is an administrator out in the field. He doesn't see the bigger picture, as I do, here at the center of power. Rely on me." The smirk this time was not vain. It glimmered with malice. "We are a great team, are we not, Herr Ambassador?"

Dan cleared his throat. He knew why Eichmann had shown him the memo from Poland. To remind Dan of his importance. To demonstrate that he needed him—the Jews needed him. And that Dan had no friends, and that there were few enough in the ss who wouldn't rather see him dead.

"We are, indeed," Dan said. "A great team."

An untersturmführer with thin blond hair knocked at the open door and clicked his heels. Eichmann beckoned to him. The young lieutenant glanced sidelong at Dan as he brought a sheet of paper with a handwritten message to his commander.

Eichmann grabbed the paper. Dan read the angular script in the moment it took the Nazi to lean back in his chair and take it out of his sight. Heydrich wanted to see his underling. The slightest of trembles in Eichmann's hand rustled the paper. Heydrich frightened everyone.

"Is there an answer, Maestro?" the lieutenant asked.

Eichmann placed his hands flat on the desk to stop them shaking. His staff called him Maestro for his virtuosity on the violin. Had Eichmann attempted to play the simplest tune now, the bow would probably have fallen from his grip.

"Cancel everything," Eichmann said. "We will prepare the statistics for the Obergruppenführer as he requests."

He collected himself as the lieutenant went out. He returned to Dan's file, but he was distracted. He put his hand to his forehead.

"New responsibilities?" Dan hated making conversation with Eichmann, but the man was in charge of Jewish emigration. His stamp on the papers in the file rescued Jews from the poverty and persecution that was their lot now in Germany and everywhere else under Nazi control. Almost all of Europe was in Hitler's hands—Greece and the Balkans, Belgium and Holland, France, Norway and Denmark, Poland, Czechoslovakia and Austria. In June, German forces had driven into the Soviet Union and seemed likely to reach Moscow by the time winter set in. Since Hitler delivered his ultimatum to Ben-Gurion at the start of the war, Dan had buttered up the anti-Semite across the desk from him, appealing to his vanity, declaring admiration for his bureaucratic skills, professing the kind of flimsy friendship that exists between a salesman and his client. He was thankful that the British had insufficient troops in the Middle East to make good on their ultimatum to invade Israel unless it joined the war against Germany. British forces in North Africa which might otherwise have driven up through Sinai to Israel were being pressed hard by the Nazis' Afrika Korps under Generalfeldmarschall Rommel. But Dan never forgot that a few British victories in the Western Desert would leave Israel vulnerable to them. The ultimatum remained in place. It might be activated any time. Until then, he had to work fast. With this ss officer.

Eichmann put aside Heydrich's note and sighed. "Turn off the music, please. I simply must concentrate now."

Dan lifted the heavy needle and took the record from the turntable. He read the label at the center. The recording was from 1933. Bach's beautiful piece being performed by Wili Gottfried. The lacquered disc seemed to quiver in his hands as if the grooves had been scored with Gottfried's rage. He turned to find Eichmann staring at him in stupefaction. He was holding one of the emigration requests toward Dan, shaking his head in disbelief.

Dan took the sheet. He scanned it and frowned. It had been filed on behalf of a science teacher from Leipzig, unemployed for six years since Jews were banned from the schools. He searched the page for something that would have prompted Eichmann's curious reaction. Then he realized it wasn't the teacher whose details stood out. The signature at the bottom of the page and on the embassy stamp were usually filled out by Dan, but the volume of requests for visas these days was so great the rest of the staff had taken to signing—no Jew was refused, after all. Most often, Shmulik's wife Devorah completed the applications in between coding messages to Tel Aviv. This one bore the perfect penmanship of a man accustomed to creating pleasing things with his hands.

"Is that signed by *the* Wilhelm Gottfried?" Eichmann whispered.

"He's my first secretary, responsible for cultural affairs." Dan laid the sheet on the desk.

Eichmann touched the signature reverently. "I must hear him play."

Chapter 23

Shmulik shot to his feet. "You're insane," he shouted. He grabbed Gottfried's shoulders. The virtuoso sat hunched before Dan's desk. "This is going too far. Don't you understand the danger you're placing this man in?"

"Certainly I do," Dan replied.

"I don't believe this. You want him to play for Eichmann? Now we're *entertaining* the Nazis?"

"Eichmann is an aficionado of the violin. Eichmann is also the man in control of Jewish emigration. As long as we keep him content, we get Jews to Israel. Gottfried is a favorite performer of Eichmann's. His music would go a long way to keeping Eichmann on our side."

"On our side?" Shmulik slapped his head. "Listen to yourself. You're so busy dodging between the raindrops of Hitler's ultimatum and the one the British left hanging over you that you don't realize someone's pissing on you."

"Ben-Gurion wants diplomacy from us, not resistance."

"You're weak," Shmulik bellowed. "You're like an old shtetl Jew, sucking up to the goyim so that they don't mistreat you, even though you know that whatever they do it won't be fair to you. Knowing that they despise you. We're Israelis now. Try to understand what that means. We don't have to kiss their asses. We're New Jews."

"But the Jews of Germany aren't Israeli," Dan shouted. "They can die just like old Jews."

Shmulik stomped to the window. The Gestapo detail loitered around the Mercedes outside, leering at the Jewish girls bringing their emigration applications into the embassy. "It's completely *fakakt*, Dan," he said.

"Well, I agree with you there." Dan looked at Gottfried. There was some new glow in the man's face. "What do you think, Wili?"

The slack skin around Gottfried's jaw drew tight. Suddenly he looked younger. "I'd like to do it," he whispered.

Dan turned to Shmulik. The Mossad chief was unconvinced. "What do you expect him to say? These performing artists will do anything for a round of applause."

"You go too far, Shmulik." Gottfried stood. He seemed to glide across the woodblock floor in a state of complete contentment. "I should merely like to shove my music down the throats of these Nazi bastards."

Shmulik laughed. "Finally you're speaking my language, Wili."

It was Dan who was uncomfortable now. He wondered if it was only his music that Gottfried intended to force the Nazis to consume. Perhaps he had made a mistake. Gottfried might decide to make a statement at his performance, to condemn the Nazis. He could ruin everything with Eichmann. Dan cursed the first secretary's signature on the documents. "On second thoughts, it might not be such a good idea," he said. "After all, Eichmann could hardly come here to listen to you perform, and there's nowhere else."

"The Countess would be happy to host us." Gottfried gestured toward the wall of Dan's room, beyond which was Countess von Bredow's mansion.

In a way he didn't quite understand, the planned performance was getting out of Dan's control. The Countess's soirees were attended by critics of the regime. The last thing Dan needed was for Eichmann to connect him and his embassy with such people.

"So, when shall we bring Eichmann over for the show?" Shmulik grinned.

Diplomatic and political risks were now the least of Dan's worries. He wouldn't put it past Shmulik to try and kill Eichmann. "I order you to take no action against that man," Dan said.

Shmulik shrugged and turned back to the window.

"I shall talk to the Countess about Eichmann," Gottfried said. "She'll want him to hear me."

"Invite them all," Shmulik said. "The Israeli ambassador deals with these Nazis as though Jews were stamps to be purchased over the counter at the post office. Why shouldn't the first secretary have friendly relations too?"

Gottfried touched Shmulik on the arm. "Perhaps I shall play for Hitler someday."

Dan jerked his head toward him in surprise.

Shmulik hugged Gottfried and kissed the older man's brow. "You and I shall make that bastard dance to our tune," Shmulik said.

Chapter 24

Bertha Polkes kneaded the mixture of diced veal and sardines, the breadcrumbs, eggs, parsley, and chopped onions. She scooped out balls of the mixture and dropped them into the simmering chicken broth while humming a tango she had heard before the nightclubs barred Jews.

Anna entered the kitchen, taking off her overcoat. "What a wonderful smell, Bertha."

"Königsberger Klopse. I have to make myself useful around here. It's good to have so much food available. For so long we've..." She stopped, reaching to wipe her tearful eyes, then remembered that her hands were covered in dumpling mix. She laughed in embarrassment. "I don't mean that you have it easy. I just—"

Anna touched her wrist. "If you read my mother's worried letters, you'd think I was already a prisoner of the Gestapo. But I can't even begin to imagine how it has been for you, Bertha."

"Let's not talk about my problems. When I'm making dinner, I should focus on how lucky we are."

"*We're* lucky to have you here. Where's Arvid?"

"He went to the Central Office for Jewish Emigration."

"To the ss?" Anna couldn't hide her alarm.

"Dan spoke to Eichmann about us. He thinks we could get some special dispensation to leave for Israel. To join our children there."

"But you're aliens. The ss would arrest you."

"I thought it was a risk too. Arvid was convinced by Dan. He thinks Eichmann wants to help us get away from Germany."

Anna tried to make her smile reassuring. "I'm sure he does. It'll be just fine. Now I'm going to change before dinner. I've been running around from patient to patient all afternoon."

Anna left behind the scent of meat and broth, but the fear stayed in her nostrils as she went up the stairs to her apartment. She found Dan dozing on the bed, fully clothed in his suit. He sprang upright when she entered.

"I just lay down for a minute and I dropped off. I've been so tired." He rubbed his face and checked his pocket watch. "So late. Almost dinner time. I must go back to work."

She stopped him on his way to the door. "You should rest."

"So much still to do."

"No." Her voice was taut. It halted him. "I think you're overtired. In fact, I think you're making mistakes because of your tiredness."

"What're you talking about? What mistakes?"

"Danny, you sent Arvid Polkes to Eichmann."

"The Sturmbannführer really wants to help. I've built a relationship with him over the last year and a half—"

"Do you even see what's happening around us?"

He recoiled, surprised by her anger. She pushed the flat of her hand into his chest. Not to hurt him, to wake him up. To shake him from the bureaucratic torpor she believed had him in its grasp.

"I know all your arguments, Danny. But every day it gets worse. I see Jews beaten in the streets. I visit patients whose neighbors have disappeared, no one knows where to. Everyone's starving, because they can't work to earn money."

"I know all this. It only makes my work more urgent."

"Eichmann is one of *them*. He is not your friend."

"I never said he was."

"Then treat him as an enemy. Don't send a sweet, naïve man like Arvid to him. What're you going to tell Bertha if Arvid simply doesn't come back?"

"Eichmann wouldn't dare."

"Why not? Are you going to lodge a protest with the German Foreign Ministry?" She spun around and went into the bathroom.

He followed her in. She took off her dress. He ran his hand over her bare shoulders. She shrugged away and removed her earrings.

"I've made mistakes, Anna. I know it." He spoke softly, watching her face in the mirror. "But I'm doing my best to follow the path Ben-Gurion laid out for me. If I'm wrong about Eichmann, then everything's a disaster. It would mean I simply couldn't accomplish what I'm trying to do. He's the man who allows me to get Jews out of Germany—out of all the other territories under Nazi control eventually too, I hope. Please don't blame me for being blind to that possibility. It's just too frightening."

She relented. Her shoulders fell and she turned to embrace him. "Oh, Danny. I'm sorry. You don't need pressure from me. You have enough of it."

"I'm happy for you to tell me what you see happening. Just please don't be angry with me. I'm doing my best."

"I know, sweetheart."

He kissed her. "What's that smell?"

"I don't know. It's not perfume. *That* hasn't been available for months."

He grinned. "I didn't mean you. It's coming from downstairs. I think it's chicken broth. Did Bertha make Königsberger Klopse?"

She slapped his chest playfully. He pulled her close.

Chapter 25

Heydrich was still, and quiet. He waited behind his desk for the head of the Central Office for Jewish Emigration to give the Hitler salute and snap his heels. He pointed toward the chair opposite and watched.

An examination by those blue eyes was like being cut by diamond. Eichmann had experienced it frequently. But he sensed something different here. He was being assessed, and Heydrich was uncertain. Eichmann had never seen *that* before. Uncertain of the task he was about to give to him. *Surely not,* he thought. That kind of confusion could never exist in the mind of the General—Eichmann believed this absolutely. Heydrich was uneasy because he needed to know that his underling Eichmann was up to the job, whatever it was. Eichmann sat down across from Heydrich, and drew himself up. He understood the General's thoughts. He would not disappoint him.

"The Führer has ordered physical extermination," Heydrich said. He paused, a long time, testing the effect of his words.

For a moment Eichmann didn't grasp his meaning. He rolled the sentence through his mind as though Heydrich spoke in some foreign language in which Eichmann was not quite fluent. *He means the Jews*, he realized. *He means all of them. To die.*

Eichmann's work had been dedicated to shipping the Jews away from Europe. That summer he had prepared a policy memo at the Führer's request assessing the possibility of sending one million Jews to Madagascar, annually. The former French colony was too far away, and transports would be intercepted by the British Royal Navy. Palestine and, since its establishment, Israel, was the most effective solution. Ambassador Lavi was extremely malleable—Eichmann was confident the man would do whatever he demanded of him. After the invasion of the Soviet Union in the summer, the option of massive deportations to Siberia had also come into play. But Eichmann understood the pressure to rid Germany of the drag on resources created by the millions of Jews in their newly conquered territories. It was to this, he imagined, the Führer and Heydrich were reacting. And now he was to share their reaction.

Extermination. Heydrich licked his lips, watching him. Eichmann hadn't considered a solution of such absolute violence before. Not out of any concern for Jews. His detestation of that race was all the greater for his work in proximity to them. But he wasn't a violent man. He hated the sight of blood.

"Go and see Globocnik," Heydrich said.

The ss-Brigadeführer in Lublin, Poland. An Austrian, but not Eichmann's kind of Austrian. Two years ago, Heydrich had busted him to corporal for corruption. Then, when he needed a ruthless governor, Reichsführer-ss Himmler brought Globocnik back to command the eastern region of Poland around Lublin.

Eichmann held still. He wouldn't move or show any reaction. He despised Globocnik, but he feared Heydrich would misinterpret any expression of dislike as disapproval of the plan to exterminate the Jews.

"The Führer has already given Globocnik instructions," Heydrich said.

The Führer. It was *his* initiative. Or at least he had approved it. Eichmann remained still, but his heart rushed.

"Go take a look and see how Globocnik's getting on with his program," Heydrich said. "I believe he's using Russian anti-tank trenches for exterminating the Jews."

"Yes, Herr Obergruppenführer."

"Report back to me after your trip to the east. We'll have to make a formal plan, of course."

"Certainly we shall need to understand the dimensions of our task. Statistically."

"We can't just shoot eight or nine million Jews in ditches. We'll need something more efficient."

Eichmann relaxed. This was his field. "If they are all to be exterminated, we will need facilities to dispose of about eleven million Jews."

"Are there that many of them?"

"Six million in the current territories of the Reich. But if one includes those in European countries as yet not conquered, or neutral, the number rises to eleven million."

"Of course, we must include all those. This is the Führer's will." Heydrich shifted his fingers over some papers on the desk. Perhaps to divert his attention from the Jews, or because he considered the matter closed, he whistled the rondo theme of Beethoven's Violin Concerto in D Major.

Eichmann bowed a little in his chair. He felt proud that he had passed Heydrich's examination and was entrusted with this command from the Führer. He cleared his throat. "Did you know," he said, "that Wili Gottfried is in Berlin?"

Chapter 26

Dan came out into the evening chill of Berlin in early fall. He waved away Draxler's Gestapo watchers, to let them know he wasn't going far, and walked along the sidewalk a dozen yards to the home of the Countess von Bredow.

The butler who opened the door looked more like a Prussian aristocrat than the Countess did. He lurched in stately fashion to the salon on the first floor, and Dan followed under the glare of the old nobles in the portraits on the walls. He settled into a sofa that gave off the delicate reek of an antique and waited for the lady of the house.

Footsteps came down the stairs fast. Not a woman's tread. Dan stood to greet whoever it was.

Brückner entered the salon in full uniform. Hitler's liaison to the Wehrmacht angled his head aggressively toward the Israeli ambassador.

"Do you have any idea of the dangers you people are creating for my aunt?" Brückner kept his voice low, but it was all the more emphatic for that.

"I certainly didn't intend—"

"She's upstairs now." Brückner's arm shot out as if in the Hitler salute. "With your—your first secretary."

Dan glanced at the ceiling. Upstairs? He couldn't exactly ask what intimacy that implied between Gottfried and the Countess, but the fury of the young officer before him signaled that more might be happening between the two sixty-year-olds than a game of bridge in the dressing room.

"And now *you* turn up. What the hell do you people expect of her?" Brückner slammed his hand down on the mantelpiece and stared into the fire.

"My dear Hauptmann Brückner, I believe the relationship between your aunt and Herr Gottfried is an old one. I apologize for the trouble it appears to cause you, but I don't see that I can do anything about it."

"You could send him back to Israel." Brückner turned to face Dan. "Get him out of the way."

Shunting people around the globe certainly seemed to be a fetish among these Nazis. Even when it concerned affairs of the heart, rather than matters of blood. "Wouldn't that upset your aunt? She's quite fond of him, isn't she?"

"She's *fond* of peach schnapps. She claims to be *in love* with this—this man."

The last word came out in a stutter. Dan knew that it had been substituted for "Jew." He had sucked up a great deal of abuse for the sake of diplomacy, to protect the chance for Jews to emigrate, to save their lives even. But this concerned love. As he watched the Wehrmacht captain tremble with rage, he thought of Anna in the embassy next door, and he knew that he would rather be dead than without love. Men like this could call him *Jew* and heap their hate upon him, but he would always find an inner strength. He'd find it with his wife, and he would feel her presence even if they were separated. Brückner could have drawn the Luger from his holster and shot him down, but Dan would have departed the world happy, and not alone.

"This man?" He shook his head. "Let's call him what he is—at least as far as he is seen in this country. Let's say *this Jew*. This Jew is the most talented musician I have ever heard, Hauptmann Brückner. And your aunt shows greater humanity than other Germans in responding to Wili Gottfried's talent and personal qualities, rather than to his race." Dan shook as much as the adjutant now. The adrenaline that he suppressed and diverted into the pit of his stomach when in conversation with Eichmann or Draxler, or even Shmulik, coursed through him freely.

Brückner caught his hands together behind his back and paced the floor. The German's breath slowed with each step. When he had control of himself, he returned to stand before Dan. "My apologies, Herr Ambassador. I hope you will ascribe my outburst to the pressures of wartime, not to any personal animus on my part." He held out his hand.

Dan shook it, but he hadn't yet regained control as Brückner had. "The pressures of wartime? I would ascribe it to the pressures of life under a dictatorship which treats all but a small segment of Europe's population as subhuman."

Brückner sucked his lips tight. "You must not assume that I am like that, Herr Ambassador."

"You are Hitler's adjutant. What should I assume?"

"That I do my duty to the German army."

"What of these reports from Poland and further east? Reports that Jews and Poles and Soviet prisoners of war are being executed by German soldiers. Are those executioners doing their duty?"

Brückner went slowly toward a portrait of Otto von Bismarck on the wall. He touched his hand to it. "I am a Prussian officer. I am concerned with my own conduct and the conduct of my family and of the soldiers I command. Perhaps you would say I am a conformist. But my code does not allow me to be one who draws political conclusions and strives to force them upon others."

"So you serve evil men?"

"I do not concern myself with their evil or their goodness." He shrugged. "I don't like the Nazis. They are vulgar boors. But that only makes it more important that I do my duty as a military man and look no further than military affairs."

"But in the case of your aunt?"

Brückner turned away from the portrait. "What of *your* duty, Herr Ambassador? Perhaps you will understand my position somewhat if I put it this way. Do you *like* to deal with Sturmbann-nführer Eichmann at the Reich's Security Head Office? My behavior toward the Führer is a parallel to your conduct toward the ss."

"There's no comparison at all."

"Isn't there? Perhaps it's all determined by the context. Some-one else may see things very differently. For example, what will other Israelis say to you when you go back home? Will they not ask you why you didn't simply take out a pistol and shoot Eichmann dead? Why you did not assassinate Hitler at your presentation of credentials? You will be asked these questions when you return, I am sure of it."

Dan was momentarily ashamed. He hadn't even considered killing Hitler when he met him. He had focused only on the many tasks involved in setting up an embassy, and the prospect of work-ing with the Nazis to transport as many Jews as possible to Israel. He knew how his explanations sounded to a man of action like Shmulik. The Mossad agent didn't seem to care that Dan was follow-ing the instructions of their prime minister. How would they sound to political opponents when he returned to Jerusalem one day? "I object entirely to the Nazi worldview, but I deal with them because I have to save the lives of Jews."

"And I too object. I deal with the Nazis because I have to save the German army. The Jews are your people. My people? The army."

A door opened upstairs. Gottfried spoke a few low words and the Countess laughed. In fact, Dan would've said she giggled, like a girl. Their footsteps and light chatter descended the staircase.

"And my aunt. She too is of my people." Brückner headed for the door just as the Countess entered on Gottfried's arm.

The Countess smiled with delight at the captain. "Hasso, I'm so glad you're still here. I was afraid you would run away while you waited."

Brückner took her hand and kissed it. "I am sorry to say that I must leave."

"It's so late. Surely you can—"

"There is much to do at the Reich's Chancellery, *Tante*. There will surely be a number of messages I must transmit to the front."

"Messages from *that* man."

He let go her hand. "Yes, from *that* man." He snapped his heels, pivoted, and bowed to Dan without meeting his eye.

Gottfried reached out to the young officer. "Hasso, come, let's get to know each other."

Brückner moved stiffly around Gottfried as though they were engaged in some ancient formal dance step. He went down the stairs. Gottfried looked after him. The Countess touched his arm gently.

"So happy you could come, Herr Ambassador." The Countess let Dan take her hand for a kiss. There was sweat on her upper lip. Gottfried's shirt was missing a button over his belly as though it had been ripped away in a passion.

Dan listened to the slam of the front door and the crisp, speedy contact of Brückner's boots on the sidewalk outside.

The Countess led Gottfried to the sofa. Dan sat in a wing chair of some vintage. He wondered if the Countess's grandfather, Chancellor Bismarck, had settled into it to formulate political ideas a thousand times more subtle and intelligent than anything circulating in today's Berlin.

"Your nephew is somewhat agitated, shall we say, by the blossoming relationship between you, my dear Countess, and my first secretary," he said.

Gottfried breathed in sharply. The Countess stilled him with a touch of her hand to his knee.

"Hasso is under a great deal of pressure because of his work at the Reich's Chancellery," she said. "Imagine being in contact with such people every day. These Nazis rub him entirely the wrong way, but he has the disease of duty. It's bred into any Prussian."

"How then do you come to be so different?"

"My duty compels me to honor all humanity, not just my family."

"There are risks in such a perspective. Are there not?"

The butler brought in a tray of hot chocolate. Dan watched in silence as the old man in the starched wing collar handed out the steaming cups.

"You may speak freely even in front of Otto," the Countess said. "He detests the Nazis. Don't you, Otto?"

"They are the shit on my shoe, my Lady." The butler bowed and left the room with the Countess shrieking in delight.

"Have you come to tell me that Wili and I are a danger to the mission of the Israeli Embassy?" The Countess took Gottfried's hand.

"On the contrary, I should like to invite a friend to your musical soiree this week," Dan said.

"Any friend of yours is welcome here, Herr Ambassador."

"Clearly you don't know the circles I move in." Dan smiled. "Wili, did you tell her you're going to play for Adolf Eichmann?"

Chapter 27

The Countess was not eager to allow a senior ss officer into her house, but Gottfried's enthusiasm, his desire to rub Eichmann's Nazi nose in Jewish musical genius, overcame her reservations. Still she would have to visit her anti-Nazi friends in a hurry, to let them know the identity of her surprise guest and to insist that they avoid any kind of scene. It was after midnight by the time Dan had convinced her of the importance of the event.

Back at the embassy, the gunfire from the basement range was sustained. Dan took off his coat. Richter, Shmulik's Mossad underling, sat behind the reception desk in the hall, the Schmeisser machine pistol resting before him.

"Sounds like Shmulik's up against an entire platoon in the basement," Dan said.

"I'd put my money on him." Richter's tone suggested to Dan that he wouldn't wager a pfennig on his ambassador.

Dan went down to the shooting range. Shmulik sneered at him and emptied his MP38 into the target.

"Don't you think it's time you called it a night?" Dan said. "The Polkes couple needs to be getting to bed, after all." He gestured at the rolled mattress and pitiful stack of belongings arranged around the suitcases in the corner.

"Bertha won't get any sleep tonight," Shmulik said. "Not unless I put a bullet through her."

He shoved a new magazine into his machine pistol and turned to fire.

Dan grabbed his arm. "What do you mean? What's wrong with Bertha?"

"You sent Arvid Polkes to your pal Eichmann this afternoon."

"To get a special pass for a second emigration. He was denied before."

"I'm glad you have such good connections in the Security Service. They're really working out well for us all." Shmulik shrugged his arm away from Dan.

"What happened to Arvid?" Dan spoke softly.

"He didn't come back."

"Maybe he went out somewhere."

"To celebrate? In Berlin? They don't let Jews do that nowadays. Even if there were a Jew crazy enough to think there's something *to* celebrate." Shmulik hammered his machine pistol onto the table. His spare magazines jumped. "They've taken him, Dan. Damn you, the poor bastard was safe here. You didn't have to give him false hope and send him into the mouth of the beast."

Dan checked his watch. It was almost 1 a.m. "I'll go first thing to Eichmann. There must be some mistake."

"Sure. You're the one who made it."

"I'm only—"

"Following orders? You make me sick. Those orders are sent to you by the Old Man. But he doesn't know what's going on here. People are just numbers to him. You send him a few thousand Jews, and he sends them to the kibbutzim or to the army. He's happy with that."

"He has a new country to run."

"You're not in Jerusalem, Dan. You're here. These people have faces. They aren't numbers. Arvid's married to a cousin of your own wife."

"Shmulik, you're the one who informed me of the *Einsatzgruppen* in the east. You told me they're dragging Jews out to be shot. They're herding Jews into synagogues and burning them down around them. Every Jew I save from that fate is a number. That's right. A *living* number who can build our new country and keep our people alive."

"One day, Dan, you're going to see a list of the dead. I wonder if you'll think this was worth it then."

"What do you want from me?" Dan yelled so loudly he wondered if his words would break through the soundproofing to reach Richter in the lobby or Draxler's Gestapo thugs in the street. "Should I go head to head with the entire Nazi regime? How do you think that'd work out for us? Do you think anyone would help us? Would the British invade Europe to keep the Germans decent? Would the Russians throw another two million soldiers into their defense to push the Wehrmacht out of their territory and rush to our aid?"

Shmulik squared up to him. Dan thought he was about to attack, such was the throbbing energy in his muscles, in the thick neck and heavy shoulders. Instead he growled, "Come with me."

He pushed past Dan and led him out of the shooting gallery into the Mossad bureau. He opened a safe in the back wall. The file he took out was stamped with the *Reichsadler*, the spread-winged eagle and laurel-enclosed Swastika of the Nazi state. Shmulik opened the file and took out a piece of paper.

"From Globocnik, the SS chief in Lublin," he said. "To Eichmann's boss, Heydrich."

Dan took the letter. "Where did you get this?"

"I have a man inside Globocnik's office, an ethnic German from Poland who pretends to be an enthusiastic Nazi. SS-Brigadeführer Globocnik was here in Berlin recently. He had a long private meeting with Hitler. From the letter, it seems Hitler told him to be in touch with Heydrich."

"About what?" Dan read over the text. "What's Zyklon B?"

"It's a pesticide, for delousing ships and warehouses. Mostly it's made up of hydrogen cyanide. It's completely lethal if you inhale it."

"Why do you say that? Why would anyone inhale it? I don't understand." Confused, Dan continued reading from the page in his hand. "'*Further to my discussion with the Führer, I suggest the use of a more sustainable method of disposal in which special treatment shall be given in the form of Zyklon B, followed by incineration. This project could be carried out on a major scale within a matter of months.*' What are they incinerating? What does special treatment mean?"

"It means they're going to have to change the name of your friend Eichmann's—"

"Stop calling him 'my friend.'"

"—department to the Central Office for Jewish Extermination. Surely you see now that this is their plan?"

Dan wanted to be quiet, to be still and take in this news. But Shmulik's aggression and, perhaps, his own shock, forced his mouth to run on. "If it *is* extermination that only makes our work more urgent. We have to get as many of our people out as we can. The letter says it could take months for this to start."

Shmulik laughed. At first Dan thought it was mockery, but soon the Mossad man was wiping tears of mirth from his eyes.

"How is this funny?" Dan said.

"It's you, Dan. I *have* to laugh my ass off. If I didn't, I'd blow my head off. You still think they're just bureaucrats. You think Eichmann's a banal little paper-pusher who's following orders. When will you understand that he's driven by ideology, by murderous hatred of Jews?"

"It's not relevant. I have a job to do. If I can use him in my interests, I'll do so until the day he ceases to be of assistance to me."

Shmulik dropped into a chair. All energy and color had leeched from his heavy frame, like a bear in hibernation. "That's how the world is, isn't it, Dan? You're used until you're no longer of assistance."

Shmulik's tone was menacing. Dan suspected that it would be the Mossad man who might decide when he had outlived his usefulness, not the Nazis. He held the letter out to Shmulik.

"I don't need it anymore." Shmulik gestured toward the file on the desk.

Dan slipped the sheet back into the manila folder. "Aren't you going to send it back to Jerusalem?"

"I already did."

Dan understood now. Shmulik had cut him out. A decision had been made without him. "And? What did the Old Man say?"

"Ben-Gurion orders you to keep on getting as many people out as you can. Until—"

"Until what?"

Shmulik gazed at the shooting gallery down the corridor. "Until I kill Hitler."

Chapter 28

Oberleutnant Schulze caught Dan's arm as he mounted the stairs to the Countess's salon for the concert. The Luftwaffe officer drew him aside, smiling nervously to the other guests as they passed. "Are you sure you want to be here?"

"I'd rather be at home with my wife, but she's out treating sick children. In any case, it was I who suggested this." Dan was eager to see Eichmann at the soiree. He had gone twice that day to the office on Kurfürstenstrasse to inquire about Arvid Polkes, but each time found Eichmann absent.

He looked past the German's shoulder. The salon was quieter than he'd expected. He heard one man, in quiet conversation with the Countess. It seemed almost that the remaining guests were struck dumb. Perhaps the anti-Nazi bent typical of Countess von Bredow's guests led them to be shocked into silence by Eichmann's presence. "Is he here?"

"Yes, *he* is. I don't know what you're thinking, but I believe this is a dreadful risk for your Gottfried. For my beloved Countess, it's pure madness."

Dan smiled. "Come now, Herr Oberleutnant. He's not so bad."

Schulze's ruddy boyish cheeks blanched. "How can you say that? He's the purest monster."

"Eichmann's an anti-Semite, of course, but I don't quite see that he's—"

The Luftwaffe officer didn't let Dan finish his sentence. He turned up the stairs, shaking his head. As Dan followed, Kritzinger, the deputy chief of the Chancellery bureaucracy, hustled past him, pale and shocked. Evidently the man was disturbed that Eichmann would see him here.

At the top of the stairs, the Countess's nephew, Brückner, hovered on the landing. He shook his head and turned away from Dan, no less angry than he had been at their last meeting and seeming, somehow, even more on edge.

Eichmann stood among the other uniformed men in the salon, a glass of champagne in his hand. His posture was upright and attentive, his face alert to the next witticism from the man who was speaking to the Countess. In his curious falsetto, Reinhard Heydrich was expounding on Gottfried's virtuosity, his style, and the delicacy of his phrasing.

Dan realized that this was the man to whom Schulze had been referring, not Eichmann. This was the purest monster.

The disquiet of the Countess at the presence of such a senior, fearsome Nazi was evident. The blood had drained from her face, a contrast only sharpened by her vivid scarlet dress and long red gloves. Gottfried stood near her, motionless and detached, seeming to gather himself for his performance.

Heydrich noticed Dan's arrival. His eyes lingered on the Israeli ambassador a moment. His expressionless features seemed to conceal a range of calculations, like the secret bidder at an auction house.

Eichmann came beaming across the room. "Herr Ambassador, good evening."

Dan had hoped that putting on a concert for the violin connoisseur would make a grateful Eichmann more favorably disposed to the cases he brought before his department for approval.

The presence of Heydrich, chief of all the Reich's dreadful security apparatuses, disturbed him.

"Why is Heydrich here?" he murmured.

The Countess went to the piano and seated herself. She removed her red gloves.

"The Obergruppenführer is also a considerable virtuoso on violin," Eichmann said. "He could hardly be expected to pass up the opportunity to hear Gottfried. But just you wait, after the performance I think you'll be still more pleased by what I've cooked up."

"I want to talk to you about Arvid Polkes."

"I keep telling you to be less German. You're too much concerned with business." Eichmann jabbed Dan's arm playfully and turned to face the piano. The Countess laid her hands across the keys, as if she hoped it would stop her fingers shaking.

In his white tie and tailcoat, Gottfried settled his Stradivarius against his jaw and gave the Countess a faint smile. At once they went into the delicate, joyous opening movement of Mozart's Violin Sonata in G Major.

This was not the tempestuous or emotional Gottfried Dan had grown accustomed to hearing when he brought the bow to his violin. This was a more buoyant music. Gottfried's instrument seemed to be in delighted conversation with the piano. Dan wondered if the choice of music carried a message for the two Nazis in the room. Did Gottfried want them to believe that he wasn't anguished, that he had found the order and liveliness of Mozart's music within himself, in spite of everything their regime did? And found it, no less, in partnership with a symbol of the ancient German order, the Countess von Bredow.

Dan watched the pair go through the second movement, the Allegro, with growing pleasure. Perhaps he ought to think of his life in these terms too. There was Zyklon B, but there was also love for his wife. There was Germany, but there was also Israel. Why be drawn into the horror? Instead he might focus on a better world.

When the applause for the Mozart sonata ended, Gottfried met Dan's gaze. There was a glint in his eye that suggested he knew Dan understood his choice of music. But then he went into the demanding opening movement of Beethoven's Kreutzer Sonata. The furious tempo presented a vivid contrast to the balance and contentment of the earlier piece. Then Dan saw that Gottfried had sprung a trap, designed to draw in both Heydrich and Eichmann. These men liked to consider themselves virtuosi of the violin, and of course they thought of themselves as connoisseurs of the German composers approved by the Nazi Party. Though even Hitler thought Heydrich had a heart of iron, these Nazis were stirred by the emotion of Beethoven's music. Men who had no reaction to the most horrific of occurrences insisted upon responding to the beauty of the violin as though they were the most sensitive of souls.

Dan watched the final Presto transport Heydrich. Eichmann too appeared to have been carried to some finer place on the six-eight beat of the tarantella. Their applause, when after three-quarters of an hour the Countess and Gottfried completed the sonata, was ecstatic.

The two Nazis congratulated Gottfried as though he were not a Jew. Dan could think of no other way to describe the admiration on the faces of the two men as they pressed around the exhausted, stooped figure of the violinist.

Gottfried wiped the sweat from his brow and held his hand to his heart in acknowledgment of their praise. Around the room, the Countess's regular guests granted themselves hard hits of schnapps to calm their nerves.

The Countess called for quiet. "We are honored to have among us such great representatives of the German Reich." She gestured to Heydrich and Eichmann.

The applause of the group was polite, necessary. The Luftwaffe man, Schulze, stood close to Eichmann. Dan wondered at Schulze's cheerful demeanor. The flier was deeply opposed to the Nazis and considered Heydrich a monster, but now he appeared friendly and relaxed. Dan sensed that calculations were being made around the room of which he was unaware. He grew nervous, as though the floor shifted beneath him. He sensed, also, that it was more than politeness that led the Countess to speak with such respect for the two ss chiefs. She held onto their hands, but didn't look at them. Her eyes were far away.

"Wili and I have so enjoyed performing the work of our great German composers together. I'm deeply thankful that Wili is here in our capital city. In many ways, it's thanks to you, Herr Obergruppenführer Heydrich. Without the work that you and Sturmbannführer Eichmann perform with the Central Office for Jewish Emigration, Wili wouldn't have come to our beautiful city on his mission, and his talents would have been lost to us."

Heydrich bowed.

"It is only right, therefore, that I invite all of you to return for our next performance. I have a surprise for my regular guests. Herr Obergruppenführer Heydrich has assured us that he will arrive here next time with another admirer of German music, a man of artistic soul who recognizes other geniuses such as Wili." She gave Heydrich a great smile.

Brückner leaned against the door beside Dan. He whispered, "What're they up to? Christ, they can't mean—"

"My dear Countess," Heydrich said, "it has been a wonderful evening, and I thank you for your suggestion of another charming event in the same vein. I can inform all of you that within the next several weeks, despite his very demanding schedule, the Führer himself will be delighted to attend the next performance of the Countess and Herr Gottfried here at the von Bredow house."

"God damn it," Brückner whispered. "This is insane."

Schulze exclaimed with pleasure. "My dear fellows, this is wonderful news."

Dan found the Luftwaffe man's response baffling. Schulze detested the Nazis. He clearly had some other motive for his enthusiasm. But however odd, Schulze was only a distraction. Dan focused on Gottfried. To play his music before Heydrich and Eichmann was a kind of revenge on them for his treatment at the hands of the Nazis. But to appear in front of Hitler? It seemed to Dan that Brückner was right this time. It was insanity.

Gottfried winked at Dan. It was like the kiss of a madwoman whose disease was the very thing that made her irresistible.

Chapter 29

Brückner drank steadily as the guests left the Countess's soiree. He barely managed to salute when Heydrich gave him a stiff Heil Hitler. Dan watched the Führer's adjutant descend from rage into self-pity. He seemed to be slipping out of his crisp uniform and polished jackboots into the lederhosen and sandals of a young boy. He was, after all, not much more than that, Dan thought. No one was truly equipped to be around senior Nazis like Heydrich. The menace they carried with them would have crushed the toughest man. Poor Brückner faced the daily presence of the arch-lunatic himself, ranting hysterically or droning monologues about his own genius. The adjutant dropped his head back onto the couch and closed his eyes, seeming to be almost in tears. The Countess sat down beside him, whispering and stroking his hair. Gottfried watched them from the piano, tripping out some dreamy jazz and waving farewell to the departing aristocrats.

Schulze, the Luftwaffe officer, was the last to leave. His collar was open and his face was filmed with a perspiration that must have been at least sixty percent alcohol. He put his arm over Dan's shoulder.

His breath was whisky and garlic. "When the day comes, I will fly you," he said. "Fly you out of here and take you to Israel."

"What day is that?"

Schulze squeezed Dan's shoulder. "Herr Ambassador, with me you have no need to pretend. I despise these Nazi bastards. They'll bring this country to absolute ruin. They don't care about Germans or Germany."

"Then why don't you leave now?"

"Because then there would be no one to fly *you* to safety when the day comes."

Dan felt toyed with, almost mocked. "You care so much about Israel?"

"Don't be angry with me. I'm quite drunk, but I'm also quite serious. My father was a Lutheran pastor. One of his posts was at the Church of the Redeemer in the Old City of Jerusalem. I spent a few years there as a boy. I treasure the Bible and the Holy Land, and I want to do my part to save its historic people from our damned Führer—and from the Heydrichs and Eichmanns."

"Then why were you so friendly with Eichmann? You more or less hugged him goodbye."

Schulze's smile was filled with secret knowledge. Dan watched his flushed, gentle face. He had been sure that not all Germans could adore the raging demagogue who lived in the Chancellery, and he had seen this man mock the Nazis at the Countess's soirees before. Schulze's words represented an expression of genuine love for Jews. Still, Dan was wary. On a night when his first secretary had agreed to perform on the violin for Hitler, the last thing Dan needed was to be caught plotting against the regime.

Then the Luftwaffe man closed his eyes and spoke with a low, firm voice, full of wonder. "'*Saneti kehal mere'im, ve'im resha'im lo eshev.*' I hate the assembly of evil-doers, and with the wicked I shall not sit."

The words of the Hebrew Psalm from the mouth of the German officer shocked Dan. Schulze opened his eyes and smiled wanly. "My undergraduate studies were in biblical Hebrew. I find it's a perfect qualification for flying a war machine while keeping a pure heart."

Dan laughed. "Perhaps that's the source of the Bible's power?"

"The sense of righteous spiritual behavior alongside all the smiting and dashing out of brains? I'd better hope so. I've marked up sixteen kills in my Messerschmitt. I'm in need of forgiveness."

"Then let me quote to you now. 'Rebellion is as the sin of witchcraft.'"

"Ah, Samuel. That book seems to me to be *opposed* to the idea of monarchy and of holding up any man as better than others. In any case, what if the rebellion is against an evil magician who's determined to take everyone around him down to hell with him?" Schulze rubbed his face. "I have to go, Herr Ambassador. I simply ask that you remember who I really am. Do not imagine that there are no Germans to aid you, in whatever project you embark upon."

With sudden gravity, Schulze reached out his hand. Dan took hold of it, feeling the steadiness and determination in it that allowed Schulze to shoot Spitfires and Shturmoviks out of the sky. Schulze went down the stairs, whistling the new Duke Ellington hit, "Take the A Train." Dan shook his head wonderingly. In Hitler's Berlin, whistling jazz was only a little less risky than reciting the Bible in Hebrew.

It was with risk on his mind that Dan turned again toward the trio in the salon. Brückner shook himself awake and hauled himself to his feet. He brushed off the Countess's solicitous caresses.

"Leave me alone," he growled. "If you want to stroke someone, you've got your Jew over there at the piano."

The Countess touched her hand to her heart. Gottfried stopped playing the piano abruptly. He spoke sharply to Brückner. "You should go to your room now, Hasso."

"So that you can slink off to bed with my aunt? Don't you know the racial laws of this country? Don't you know the trouble you could cause her?"

"I know the laws perfectly well. I was one of their first victims."

"You seem determined once more to be a victim, only this time you want my aunt to go down with you."

Countess von Bredow reached for Brückner's arm. "Please, Hasso. Don't fight with Wili."

"Wili? You call him Wili, as if he were still a German. You know he's Israel now. Every Jew must take the name Israel, and the women must call themselves Sara. How does it feel to take Israel to bed, Auntie?" The young man sputtered like a child in his rage.

"How dare you?" Gottfried spoke quietly, but Dan saw what was building in him. He approached the musician, but Gottfried waved him away. "In this house? How dare you, Hasso?"

"How dare *you* call me Hasso? I'm Herr Hauptmann Brückner to you." The adjutant reeled toward the piano, his aunt grappling with him as he went. "You're going to bring the Führer here to listen to your damned music. The Führer, in the name of God. In my aunt's house. To listen to a Jew. It's insane. You're going to get her killed, just for the sake of your shitty career."

"My career? That isn't why I'm playing for him."

"Then for what? For some kind of revenge? You're sick. Heydrich and Eichmann are mad about music. They detest Jews, but they'll use you to wring a little bit of favor from the Führer. For them it's worth the risk. That's how things are with that gang. For the Nazis it's all about infighting and gaining any advantage over the other thugs and bullies who lead the party and hold ministerial positions. But Hitler doesn't have any limits and he doesn't need to mark up any points. If he finds out you're a Jew he'll send you to your death for the insult of being in his presence and my aunt will go with you. You old bastard, don't you care about my aunt?"

Gottfried slammed the lid of the piano down and yelled, "She's not your aunt."

"Wili." The Countess rushed to Gottfried. "Please. Don't."

Brückner grabbed wildly at Gottfried's lapel. "What did you say, you shitty old Yid?"

The Countess pushed between the two men. Dan hurried toward them. He reached for Brückner, but the captain slapped his arm away. "Shitty Yids," Brückner muttered. "Get your hands off."

"She's not your aunt." Gottfried struggled forward against the Countess's body, pulling Brückner toward him. Over the shrieking protests of his lover, he bellowed, "She's your mother."

The wrestling stopped. Brückner stumbled backward. The Countess collapsed, sobbing, against the top board of the piano. Dan stood, rigid, feeling like an intruder.

Gottfried spoke quietly now. "Thirty years ago, it wasn't illegal for a Jew and an Aryan to be in love. It was frowned on, particularly if the Aryan happened to be an aristocratic Prussian. But illegal, no."

Even had Brückner been sober, he might have found it hard to take this in. He was so shaken by Gottfried's assertion about his aunt that he didn't realize the full implications of what he had said. His befuddlement seemed to overcome his entire muscular system. He dropped onto the sofa, shuddering.

"Hannah became pregnant," Gottfried said. "She left Berlin, went to the estate in the Sachsenwald where her married sister lived. When she gave birth to you, she left you there with her sister. Maria raised you as her own."

"No, this is not true." Brückner begged the Countess. "Aunt?"

The Countess wept. Gottfried went to her. He laid his hand on her bare shoulder.

"Don't touch her, you shitty Yid." Brückner struggled off the couch, fumbling with the holster on his belt.

"Hasso," the Countess screamed, as the young man brought out his pistol.

Dan leapt at Brückner. He shoved the German's arm down. The pistol fired into the piano. The bullet sheared through the wires of the highest notes. He grappled with Brückner, trying to wrestle the gun from him.

The Countess moved swiftly toward the man who now knew he was her son and stood before him. "Don't do this, Hasso."

"I'll kill the Yid bastard." Brückner swung his arm against Dan's grip. He hammered the butt of the pistol onto Dan's head. The pain was sharp, but Dan held on.

"You can't, my darling. Haven't you been listening? Don't you understand what he's telling you?"

Brückner snatched his arm away from Dan, then elbowed him on the nose. This time the blow sent him to the floor. As he fell, he smacked the back of his head against the raised marble of the hearth. His vision exploded into bright colors. He blinked hard and opened his eyes to see Brückner raise his pistol.

Gottfried stepped toward the adjutant. He stood before the gun unafraid, as if he knew there existed some natural law to protect a father from death at the hands of his son. Brückner's face contorted. He stared into the calm face of the man he intended to shoot. His hand shook, and then it was no longer rage that twisted his features.

Gottfried reached for the pistol and took it out of Brückner's hand. The officer doubled over as though he were retching. He pounded his fists against his thighs and bawled his frustration and loss.

Gottfried put his hand on the young man's pomaded hair. "Don't worry, my boy," he said. "My son, calm down."

Peace came over Gottfried's face. Dan had seen that expression on his friend's face only in the moments during which he played the violin. He had never seen it otherwise.

The Countess took Gottfried's hand and kissed his fingers.

But Brückner wasn't quite ready to accept such a parentage. He wrenched himself away from them and wiped his sleeve across his tearful face. He shook his head, disbelieving. "I won't...I can't—"

"Hasso, it's true," the Countess said. "My sister wanted you to know the truth before she died, but I was too much of a coward. I begged Maria not to tell you."

"Don't call her Maria. You must call her Mamma. She's still my Mamma." He wept. "Mamma."

The Countess moved toward Brückner, but he held up his hand. "Stay away from me." He drew himself straight and shrugged his tunic back on his shoulders. "I refuse to accept this. I am more determined than ever to serve my Führer."

"Hasso, you can't possibly—"

"You're a whore who sleeps with Jews. You should be made to stand in the street with a placard around your neck so people can see you for what you are. I am the Führer's adjutant and I shall do my duty, regardless of the slurs you cast on the name of my mother, may she rest in peace."

"Maria would rest a lot easier if you'd accept who you really are." Gottfried's calm was gone. Now that Brückner had reverted to the posture of a stiff Prussian officer, Gottfried trembled as the young man had done moments before.

"Are you going to ask me to immigrate to Israel?" Brückner snorted a contemptuous laugh in Dan's direction. He had picked himself up from the fireplace and stood, wavering, against the mantel.

"I'm asking you not to play a role in the destruction of your people."

"I am not a Jew."

"That's not what I meant." Gottfried's voice was raw. "Hitler will destroy the Germans. Within a couple of years, your mother's Germany—whichever mother you choose to accept—will be no more. It will be buried in the shame of Nazism. Perhaps it will even be overrun by Bolshevism. Surely you can see that? The attempt to invade Britain failed. Now look how the campaign in Russia is collapsing."

"The Führer will be victorious in Russia, and lead the German people from strength to strength." Brückner spat on the carpet and sneered at his father. Then he turned and stamped down the stairs to the front door. It slammed behind him.

The Countess sobbed quietly on the sofa. Gottfried reached for her arm and helped her to her feet. Their son's rejection must surely have devastated the two old people, Dan thought. Gottfried touched the Countess's cheek and she laid her head on his shoulder. They left the room without a glance at Dan.

Dan took a shot of schnapps to clear his head. The sudden silence in the room disturbed him, as though he might be caught alone there and blamed somehow for the lies that had been exposed. The soundboard of the piano tinkled lightly as the tension of the instrument worked at the shattered bridge. He put his shot glass on the coffee table and left the house.

Chapter 30

Anna cut across the Monbijou gardens on her way home from her last call out of the day. She felt exhaustion and accomplishment, the two main emotions she always experienced as a pediatrician in Berlin. Tonight it had been a six-year-old who lived with her penniless parents on a street behind the Hackescher Market. The girl had a pitted white strawberry tongue and red cheeks, an itchy rash across her back and a sore throat. Scarlet fever. Penicillin was the latest treatment, but Anna had none. She gave the girl an antitoxin preparation and left her to rest.

The park was quiet and dark. Berliners were home, awaiting another British night raid. The sky was empty for now and Anna's quick footsteps the only sound in the hush. Beyond the lawns, the rears of the embassy and the Countess's house were black masses against the cobalt sky.

But Anna wasn't alone. The perverse Nazi regime trailed her even as she let out the tension of her long work day. She passed a sign that read: *Jews and Dogs Prohibited.* She imagined many Nazis might consider that an insult to their canine friends. It was two days since Jews had received the order to sew onto their clothing a yellow Star of David bearing the word *Jude*. Dogs wore no badge. Neither did she, or the diplomats accredited to the Israeli Embassy. Not yet.

The thin light of a crescent moon lit the yellow benches marked *For Jews Only*, as though a Jewish backside spread infection in the same way that Streptococcus pyogenes carried scarlet fever. She pictured herself crossing the park in Copley Square to the Boston public library and the sense of threat lifted. For sure no one would ever make Nazis out of the Boston Irish. Her family was only three generations distant from Central Europe, but she felt intensely American. Jewish, too, because after all she was observing the persecution of a people with whom she was kin. But the destruction of democracy and freedom in Germany left her with a deeper appreciation for her native country. As an American, she realized that politics needn't be the focus of her life. She could put it aside and focus on the role she was able to play in improving the lives of her patients. It was the world's microbial pestilences, not the political ones, that were her concern. She would leave the Nazis to Dan and Shmulik.

Another set of footsteps approached on a path perpendicular to hers, from the direction of the river. Probably a police patrol, Anna thought. She felt for the American passport she kept in her bag, in case she was asked to show her papers, and experienced a moment of guilt. Why didn't she carry her Israeli diplomatic passport? Because, of course, the us document didn't show that she was Jewish. It often elicited a cheerful remark from policemen about some cousin in Cleveland. An Israeli passport, she imagined, would have an entirely different effect.

The footsteps came closer. Anna saw that it wasn't a uniformed police officer. It was a heavy figure in a long coat, wearing a fedora low over the face. Even those who carried American passports knew that this was a Gestapo agent. She lowered her head and walked faster.

At the junction of the two paths, the Gestapo officer fell in beside her. She glanced at him and felt relief.

"Good evening, Herr Draxler," she said.

Draxler lifted his hat. "Your diagnosis for the little girl, *Frau Doktor?*"

Dan's Gestapo escort was evidently keeping track of Anna, too. "It's scarlet fever. If I had penicillin, I would be sure of a recovery. But most likely in ten days or so she will be free of the disease and she will be safe."

"Safe? Did you give her a medicine that makes her no longer a Jew?" Draxler's teeth gleamed in the moonlight. There seemed to be no malice in his joke. Anna thought perhaps she heard even a touch of regret.

"You ought to ask a rabbi, Herr Draxler. I'm unaware of any such treatment."

"I believe one has been found." Draxler looked toward the Spree. Anna watched him curiously. "Though it's not to be wished upon anyone."

They turned onto Monbijoustrasse. The Gestapo Mercedes sat outside the embassy, a curl of smoke rising from the open window. The watchers were hard at work on their cigarettes.

"You are a good doctor and a good woman," Draxler said. "You saved my Traudl. On Kristallnacht. I haven't forgotten that."

"I hope she's well."

"She's a good little girl and I'm..." Draxler hesitated. "I love her very much."

The humanity of Draxler's statement disturbed Anna. She felt repelled by her own lack of empathy for the man. He was a father, after all.

"I will always be grateful to you for treating my girl," he said. "More than grateful, in fact."

Uneasy, Anna detected an emotion in his voice that she didn't wish to name. Draxler moved his hand as though to reach for her, then pulled it back. "My...my concern for you dictates that I must advise you to leave Germany."

Anna stopped at the foot of the embassy steps. She wanted to be away from him and his need, but she had to know what he meant. She looked along the empty street. "I don't understand."

"It is best that you leave Germany *before* you understand. Once you understand what I mean, it may be too late for you."

"Herr Draxler, I have my patients. My work with them is important. My husband's work here is even more vital."

"Is your life not important to you?"

"My life is threatened? Are *you* threatening me?"

"Not me." He hesitated and glanced at his men in the Mercedes. He lowered his voice. "Arvid Polkes is gone."

"Gone where?"

"To the cellars under the Gestapo headquarters."

She gasped and brought her hand to her mouth.

"Damn it, it's dangerous for you to keep people like that in the embassy," Draxler said. "You should tell your husband to kick out Polkes's wife. Yes, I know she's hiding in there."

"I can't ask Dan to do such a thing—she's my cousin."

"Is she, indeed." Draxler paused, as though calculating the significance of this knowledge. Anna wondered if it had been a mistake to tell him.

"Soon," Draxler said, "Arvid Polkes and everyone like him will be going east."

"Why east? To fight against the Russians?"

Draxler raised his hands and let them fall to his sides. "In the east, the Jews are being…removed."

"To where?"

Draxler brushed his palms against each other as though wiping away crumbs. "To nowhere."

Anna clasped both her hands over her face and shook her head. "Arvid. No, it can't be."

"I'm informing you of this because I want you to understand that, eventually, it may happen to you."

"But I'm the wife of a diplomat. I'm American."

He spoke slowly, as if he were explaining an adult concept to a small child, thinking at once of the clearest way to express himself and also of the innocence his words sullied. "You are a Jew. You told me yourself, there's no medical cure for that. And in the German Reich, it's the worst disease to carry. Believe me, if only you knew how truly I wish that I could—"

The door of the Countess's mansion slammed shut. Dan came down the steps. He saw Anna and Draxler on the sidewalk and paused a moment, before marching toward them. He took Anna's arm. She saw that he sensed her agitation.

"Good evening, Draxler," he said.

Without a word, the Gestapo man turned and climbed into the back of the Mercedes. A small point of orange light flared as he took a cigarette from one of his men and inhaled.

"What was that about?" Dan said.

Anna shook her head. Polkes, it was too terrible. What would she tell Bertha? She opened her mouth to speak, but Dan didn't notice.

"Well, I've had a hell of an interesting night," he said. "How about you?"

Anna shivered.

"You're cold. Let's go inside, darling." Dan guided her toward the steps. "How is the little Frankel girl? Will your patient live?" He smiled.

Anna's mouth was dry. She cleared her throat and croaked, "She'll live." She heard no conviction in her voice. *She'll live. But for how long?* She thought Dan might detect her doubt, but he was ringing the night bell.

"Danny, Arvid is gone," she said.

Now Dan paid attention. "Where?"

"To the Gestapo cells. They arrested him when he went to Eichmann."

"I'll take care of it in the morning."

"Draxler said soon Arvid would be sent east. And everyone like him. What does that mean?"

"I'll handle it, sweetheart."

Richter opened the door for them. As Anna passed him, his machine pistol caught the moonlight.

Chapter 31

In the morning, Richter was gone. So was Yardeni. Dan went down to the basement and found Devorah at her code books. She laid her hand over the note she was transcribing when the ambassador came to her.

"Where are the boys?" Dan said. "Where's Shmulik?"

The Mossad chief's wife shrugged and stared at him, waiting for him to leave so she could get on with her work. Dan grinned bitterly. The woman didn't even bother giving him an insolent brush-off anymore. He glanced down at the desk. She pulled the paper away and brought her elbow across to cover it too.

"Devorah, I'm on your side, you know."

"Then you ought to stop bothering me and realize that Shmulik's doing exactly what you ought to be doing, instead of sucking up to the ss."

Evidently it wasn't only his secrets that Shmulik shared with his wife. She knew just how her husband felt about the ambassador. Dan took a long breath. He turned toward the stairs and his foot caught painfully on a sledgehammer that had been leaning against the wall. It dropped to the floor.

"What's that doing there?" he said.

"Escape tool," Devorah said. "You made the mistake of putting your Mossad team in a basement with a wall adjoining that of a German's cellar. Shmulik decided to turn it to our advantage. If the Nazis ever try to barricade us into the embassy, we'll break through into the Countess's home and get out that way."

Dan left the basement. Shmulik's constant anticipation of disaster vexed him.

He waited at his window with his morning coffee, watching the street. He had to go to Eichmann with a new set of papers soon. Meanwhile, his associate, the Mossad bureau chief, was out with his men, no doubt scouting locations for the assassination of Adolf Hitler. Dan was accustomed to fear. What Jew wouldn't be, when he kept such close contact with Nazi officials? Routine was only a screen for extreme danger, like the procedures a zookeeper might have for cleaning out the tiger cage. But, underlying his trepidation, Dan detected something more sinister, perhaps even more threatening. It was fear of Shmulik, and of Devorah, and of all his own people. When he returned to Israel, what might they accuse him of? Collaboration with the Nazis? Jews worldwide had lambasted Ben-Gurion as a collaborator for fixing the transfer deal. Dan was here, in Berlin, in daily contact with the ss and Gestapo. He signed documents that held the stamp of the Nazi government. They could be filed away for use against him later. Ben-Gurion would protect him, but what if a different prime minister came to power, one who felt no debt to Dan? What would he say then, when people demanded of him why he hadn't helped Shmulik kill the monster?

His reasons seemed thin to him now, more like excuses. He took a sip of coffee and the cup trembled in his hand. He put it down. It wasn't real coffee anyway. He spat the mix of wheat bran, molasses, and starch back into the cup and vowed to get something more drinkable, no matter the cost. No more substitutes. Maybe that was what *he* was, too—a counterfeit of the strong New Jew of Israel. He had a country now, but here he was nevertheless, fawning before the European oppressor as generations of Jews had done, scrabbling to fend off the pogrom that everyone else knew was inevitable.

Gottfried knocked at the door. He carried a stack of papers to Dan's desk. "These are for Eichmann too," he said.

"Thank you, Wili."

Dan packed the papers into his briefcase. They seemed heavier than usual. He shrugged on his overcoat and went out onto the steps. The morning was cold and misty. It reminded him of walks to school with his father when he was a small boy, before they went to Palestine. He remembered discussions of history and Talmud and law, and word games that had made him laugh. Despite his nostalgia he found it hard to believe that he had ever been carefree in Berlin.

He passed the indolent Gestapo detail loitering outside the embassy and headed toward the bridge over the Spree for the walk to Eichmann's office on Kurfürstenstrasse. It was an almost daily trip now, so the Gestapo didn't even bother to track him. Certainly the guards had given up all pretense at protection.

Dan crossed the first section of the bridge onto the island where the city's great museums stood. As he approached the great dome of the Kaiser Friedrich Museum, he saw three men gathered, hands thrust into the pockets of their overcoats. They kept their bodies very still, but it was clear to Dan from the subtle tipping of their heads that they were marking out points on the road and the sidewalk.

As Dan came closer, he saw that he knew the men. Shmulik and his two Mossad underlings. He recognized the aura of conspiracy and knew why they were there.

"So you're going to kill him here?" Dan whispered. "Right in the middle of Berlin?"

"Respectfully, Your Excellency, Mister Ambassador, shut your big mouth," Shmulik replied.

"Hitler's coming to listen to Gottfried play at the Countess's home next week and you're going to kill him en route?" Dan caught Shmulik's arm. "They'll connect the assassination to the embassy. Don't you see that? Our first secretary performs. Hitler dies on the way. How will that look? They'll arrest all of us. They'll shut down our emigration operation."

"Dan, thank heavens I've caught you." Gottfried hurried onto the bridge, breathless, waving another stack of emigration forms.

"I forgot to give you these. Can you add them to the papers for Eichmann?"

Gottfried seemed frail, resting against the railing of the bridge to catch his breath. And Shmulik intended to use this naïve musician as bait for his hit on Hitler. Dan couldn't let it happen. More importantly, he refused to allow Shmulik to put his entire emigration program in danger. "You're not to play for Hitler, Wili. That's an order. Do you understand me?"

Gottfried's features darkened. "I don't understand, Dan. I *must* do this."

"You work for me. I'm your ambassador. I'm instructing you, in the presence of these men, not to perform for the German Führer at the home of Countess von Bredow. Do I make myself clear?"

"But I need to make the Nazis understand what Germany loses by expelling its Jews. To see that we are part of their culture too."

"If you do not follow my orders, I shall have you sent back to Israel. Immediately. Do you understand?"

Shock and anger replaced Gottfried's confusion. "My place is here, Dan. Please. You cannot take me away from—from the people I love."

A sting of bile cut across the back of Dan's throat and he knew it was his body rebelling against him, disgusted by the fear he was instilling in Gottfried with his threat. He had to make this man do his bidding, but he hated himself for it. Poor Gottfried wanted only to be in Berlin, with the Countess—perhaps even to build a relationship with Brückner, the son who had rejected him. But here was his boss, his *friend*, menacing him with the prospect that he might take it all away. The voices of the souls who would be destroyed or whom he might save clamored around Dan and hardened him. "Your duty is to the state of Israel, and I am the one who decides how you must carry it out. Clear?"

Gottfried leaned harder on the railing, as though he might collapse into the gray waters of the Spree. He murmured, "You are clear, Dan. I understand."

Shmulik tipped his head at Yardeni. The young man took Gottfried's arm and spoke gently, "Come on, Wili. Let me help you back to the embassy." He took the musician, shuffling, back along Monbijoustrasse. Richter gave Dan a disapproving look and followed them.

"Gottfried works for Ben-Gurion." Shmulik came close to Dan and growled at him. "Ben-Gurion wants Hitler dead. But you don't. Why not?"

Dan stuffed Gottfried's papers into his briefcase. "You know I'm utterly loyal to Ben-Gurion. But I have to stop this, Shmulik. In the name of God, we have to get as many Jews out of this country as we can. Look at all these applications for emigration. Every one of them means a life saved, a new life in Israel. I'll talk to the Old Man again, but in the meantime I won't allow Gottfried to participate in your plan. You too should call a halt to what you're doing or I'll—"

"You'll what? Rat us out to your pal Eichmann?"

"My God, you can't think I'd do that?"

"You have your mission and I have mine. I won't let anything stop me from completing it. Perhaps you're prepared to do unthinkable things to get your job done too."

"To betray you to the Nazis? Shmulik, get a grip on yourself." But it was Dan who felt shaken by doubt. The Mossad man was right—Ben-Gurion had ordered Hitler's death, so why didn't Dan want it done? It was because he knew, better than anyone, better than Shmulik and the Old Man, that he could still save people from the Nazis. He just needed a little more time. Every day that he could put off the big confrontation, every hour that he could maintain his working relationship with the Nazis, lives were preserved, families reunited. Why couldn't they see it as he did? For the first time he found himself determined to oppose the Old Man. He had to buy himself a few more days.

Shmulik started away from Dan, back to the embassy. "If this thing goes wrong, we'll know who to blame."

Dan cast his eyes down to the cobblestones. He walked toward Eichmann's office.

Chapter 32

Up the marble staircase at Kurfürstenstrasse, Eichmann greeted Dan at the door of his office. "*Baruch haba, adoni hashagrir,*" he said. Welcome, Mister Ambassador. Dan's contact with the Sturmbannführer was substantial enough for him to know that when Eichmann dropped a Hebrew phrase into conversation it was a sign of extreme good humor—except when it reflected insecurity and the need to show off his superior knowledge of Jewish culture. This instance was clearly a sign of the former. Eichmann's face shone like a teen in the afterglow of his first sexual experience. The approval of his commander, Heydrich, seemed to linger deep within him after the successful concert at Countess von Bredow's home. He clapped his hands and ushered Dan inside the rooms where the Jewish Brethren Club used to dole out charity to the community.

Dan took the day's new set of emigration papers from his briefcase. He laid the stacks on the desk as Eichmann settled into his chair and slung a shiny jackboot over his knee.

"Come now, Herr Ambassador. Let's not be in such a hurry. Sit, please."

Dan had never before been invited to take a seat. He pulled up a swiveling office chair from the empty clerk's desk in the corner. It left him lower than Eichmann, even as the Nazi reclined and lit a cigarette.

"Was it not a magical performance last night, Herr Ambassador? The Obergruppenführer was quite enchanted with your Herr Gottfried."

"He's an extraordinary musician, yes." Dan slipped the pile of new applications across the desk.

Eichmann measured the stack with his thumb and forefinger. "Quite a collection you have for me once again."

"We have our quotas to keep to."

Eichmann pursed his lips. "Indeed you do." The quota was Eichmann's invention. To force Jews out of Vienna, in 1938, he had informed the local Jewish Council that they were to find four hundred of their people each day who were prepared to emigrate. He had instituted the same kind of system in Berlin. He required the city's Jews to put forward the names of seventy families each week. Because of Nazi laws against the employment of Jews and restrictions on Jews in the professions, most were now destitute and couldn't meet the minimal capital requirements necessary to obtain visas to Western countries. The advantage of immigration to Israel was that there was no such capital requirement. Any Jew could go, no matter how much of his wealth had been stolen by the Nazis. Which was why Dan's pile of papers grew as opportunities for Jews to flee to the US or Western Europe diminished.

"This lot—" Eichmann flicked at the new papers on his desk "—will no doubt take me until Herr Gottfried's next concert."

Dan cleared his throat.

"The Führer will be enchanted by the performance," Eichmann said. "I'm sure of it. The Obergruppenführer Heydrich is extremely gratified by the prospect."

"Do you not think that it's something of a risk?"

Eichmann frowned.

"The Führer has an…antipathy toward Jews," Dan said. "I believe I do not go too far in saying such a thing."

Eichmann dropped the corners of his mouth, as though Dan had suggested merely that the Führer wouldn't wish to be served liver, or tinned fruit.

"Do you not think, Herr Sturmbannführer Eichmann, that perhaps it is a risk for you and for the Herr Obergruppenführer Heydrich to present a Jew as entertainment for the Führer?"

"You concern yourself with issues that are beyond your understanding, Herr Ambassador."

Dan wondered what was in this for Eichmann and Heydrich. If he could figure that out, he'd know how forcefully he could oppose the concert. "Of course, you know better than I, but—"

"The Obergruppenführer measures all his actions carefully, believe me."

"But why—why do you want to bring the Führer to listen to this music?"

"Do you not attempt to provide your Herr Ben-Gurion with certain entertainments to curry his favor?"

Herr Ben-Gurion. It took Dan a moment to get past that, and the notion that anything other than work and no-holds barred debate provided diversion for the Israeli prime minister. He played along. "Naturally."

"This is our purpose. In this I can be frank with you, Lavi. To entertain the Führer and thus to earn a little more of his good will."

"Might the Führer perhaps react negatively?"

"The Führer overlooked the race irregularities of the baritone, Hofmann, at the Bayreuth festival, because the Führer is a music lover. He even had the fellow come to him in his box. The Führer's favorite singer in the truly Germanic role of Siegfried is Max Lorenz, in spite of the fact that the singer is married to a Jew. Rest assured, Lavi, that the Führer will see this as an excellent entertainment. It doesn't represent a shift in policy. Herr Gottfried is, after all, within our power. We wish to hear him play. It will gratify the Führer's own creative faculties, which, as you know, are considerable. One might even describe them as on the level of genius."

"Gottfried works for me at the embassy. We're extremely busy. His duties are quite onerous."

"It would appear, in fact, that Gottfried works for *me*." Eichmann lifted the pile of emigration applications from his desk. He dropped them down with a thump. "As do you."

Dan imagined Ben-Gurion sitting in his place. He tried to bring the prime minister's scrappiness into his own actions now. "I have instructed Herr Gottfried that he is not to perform at the concert."

"Have you, indeed?" Eichmann's voice was quiet. He stubbed out his cigarette, not looking at Dan.

"I believe it presents a risk to the operation of our embassy and to our mission as diplomats, which is to save—"

"Save? Who do you want to save, Herr Ambassador? Surely you don't suppose my Jews are in danger here in Berlin?"

My Jews. Eichmann's possessions. To be disposed of as he wished.

"Gottfried, as I said, is in my power," Eichmann said. "And so are you, Herr Ambassador."

"On this matter, I cannot alter my instructions. I refuse to allow Gottfried to perform for the Führer."

"How dare you, you sack of shit." Eichmann's voice lost all its poise and restraint. He grabbed his riding crop from the desktop and slapped it across Dan's face. "I'll ride you like a sled."

The whip bit into the skin of Dan's jaw. The uncouth idiom Eichmann had flung at him meant that the Nazi was ready to control and crush him. Like a boy throwing his weight onto the frame of a sled and speeding wherever he cared to direct the runners. Dan lowered his eyes. He took out his handkerchief to staunch the cut on his face.

Eichmann stared at him, breathing loudly through his nostrils, his mouth pursed and hard. He opened the drawer of his desk and took out an index card. The corner of the card was marked with a red tab and the letter *A*. He set it on top of the pile of papers.

Dan read Eichmann's neat handwriting along the top line of the card. *Polkes, Arvid.* "What does this mean?"

"The red tab signals an immediate danger to the Reich. *A* is for arrest."

Dan remembered Anna's fear the previous night. He thought of Bertha, huddled in the basement waiting for her husband to return with their emigration papers. He had sent Polkes to Eichmann. Now the man's card was marked with an *A*. "Polkes came to you at my request. His case is a very simple one. Why have you arrested him?"

"His case *is* a very simple one, indeed. He left the country some years ago, but he returned. Emigration is supposed to be final. When a Jew comes back to the Reich, he does so illegally. He is not wanted here. So this Polkes fellow has been arrested."

"I must protest that—"

"The card mentions that Polkes has a wife. Do you know where she is?" Eichmann flicked at the index card.

"I have no idea."

"Of course you don't." Eichmann put the card back in his drawer. "I don't have time to deal with your pettifogging. I've made arrangements for a concert at which the Führer will be in attendance. The matter is done. I have to take a brief working trip to Poland, which will occupy me until next week. Meanwhile kindly rescind your order to your first secretary. I should be very disappointed if Gottfried failed to perform for the Führer. I hope you will allow him time off from his regular diplomatic duties to rehearse his pieces. Do not disappoint me, or this Polkes fellow shall suffer for it most grievously."

Dan watched the card-file drawer slide shut. Arvid Polkes was in the Gestapo cells on Prinz-Albrecht-Strasse. If Gottfried didn't play for Hitler, the best Polkes could hope for would be to remain in those cells. The worst? Dan knew what they could do to him.

"Gottfried will play," Dan said. "As the Herr Sturmbannführer wishes."

Chapter 33

The walk to the Berlin Philharmonie took Gottfried through the government district. He could have skirted around the ministries to Askanischer Platz, where the concert hall stood across from the Anhalter Station. Instead he strode down Wilhelmstrasse, passing almost every major government institution, the Ministries of Justice and of Propaganda, of Finance, Transportation, and Aviation. Past Hitler's Chancellery and the Gestapo headquarters. He felt like a wild animal on the loose because he was a Jew, seemingly the greatest fear of those who inhabited these looming palaces of destruction. He imagined the Germans on the sidewalk fleeing in terror as a beast of prey loped toward them, rather than a violinist. The instinctual rage of the tiger dwelled in him now.

He passed the old concierge at the stage door. The man started to greet him with a Heil Hitler, but stuttered and went silent when he recognized Gottfried. As he approached the hall, he smiled at the sound he had heard so often before—Furtwängler in a tirade about the musicians' performance.

He reached the corner of the stage. Furtwängler saw him over the harp and the first violins. Gottfried gestured for him to carry on.

The orchestra played the D minor Scherzo of Schumann's Fourth Symphony. As the piece developed, Gottfried heard again so much of what he had always loved about Furtwängler. The conductor never knew until the performance exactly how the piece should sound. Others in his role tried as quickly as possible to let the orchestra grasp exactly what was required of it, so that the music could be perfected. Furtwängler needed to explore the symphony, to enter into it and engage with every possibility and emotion in its structure.

He brought Gottfried along with him. Schumann's music pulled the violinist's heart from his body and tossed it around in the orchestra, returning it to him when the piece ended, energized, beating more strongly.

Furtwängler crossed the stage to Gottfried. He was sweating and flushed, and he might have appeared irritated to someone who didn't understand that the musical score continued to surge through him. His very footsteps seemed to mark out a new coda to the music.

"I need your help," Gottfried said.

Furtwängler took him to his dressing room. The conductor dropped into a sagging wing chair and waited.

Gottfried shut the door. "I am to play a private concert. I wish for you to accompany me on piano."

Furtwängler started to speak. Then he stopped, holding himself back. Gottfried couldn't tell if he had intended to refuse or to ask for more details. It hadn't looked as though he would agree. Instead he motioned for Gottfried to continue.

"The performance is at Countess von Bredow's home. At her regular soiree, where we met the other week."

"I see. Why do you need me?"

"I want us to play together. I want us to show that German music is at its best when performed by those whose spirits are clear."

"What do you know about my spirit?"

"Don't be obtuse. I've heard your music. I know all about your spirit."

Furtwängler let his head loll forward. He could make no counterargument on that point. "I appreciate, Gottfried, that you have not carried a grudge against me since your return to Berlin."

"A grudge? I came back for two reasons. One of them was of a personal nature. An affair of the heart. The other was you."

"Truly?"

"You carry the soul of German music. But so do I. I want Germany to understand that when it expels the Jews, it expels a part of its soul. Your music is lessened without me. Just as I am a lesser musician when I perform in Israel, without you. I want Germany to feel in our music how the country is being robbed of its own soul without the Jews that it believes to be so alien to it."

Furtwängler frowned a moment. Then he stared at Gottfried in shock. "Germany? Who are we supposed to play before?"

"Adolf Hitler."

"You're mad. Damn it, Gottfried, do you know how carefully I've had to tread each time that lunatic attends a performance here? Now you want me to play for him as the accompanist to a Jew?"

"The concert is being organized by Heydrich."

"The Hangman?" Furtwängler laughed sarcastically. "Is that supposed to put me at my ease?"

"You will do it."

"Don't be so sure."

"I'm utterly convinced of it." Gottfried went to the door and smiled. "Because you want to rub that bastard's nose in your genius just as much as I do."

Chapter 34

Rudolf Höss wore the Iron Cross and Gallipoli Star on his tunic and the Death's Head on his gray field cap. Trim and energetic, he led Eichmann across the churned mud where Soviet prisoners of war and Polish schoolteachers and journalists were at work renovating the single story buildings. The cavalry barracks of the old Austro-Hungarian Empire times were being transformed into the central buildings of a sprawling camp.

"The Reichsführer chose the location primarily because of its access to intersecting railroads," Höss said. "Shipments of inmates can arrive with unfettered regularity from any part of the east."

Eichmann glanced across the dirt yards to the rails. "We will need to install considerably more track."

"There's space for as many as you like. We can run them parallel."

"I've yet to conclude exactly what numbers will be involved. But I estimate at least forty tracks. Perhaps forty-four."

Höss murmured his approval. "My main concern is that we should improve on some of the processes I observed at Dachau. I believe we can greatly increase the efficiency of the entire camp."

They walked in parallel to a herd of two hundred bedraggled Russian POWs. A half dozen Death's Head men bullied them across the mud toward a low building at the edge of the camp furthest from the gate. It was the only new structure.

"I was in Lublin this week," Eichmann said. "With Globocnik."

Höss lifted his chin, approving and thoughtful. "He has been very eager to press ahead with the special treatment program."

"It's a matter of discipline among our troops for him. The *Einsatzgruppen* have disposed of hundreds of thousands of Jews, as well as many Russians and Poles, in the last two years. But there's a negative effect on morale."

One of the Death's Head men cracked his whip. A Russian stumbled and fell. The SS overseer kicked him until he got back to his feet.

"In my discussion with Globocnik we touched on the danger with the *Einsatzgruppen* that the men will run amok," Eichmann said. "They dispose of so many people at rifle point and suffer such terrible dreams that it's only a matter of time before discipline breaks down. We can't have that here."

"Certainly not." Höss drew Eichmann on by the elbow. "The process must be mechanized and streamlined so as to have greater efficiency and less potential for damage to our personnel. That is the whole purpose of my operations here."

The Russians tripped down the steps in silence, into the new built chamber. A Death's Head man slammed the door shut and pushed home the locking arm.

Höss led Eichmann to the door. "I understand exactly Globocnik's point about the *Einsatzgruppen* and their morale. I must admit that the gassing process you're about to witness has a calming effect on me. I always had a horror of the shootings, thinking of the number of people, the women and children. I am relieved that we are to be spared those bloodbaths."

The Death's Head men were on the roof of the building. Höss gave a signal to one of them. The trooper stumped away, calling to his comrades who had spread along the length of the chamber. They unscrewed the lids of the yellow tubs at their feet.

"Zyklon B?" Eichmann asked.

The Death's Head men tipped the contents of the tubs into trays set in the roof and kicked the lids shut.

"They're feeding the pellets in now. Much better than the diesel engine they've been experimenting with at Treblinka. That simply doesn't work much of the time, and anyway we need the diesel for our Panzers. This stuff is quicker, too. Drop it in, and death comes within moments. See for yourself."

Eichmann put his eye to a window the size of a slice of bread. Through the door he saw the Russians grouped tightly in the center of the large chamber, jostling each other.

"By a quite splendid irony, Zyklon B was developed for pest control," Höss remarked. "That's rather good, isn't it?"

The Russians shouted, their voices emerging only faintly, muffled, from the chamber. "*Gaz, gaz.*" They ran for the door, trampling each other, every man desperate to save himself. They charged against the door, hammering at it with their fists.

Eichmann recoiled. "They'll break the door down," he said. "The gas, we'll breathe it."

Höss looked alarmed. The door shuddered, but held. The screams of the men inside became a low hum, like an approaching swarm of bees. Gradually, the sound dropped off.

Höss glanced through the window. "It seems to be all right. Take another look."

Eichmann watched the men writhe on the bare concrete. He rested a hand on the door and let it take his weight. His knees wouldn't hold him. The death before him was too much. He whispered to himself, "I believe in Jesus Christ. He was conceived of the Holy Spirit and was born of the Virgin Mary. He was crucified and rose again and shall come to judge the quick and the dead."

Höss slapped a hand on Eichmann's shoulder. "I can read your lips, Herr Sturmbannführer, and I, too, was raised a Catholic. Don't worry. It hits you hard at first. Try to think in terms of the process, rather than the individual suffering. And imagine how much worse it would be for these wretches if they were being buried half-alive in a pile with naked women and children all around them."

Eichmann shuddered. "You're right, of course."

"I draw your attention to the economy of this entire process," Höss said. "Thirteen cases of Zyklon B weighing 195 kilos cost 975 reichsmarks. Five kilos is sufficient for special treatment of 1,500 people in a single gas chamber. Thus, for a little less than one thousand reichsmarks, we can dispose of 42,000 Jews."

"Very good."

Höss unfolded a blueprint. "Based on the preliminary numbers you sent me—and I accept that they're only preliminary—we ought to consider dividing the camp into three. Here we will construct the extermination chambers for the camp as a whole. You have observed the gas chamber. I propose to construct three more immediately. We also need to improve on the disposal of the bodies. You and I must consult on the design of crematoria to incinerate the bodies. They must be extremely powerful because of the sheer numbers involved. One point on that score—the Zyklon B works optimally at twenty-six degrees Celsius. My suggestion to the engineers would be to funnel the heat from the crematoria back to the gas chambers, thus warming them to the correct temperature for the Zyklon B to function at maximum efficiency." He gestured to the southeast. "May we now address the factory for IG Farben?"

"The tax exemptions have gone through for IG. The Reichsführer-ss is most eager for German companies to receive incentives to expand into the east. These, after all, will constitute the ss lands, our state. Where do you intend to build the factory?"

"Just beyond the Vienna-Krakow rail line and the village of Auschwitz. The factory is designed to be operated by slave labor, of course."

"Good. Construction can begin right away. IG is the biggest industrial company in the Reich. Reichsführer Himmler is sure its involvement at Auschwitz will set a precedent for other German companies to work either in the east or with slave labor. Thyssen and Krupp are interested, for example. There is also a possibility of involving the German subsidiaries of Ford and General Motors."

Malnourished, middle-aged Poles dragged the dead Russians out of the gas chamber. Eichmann turned away.

Höss folded the plans. "You can take these back to Berlin to show to the Reichsführer."

"Very good." Eichmann gripped the blueprints hard to steady his shaking hands.

Chapter 35

The air-raid sirens wailed from the flak towers just after midnight. Dan and Anna dressed hurriedly and went down to the embassy basement. They joined the rest of the staff in the shooting gallery, dragging out the cushions and thin mattresses that Yardeni had rustled up after the first raids, more than a year earlier. Only one of the Israelis was absent.

"Where's Wili?" Anna said.

"He's with the Countess." Devorah smirked. "If a bomb lands anywhere near here, our Wili will think it's just the earth moving for him."

Shmulik laughed at his wife's ribaldry. Anna blushed.

They settled down, listening for the first blast. When it came, it was distant, a low grumble like thunder amid the popping of the anti-aircraft guns.

"Charlottenburg," Shmulik said. The bombs were falling to the west, on the bourgeoisie, the nightclubs, the department stores.

The next impacts were closer, moving like giant footfalls down the center of the city.

"What are they trying to hit?" Anna said. "What's the target? There are no factories here. No armaments works."

"The Germans bombed London to sew terror. I'd say the Royal Air Force is content to let the Germans know, in return, that they aren't safe anywhere. Except down in the Führer's bunker."

Dan hugged his shivering wife. It was because of him that she was in a basement under bombardment from the air. She might have immigrated to Israel anyway had she never met him in the Harvard library, but most likely she'd still be in America, treating the sicknesses of small children at a hospital in New England. The worst discomfort she'd have faced would have been indigestion after too many pancakes at the diner.

"It's okay, sweetheart," he said, in English.

She pressed her head to his chest as the bombs crept across town.

The sirens carried on, but the explosions halted. Then the all-clear came. Shmulik got to his feet and stretched his back.

"A sound more welcome than the shofar at the end of Yom Kippur," Dan said.

"If God has inscribed you in the book of life for another year, you're the luckiest Jew in Berlin." Shmulik reached for Devorah's hand to help her to her feet.

A massive blast sounded above them. The pound and roll and thud of falling walls and crushing wood and flying glass echoed through the basement. The lights went out and Dan felt a spray of dust enfold him. Anna gasped and held tightly to him.

Devorah shrieked. Shmulik grabbed her. "Get out of here," he yelled. "The embassy must've been hit."

Dan took hold of his wife and they stumbled to the stairs. Once upstairs in the lobby, they found the building was still intact.

"But it was so loud," Anna said. "Didn't it hit us?"

The sound of sliding masonry continued nearby. Dan rushed to the door and went out into the street. The hood of the Gestapo Mercedes had been crushed by a chunk of granite the size of a man and was almost enveloped by debris. Dan and Shmulik forced the door open and dragged Draxler out of the car. Blood ran from a wound on his head. They laid him on the sidewalk. Anna crouched over him, tending to him. Her hand trembled as she stanched the bleeding. Draxler opened his eyes. He looked up at Anna with longing.

Rubble had folded a second Gestapo man forward in the passenger seat. Shmulik and Dan wrenched at the stones. When they came away, they found the man's head crushed inside his fedora.

Dan turned away from the sight and blinked through the cloud of dust. His embassy was standing, though the windows of every floor were shattered, but the house next door lay in ruins. The walls they had heard tumbling belonged to the Countess's home. The bomb seemed to have landed at the furthest corner of the building, carving it into an ellipse, with the tall side buttressed by the embassy.

"Wili and the Countess—they'll be in the basement," Dan said. "We have to get them out."

Shmulik stared at the destruction of the von Bredow home. At its lowest, the pile of stone was deeper than a man's height. "We'll never get through that."

"Let's go in from our basement." Dan ran back up the steps to the embassy.

"That's my office," Shmulik called. "There are classified items in there. We can't just smash a hole in the wall. It's not safe."

Dan shook his head. Shmulik worried more about security than his colleague's life. But the Mossad man was never swayed by anger—he had enough himself to outlast anyone who tried to berate him into conceding. So Dan shut his eyes a moment and calmed himself.

He turned back and took hold of Shmulik's shoulder. "You want to kill Hitler?"

"At a time like this you're still trying to talk me out of—"

"I don't know how you're going to kill Hitler, but I *do* know that you're going to do it somehow when he's on his way to or from Gottfried's performance."

Shmulik stared at the rubble, a scowl on his face, and Dan knew he had guessed right. The plan to assassinate the Führer was in the same state of collapse as the von Bredow mansion, unless they could get Gottfried out alive. "All right," Shmulik said. "Let's go."

They returned to the embassy. Shmulik called Yardeni and Richter after them. They descended to the basement. Devorah followed.

"Get out of here," Shmulik called to her. "We don't know if the building's safe yet."

"You don't know how to handle my code books. And I'm not so delicate. I'll take care of this." Devorah gathered the thick pads from her desk and bundled them up.

Shmulik called to Richter, "Yossi, get all the documents from down here and burn them in the garden."

Yardeni braced his feet as he stood beside the connecting wall to the basement of the Countess's house. He swung the sledgehammer at the center of the wall again and again. Within minutes, he was through both layers of brick. A thick puff of dust blew out of the hole he created, heavy air that lingered in the von Bredow mansion after the explosions.

Dan called through to the Countess's basement. "Wili, Countess, are you there?"

Someone coughed in the dust beyond the breach.

"Make this hole big enough for me to get through," Dan said.

Yardeni hammered away another section of brick. Dan slithered though and rolled onto the floor. Chunks of fallen masonry dug into his back. He came to his knees.

"That hole has to be bigger," he said. "We need to get them out that way. Keep at it."

Yardeni went back to work on the bricks.

Dan crept through the dark space by the dim light from the embassy basement, then entered a second room where he had to move by feel only. Stepping forward, he bumped into a large, upright wine rack. Off balance already because of the bombing, the bottles tumbled to the floor and smashed. The tannins of the spilled wine attached to the dust and made him sputter.

But the noise caught the attention of someone across the room.

A woman mumbled, "Who's that?"

Dan shuffled toward her. "Countess von Bredow?"

"Here."

He came to the woman. She clutched at him. "Wili. Help Wili."

"Was he with you?"

She directed her eyes down along her body to the rubble that covered her middle. "There. He's there."

Dan fumbled to clear the fallen bricks from the woman. A man lay over her, pinning her to the floor. Wili Gottfried's features were coated in dust, and still. He must have thrown himself across his lover to protect her as the bomb exploded. Dan lifted him and lay him beside the Countess.

"Is he alive?" she said.

The violinist's pulse was dim. But it was there. "He's alive."

"His hands? Are his fingers injured?"

The fingers that played the violin. Her insistent grip on his shirt forced Dan to reply. "I believe his hands are undamaged, Countess."

He picked up a glimmer of light reflected back from Gottfried's eyes. They were open. A ragged breath caught in the man's throat. He lifted his hand and pointed beyond the Countess.

"My Stradivarius," he croaked. "I must save it."

Dan half-smiled. He would have been only mildly surprised if Gottfried's dive in the dark basement had been intended to save his violin, rather than his lover. Dan picked up the Countess. Gottfried lifted his violin case and came to his feet unsteadily. He held the case to his chest and swayed in the darkness as though cradling a restless infant. Then he followed Dan through the dust, into the embassy basement.

Chapter 36

Anna tended the Countess on the couch in Dan's office while Gottfried stared out of the shattered window at the dawn illuminating the rubble on the street. His violin case lay on the desk. Dan ran his fingers across the leather, pitted and scratched from the collapse of the building next door. From the basement came the dull sound of trowel on brick as Yardeni and Richter resealed the breech in the wall.

Devorah dragged tiredly up the stairs. She looked about for her husband.

"He'll be back soon, Devorah," Dan said. "Don't worry about him."

"He took Draxler to the hospital, and you think I shouldn't worry?" She rolled her lip with her customary disdain. "I'm going to see if there are any documents that didn't burn." She left in the direction of the garden.

Dan smiled. At least the embassy hadn't burned. That was something to be grateful for. The bombs hadn't been incendiaries that light up their targets and start a firestorm across an entire city.

He heard heavy footsteps running down the street. Shmulik lumbered to the front of the embassy, out of breath. He saw Dan's face in the window and shook his head, grimly. Dan met him at the door of his office.

"It's starting," Shmulik said.

Dan didn't have to ask what "it" was. He had known it would come. "Deportations?"

"The Nazis are rounding up Jews. On my way back from St. Hedwig I saw some people being loaded into trucks, just round the corner."

"Draxler?"

"The hospital says your friend's going to be just fine."

Dan didn't bother to react to the sarcasm. "The roundup—how many people?"

"I asked the driver. He told me they'd picked up a lot of people in Friedrichshain already. He reckoned they'd have a few thousand before Berlin wakes up to go to work. They're trucking them to the Anhalter Station."

"We need to find out how many people."

Shmulik fixed a look of pain and disgust on Dan. "You're getting more and more like *them*. Like Eichmann and his Nazi bureaucrats. What does it matter *how many* people are being taken away?"

"Some of them might have made applications for emigration to Israel. We could be able to stop it that way. To go and pull them out of there."

The Countess whimpered. "I'm ashamed. Ashamed to be a German."

Anna stroked the exhausted woman's face. "You need to stay calm now, Hannah. Please, relax. You've had a big shock."

"How can I relax when my people are doing such things?"

Shmulik glared at the Countess. Dan understood. For his Mossad chief, there was no German left untainted by this persecution of Jews. No German who could be redeemed by their professions of shame. They were all in it, just as all Jews were on the receiving end of it.

The Countess reached out her hand toward Gottfried. "Our boy, Wili. Our boy must help."

"*Our boy* is locked away with his Führer." Gottfried turned from the street. "Locked away from us."

"Then we are the ones who must take care of this."

"What on earth do you mean, Hannah?"

The Countess glanced at the violin case on the desk. Though her home lay in ruins, she clearly hadn't given up on the idea of a concert for the Führer.

Shmulik stomped to the door. "I'm going to the Anhalter Station to see what I can do there."

Dan grabbed his jacket. "Very well. I'm going to Eichmann."

He ran out of the embassy and sprinted toward the river. How many people were being taken away? A few thousand, as the ss driver told Shmulik? There was no number that would surprise him. There was no limit to the horror he believed the Nazis capable of. He would try to find out an exact figure later. He'd send Richter and Yardeni out to canvass the communities. It wouldn't be easy. Berlin's Jews had never been segregated as they were elsewhere in Germany. There was no Jewish Quarter and certainly no ghetto. There were 160,000 Jews in Berlin and they lived everywhere. Soon, Dan thought, they might live nowhere.

Exhausted from his night digging through the rubble of the Countess's home, he lost his strength on Unter den Linden. He leapt into a cab for the last stretch. "Kurfürstenstrasse 116, quickly," he called.

It was 6 a.m. The cab pulled away, driving swiftly under the camouflage netting. The central East-West boulevards that Hitler had intended to use for grand parades were perfect orienting devices for British bombers, so they had been disguised. To drive along them under the green and gray nets brought the war home, even if you were on your way back from a show at the Metropol or the Kadeko.

They passed a truck with a pair of ss men in the cab. Dan twisted around to see inside its covered rear. It was crowded with civilians. They looked like all other Berliners, but Dan knew they were Jews. They stood, huddled, holding each other against the rocking of the vehicle as it turned south. Half of Berlin lay that way, but Dan knew the truck was headed for the Anhalter Station and the lines to the east.

"Picking up a lot of Yids this morning," the driver said.

Dan cleared his throat. "Where are they going?"

"Well, they aren't off to Prora for a vacation." The driver laughed. Prora was the Nazi beach resort on an island off the Pomeranian coast, a reward for good behavior to German workers, an incentive that made people feel the Reich valued their happiness.

The taxi rattled through the leafy Tiergarten Park. When they reached the Siegessäule, Dan saw that the Goddess of Victory on her tall pillar had been stripped of her gold leaf. Another precaution to deprive British bombers of landmarks to orient themselves. She was painted a dull bronze. The driver rounded the monument and headed south, past the zoo.

At the Central Office for Jewish Emigration, Dan encountered an atmosphere of joyful activity. The ss man at the front desk sent him up to Eichmann.

He found the Sturmbannführer on the phone, at attention, his assistant, Günther, at his side. "Yes, my Obergruppenführer. Heil Hitler," Eichmann barked into the phone, snapping his heels together and raising his arm. He hung up. So it had been Heydrich on the line.

When he saw Dan, Eichmann checked his watch. "Good God, it's already six. But, look, not today, Lavi. We're very busy."

"What are you doing? Where are you taking these people?"

Eichmann rolled his tongue across his teeth. He nodded for Günther to leave. The sweet-faced young ss man gave the Nazi salute and slipped past Dan into the stairway.

"There are several factors operating in this morning's transport," Eichmann said. "We have worked together for some time. I shall do you the honor of explaining. This shall assist you in accommodating your work to our new priorities."

Dan tried to calm himself. He needed to think straight. He was in no position to make demands.

"As the Reich expands eastward, there is a need for labor in certain new industrial ventures being prepared in the *Generalgouvernement* of Poland." Eichmann reclined in his desk chair. "Jews are largely idle here in Berlin. They aren't permitted to engage in most trades." He picked up a sheet of paper and checked it. "Our statistics show three-quarters of Jews in Berlin are unemployed."

Because of your anti-Semitic laws, Dan thought. "What kind of employment are you sending them to? How were they selected? Are there among them people who have requested emigration to Israel?"

Eichmann made his face register mild shock. "What do you take me for, Lavi? If you have filed papers for emigration on behalf of some Jew, why would I go to the bother of sending him east? Once *you* have them, they are off my hands, and that's my aim. Furthermore, this morning's transport is intended to create housing for Berliners who lost their homes in the British bombing."

"You're stripping these deportees of their homes?"

"They won't need them where they're going."

"It's their property."

Eichmann steepled his fingers. "The Reich's leadership considers that it is because of the Jews that this war is being fought. The Jews started it—"

"Surely you don't believe—"

"Don't concern yourself with my beliefs. I'm telling you the answer to your question. That's all. The Jews started the war and so they must pay the price."

"I suppose they have to pay for their train tickets to the east."

Eichmann looked puzzled at Dan's sarcasm. "Of course. Four pfennigs per kilometer of track. The ss must pay the Reichsbahn for the use of its trains and for its track. Jews must reimburse the ss for this outlay, particularly as we are transporting them to gainful employment."

"Four pfennigs?"

"Half price for children. Look, you're making quite a fuss over about four thousand people. You and I have seen to the emigration of tens of thousands of Jews to your state. Look at the big picture, Lavi."

"Each of those people you've sent away is a Jew and ought to be given the option of emigration before they're deported as slave laborers."

"Slave laborers? I forbid you to use such a term. When work is found for them, they shall be looked after very well. You will see."

"*When* work is found? I thought they were deported because you needed them for the new factories. Now you're telling me they don't have work to go to?"

"Work is the aim. It shall be found for them. Work makes you free. This is our belief and we shall impress it upon those Jews who have been lounging without jobs here in Berlin for the last several years. In the meantime, they will be sent to the Lodz ghetto to await instructions."

"A ghetto?"

"Don't worry about them, Lavi. The Führer wants all Jews out of Europe. For the time being we have need of these people as potential workers, but you'll get your hands on them in the end."

Get your hands on them. Eichmann's phrase disturbed Dan. It made it seem as though he was acting with as little concern for the humanity of the Jewish refugees as the Nazis. As though they were merely instruments of strategy, to be shipped to Israel and distributed to farms and factories and military units.

"Now, Lavi, I really must get back to work." Eichmann opened the next file on his desk. "I have a lot to get through before the concert for the Führer."

Dan felt relieved that at least on this matter Eichmann wouldn't get what he wanted. "You will have to cancel it."

"Explain yourself."

"The Countess von Bredow's home was destroyed by a bomb last night."

"Gottfried?"

"Survived."

"Thank God." Eichmann surveyed the paperwork spread across his desk and murmured, "I shall have to find another location for the concert. It may take a few days, perhaps a little longer." Then he clapped his hands. "I know of just the place. Tell Herr Gottfried the ss will be delighted to host him."

Chapter 37

Shmulik's staff were hunkered down by the remains of their document fire in the garden of the embassy. The gray sky drizzled a weak rain. Dan walked across the soft grass. "Any luck at the station?" he asked.

Shmulik shook his head. He pulled a scrap of paper from his pocket, gave it a last glance, and torched it with his cigarette lighter. He tossed the paper onto the hump of charred files.

"Sorry that you had to burn everything up for nothing." Dan crouched beside him. "Better safe than sorry."

"We'd have needed to destroy everything soon anyhow." Shmulik stood up and took a spade. He turned over the documents to be sure they were all ruined.

"You're ready to do it?" Dan said. "You're ready to kill him?"

Shmulik did not answer.

Dan grabbed at the tail of his jacket. "Look at me when I'm talking to you. You're going to bring the whole of the Nazi security forces down on us. They'll take us away. At best, they'll kick us out of the country. They might just kill us. How can you be so sure that killing Hitler would stop the Nazis anyway? What will happen to all the people we could still save?"

"The British bombers nearly brought the entire building down on us last night." Shmulik stepped on the edge of the spade to drive it into the pile. "Then where would your poor refugees have been? And, yes, it would've been the end of my plans too. That's why I have to get things done as soon as I can. Waiting doesn't help anyone. It only makes it more possible that we'll be found out and stopped, or that a British bomb will put an end to us before we get a chance to act."

"We have to think of another way."

Shmulik sneered as he lifted a wad of charred paper and flipped it over, nudging it around to see if any memos or messages remained intact. "I sent Ben-Gurion an update about what's happening in the east. I gave him locations from my resistance contacts. Told him where the camps are being constructed."

"The labor camps?"

"Let's hope labor camps is all they are."

"It couldn't be for...." But Dan was through with making excuses for the Nazis. It could be for anything, and he and Shmulik knew it. They had both seen the Zyklon B document. Jews would be sent for extermination.

"Ben-Gurion contacted the British. Asked them to bomb the rail lines to the camps. That'd stop the construction materials getting to the camps. It'd also prevent the Germans from shipping Jews out there." Shmulik dropped the spade and leaned on the garden fence. "But they won't do it."

"Oh God. Why not?"

"For one thing, we haven't declared war on Germany, as they demanded we do in their ultimatum. Most importantly, though, it doesn't accord with their war aims. Those railways are not a military target."

"But the same railways are used by German troops going to fight the Russians, Britain's allies. And these slave labor camps are for military manufacturing, we can assume. They're not going to be making lace underwear, for God's sake."

Shmulik's voice was low, exhausted. "Your balancing act hasn't worked, Dan. You've tried to make the Germans happy and to keep the British off our backs. But events are moving fast—faster than you can sign the transfer papers."

"What did Ben-Gurion say? Am I to halt the emigrations?"

"Speed them up, he says. Before it's really too late. Get out as many people as you can. Until they come for *you*."

Chapter 38

The embassy filled with desperate Jews every day that week. The trucks that had taken their neighbors away in the early morning galvanized even those who had been paralyzed by fear, or who had clung to the hope that the Nazis would never actually deport them. Dan enlisted Anna to guide people through the forms they needed to fill out for Eichmann's office. Gottfried exhausted himself at his desk in the back of the building, constantly surrounded by a voluble crowd. The excitement was so different from the happy tumult his presence used to provoke at concerts. Even Richter and Yardeni were forced to assume the consular duties which were usually only covers for their Mossad roles. Dan hoped their involvement with the emigration process might hold up the assassination of Hitler and the awful consequences he feared.

He barely lifted his eyes from the mass of paperwork, or rose from his office chair, except to comfort some broken man. The women were tougher, he noticed—or at least they recognized the need for strength and purpose, despite the emotional turmoil seething within.

As darkness descended on Berlin at the end of another day, Dan stamped one more application and then looked up to find that he was alone in his office for the first time since the roundups. It had been three days of constant work. The pile in his in-tray remained substantial, but he thought he could spare a few minutes to stretch his legs. He went into the lobby. Richter and Yardeni were gone. Anna was at the desk by the door. She seemed barely awake.

"You're our security guard now?" Dan tried to smile, but the absence of the Mossad men worried him. Was tonight the night that Shmulik would attack Hitler?

"You could do worse. Everyone's scared of America coming into the war. Besides, I can do a good tough guy." Anna spoke with her best clipped James Cagney accent. "Anyone tries to get by me, I'll push a grapefruit in their face."

"You're a real public enemy."

He went to Gottfried's office. The desk light illuminated a spray of papers, but there was no sign of the first secretary. He walked back to the lobby and asked Anna, "How's the Countess?"

"The bruising on her ankle is going down nicely. She and Wili went out for some air a while back."

"If they can breathe in Berlin, they must have some kind of natural gas mask built into their systems." He bent to kiss his wife's cheek and touched her neck. "How about you?"

"I'm all right. I guess I've just had so much to do since they started taking people away that I haven't had a chance to really think about what's happening." She stood and pulled him to her. She was shaking almost imperceptibly, like the shifting blue outline of gas burning on a stove.

"We're going to be fine, sweetheart," he said. "No matter what happens, you and I are going to be together. That's all the protection I need from the world."

"That's sweet."

It's stupid, too, he thought. He could hear Bertha Polkes chopping vegetables in the kitchen. He hadn't been able to defend her husband. The world could strip away anyone's protection. Many of the people who clamored for his signature on their emigration papers had once been wealthy. Some had been powerful. None had been able to guard themselves against the assault of pure madness.

A fist battered against the door of the embassy. Anna gasped in fear. Dan stared at the dark wood. The blows fell faster. He ushered Anna toward his office.

"Who is it?" he called.

"Open up, God damn it. It's Brückner."

Dan unlatched the door. Hitler's adjutant stumbled inside, angry and agitated.

"Where are they?" His greatcoat flopped open and when he pulled off his cap his hair was damp with sweat.

"Do you mean the forms for emigration to Israel? I'm glad you've come to terms with your Jewish heritage, Herr Hauptmann Brückner."

"Don't toy with me, you bastard. A moment ago I thought my…my aunt was dead. The Gestapo man outside says she's alive."

"Your aunt? You mean, your mother. And your father. He was in there too."

"I got back from East Prussia an hour ago. Why didn't you alert me about the bomb?"

"I assumed you had other sources of intelligence. Besides, your parents are unhurt."

"Where are they?"

"They were here, but they're not now. They've gone."

"Where to?"

"To get some air. We've been busy this week, thanks to your Führer's orders for the deportation of Berlin's Jews."

"That's his office, right?" Brückner strode across the lobby to Gottfried's room and went in.

Dan followed him quickly. "This is a diplomatic facility. I insist that you—"

"There must be something here that can tell me where they are."

"I told you, they're just taking a walk."

Brückner went around the desk. He shuffled the papers clumsily.

"Don't touch those." Dan shoved the German away from the desk.

Brückner pushed back at him, but Dan stepped away and let him stumble against the filing cabinets.

"What the hell are you looking for, Brückner? Wili will be back soon enough, and your mother will be with him."

Brückner became still. He glared at Dan with sudden focus. "You've hidden them. Where have you taken her?"

"I'm not the one who's *taking* people."

Brückner rushed at him. "Where is she?" he shouted.

Anna came to the door. "Dan?"

The men wrestled against the desk.

"Stay out of here, Anna," Dan called.

"Where is she?" Brückner's voice was raw. He bawled the words over and over, raging and sobbing.

When he pulled himself together, he wiped his eyes against the sleeve of his gray Wehrmacht coat. "I saw the house...the rubble..."

Dan straightened his tie. The German officer wasn't the first person he had seen collapse in desperation and fear for a loved one that week. His stock of sympathy was severely depleted. He watched him with a stiff, resentful jaw.

Anna touched the young man's shoulder. "She'll be back soon," she said. "You can wait here."

"Thank you, Madame."

"After all, Wili can't go more than a half hour without checking that his Stradivarius is safe." She grinned.

Brückner sniffled a polite laugh. "Yes, you're quite right, of course."

Dan glanced around the office. Gottfried's violin wasn't in sight. He must have put it in a cupboard, away from the crowds that came through here during the day. Still, the presentiment of danger he'd experienced when he saw the Mossad men were gone returned to him now. It made him open the stationery cupboard and look inside. No violin. He went to the adjoining documents room. Nothing there either.

The Stradivarius might be in Gottfried's bedroom on the third floor. Even as he rushed up the stairs, Dan knew he wouldn't find it. The Countess's home lay in ruins. But Gottfried was determined to play for Hitler.

In Gottfried's bedroom, pillows were set in a triangle against the bed's headboard, where the Countess had rested while her injured leg recovered. The cloth suit bag in which Gottfried kept his tuxedo lay across the bed. Dan rushed over and saw that it was empty. There was no violin in the room. On the vanity lay a cardboard box the size of a bag of flour. The blue label had been ripped away and the side pulled open. Nine-millimeter cartridges had spilled out of the box onto the glass tabletop. Dan didn't have to count them. There would be enough missing to fill the magazine of a Luger.

As he dashed down the stairs, Dan's heart seemed to beat as loud as his footsteps. Gottfried would play for Hitler. Not in the Countess's demolished house, but somewhere else. And after he played, he would kill him.

"Where's your Führer tonight?" he yelled as he descended the last flight of stairs.

Brückner came past Anna into the lobby. "He's gone to a dinner in Wannsee."

"Dinner with whom?"

"Obergruppenführer Heydrich. At a villa by the lake."

Wannsee was a suburb southwest of Berlin, within the interlocking system of lakes and inlets off the River Havel, about ten miles from the embassy. Dan remembered Eichmann's remark that the ss would be glad to host Gottfried's concert. It had to be there, tonight. He checked the drawer of the security desk in the lobby. The Luger was gone. He opened the front door and turned to Brückner. "Can you get me into Heydrich's villa?"

Chapter 39

Brückner sped his BMW through the quiet evening streets toward Wannsee. Dan imagined Shmulik preparing for the assassination. Hiding somewhere out in the wealthy suburb. He'd have an escape plan, surely, if things went wrong. For the first time, Dan realized that by trying to prevent Hitler's assassination, he might be betraying Shmulik, handing him over to the Nazis. But the sidewalks were filled with the Jews of Europe, watching and silent, their faces expectant. Shmulik would give up his life for Israel. *What about you?* Dan asked himself. *Would you give up Shmulik to save these souls who follow you through the dark?*

The long hood of the cabriolet nosed over the bridge into the village. The car slowed almost to a halt as Brückner made the hairpin turn along the lake. From the passenger seat, Dan caught a glimpse of a black Adler Trumpf limo. It was pulled backward into a driveway. Its lights were out. It was the same car the embassy used, but it bore regular plates, without diplomatic designations.

Brückner rounded the curve and sped onto Am Grossen Wannsee, the leafy street on the edge of the water down which stood the ss villa.

He pulled the BMW up at the iron gates. A pair of SS men strode toward each side of the car. Brückner brought out his Wehrmacht identity card and his Chancellery pass for Hitler's office. He slipped Dan's diplomatic pass and identity card under them.

"You're not on the list," the SS man said.

"I *wrote* the list, Scharführer. And it's *Herr Hauptmann* to you."

The guard was only mildly impressed by Brückner's forceful attitude. The SS didn't care for the army. He picked at his front teeth and gave the cards another look.

"Sturmbannführer Eichmann is inside," Dan said. "Am I correct?"

The SS guard went to work on his back teeth. He shrugged.

"Tell him I'm here with urgent information."

The guard jerked his head toward his comrade. The second man sauntered to the gatehouse.

"Wait here," the guard said.

Chapter 40

Heydrich concluded his introductory remarks and moved away from Gottfried, clapping politely. The small group assembled in the banquet room of the Wannsee villa joined in the applause. Tall bay windows framed the virtuoso as he brought the Stradivarius to his shoulder. It was his moment.

Gottfried looked at the man of moderate height sitting in the center of the front row. That man, giggling and slapping his thigh at some joke, issued orders to an entire nation. He sent armies to take away people's countries. He commanded prime ministers and presidents to attend on him at the Chancellery. He ordered that Jews be stripped of their rights, their homes. Soon their lives would be forfeit at his word, Gottfried knew. But now, this madman would have to sit in silence and stillness. He would listen, and feel the assault of Gottfried's beautiful music on his soul. Not because Gottfried had any hope that it would cure him, or drain him of the murder lust that ran through his veins. Just so that, for a few minutes, Gottfried would force Hitler to understand that creation, not destruction, carries all the power of the universe within it.

One day, a vengeful enemy army would approach and Hitler would contemplate his end, and as he swallowed his cyanide capsule or raised a gun to his head this lunatic would hear the strains of the Stradivarius rising out of his memory to claim him, and he would realize that the *true* final solution was love, and great art. That message was all that an artist could bring to the universe, and Gottfried was content with it. He wasn't a general or a politician. Not even an ambassador. This was the démarche he carried to the world, and it found expression in the melding of musical notes scribbled across a page more than a century ago by Ludwig van Beethoven with the artistry of a Jew named Wilhelm as he played the score on his violin. The British prime minister had waved a piece of paper and said it meant peace in our time. *No*, Gottfried thought. *Listen everyone, here is peace.*

He played Beethoven's Romance in G Major. The only presences in the room were the long-dead maestro, who had written the work when he broke off his engagement, to spare his beloved the indignity of marriage to a deaf man, and Gottfried, who brought his own tragedies to the performance. There were others in the room. The person he loved more than any other, his Countess, and the one he most reviled, the Nazi Führer, were there. So was Furtwängler, waiting in his chair to accompany Gottfried in a Mozart violin sonata after the Beethoven piece. But the room was so full of music that nothing else seemed real. The A-dominant-seventh that took the piece into a melancholy D minor, the laboring half-steps that returned the piece to the romantic theme, the sweet high passionate notes—all this emptied the villa of that dreadful madman's evil.

There was movement to his left. A young ss officer quietly approached the end of the front row. He whispered in Eichmann's ear. A nod from the seated man, and the young officer left the room.

Gottfried moved into the coda.

Chapter 41

The ss guard handed the identity papers through the window of the BMW to Brückner and snapped his heels. Brückner drove the car through the gate and down the drive, stopping in the small turning circle in front of the villa. Dan jumped out and ran with Brückner between the columns of the entry portico. A young ss officer greeted them with a Nazi salute. Brückner returned it hurriedly. Dan didn't respond. The ss man stared at him with surprised blue eyes.

"Where is the Countess von Bredow?" Brückner demanded.

The young officer turned his attention from Dan. "This way, but keep your voice down. Herr Gottfried is performing now. The Führer is listening."

They crossed the oval foyer under the curving stairway. The ss man almost padded along in his jackboots. He opened the double doors.

The transcendent refrain of Gottfried's violin weaved toward Dan as though it came on the heartbeat of a man whose struggles were all behind him. Who had found peace.

He isn't going to kill Hitler, Dan realized. Gottfried truly did want only to play for the dictator. To show him the beauty that was being run out of Germany by his insane policies. He relaxed a little, but only as much as the Israeli ambassador could upon arriving unannounced in a room that contained the head of the Gestapo *and* the German Führer.

The ss officer pulled the double doors behind them. A sudden draught gusted past them and the young man's hand slipped. The locks snapped shut, the noise like a shout over the melancholy finale of Beethoven's Romance.

Hitler's eyes shot toward the door. With his receding forehead and wide cheekbones, he looked like an aggressive eastern peasant glaring out of his hovel at some wanderer come to beg a potato, defensive more than furious. He recognized Brückner, his adjutant, and made a questioning, affronted face. Then he noticed Dan and a flash of confusion passed over his features. He couldn't place the newcomer, it seemed.

Gottfried played the final notes of the piece, quiet, falling tones that reflected devastating losses, of Beethoven's hearing and of his fiancée.

At the back of the room, Countess von Bredow rose from her seat. She moved slowly along the wall, her eyes fixed on the Führer.

When she reached the front row, she raised her hand. She aimed the Luger at the dictator in his chair.

Hitler was still turned toward the newcomers. Suddenly his face transformed. He had recognized Dan. The Israeli ambassador. A Jew. "You," he roared, rising to his feet.

The Countess's bullet slammed into the chair where Hitler had been sitting only seconds before. It shattered the wood and bore into the leg of his Naval adjutant in the second row. The officer screamed and tumbled forward.

Hitler bellowed hysterically to the ss men around him. "Kill the bitch."

Heydrich and Eichmann came to their feet. A dozen military men rose from among their womenfolk, scrambling to unholster their weapons.

"Exterminate the traitors."

Brückner ran across the room and hurled himself at the Countess before she could shoot again. He took her off balance and shoved her against the wall. She dropped the pistol.

The SS men raised their weapons hesitantly as the Führer's adjutant held the assassin still.

Gottfried emerged from the capsule created by his music and saw what was happening. He tossed aside his Stradivarius and rushed forward. Furtwängler threw himself from his piano stool and scrambled toward the violin as though it were an endangered life.

All attention was on the Countess. It seemed the Nazis had forgotten all about the virtuoso performing for them. Quietly, Gottfried grabbed the Countess's fallen Luger from the floor.

"Wili." Dan hissed to him. "Put the gun down."

The momentary glance Gottfried gave him was commanding. It directed him toward the violin, as if he were ordering the ambassador to save what could be saved. The instrument, not the musician.

Gottfried reached Brückner. He frowned softly, pityingly. "I'm sorry." Then he smashed the butt of the pistol across the young man's jaw. Dan realized that Gottfried's apology hadn't been for the blow—that would protect Brückner, make it clear that he had fought against Hitler's assailants. Instead it was a doomed man's remorse for this sudden farewell to his son.

The blow also galvanized the SS officers. As Gottfried reached the Countess and stepped in front of her, the first bullet took him in the shoulder. The second pushed him back against the wall. Gottfried staggered and fired the Luger, but the shot went into the ceiling. A volley smashed into him and he went down.

Heydrich edged quickly past the dead man. He leaned over the Countess. She looked up at him with defiance and hate. He laid the muzzle of his pistol against her forehead. She pressed up toward the gun and closed her eyes. He fired. Her blood spread across the prone figure of her son.

Chapter 42

Shmulik checked his watch as he sat in the dark interior of the Adler Trumpf. The limo was cold. Or maybe it was just his blood. Gottfried was going to play a Beethoven romance and a Mozart violin sonata. The first piece would be over about now. The Mozart would take another ten minutes. Hitler would return this way soon after. His limo would come almost to a halt at the sharp corner that led onto the narrow bridge out of Wannsee. He glanced at Yardeni. When the time came, the agent would go to the far side of the road and wait behind the hedge with his machine gun.

Shmulik had no illusions about how the night might end for himself. A cyanide capsule lay tucked between his left lower molar and his cheek. But he couldn't bear to think that either of these boys would die. He and Devorah had no children. Richter and Yardeni were his sons. He had brought them here, into danger. He would see that they got away.

"How long?" Richter asked from the backseat. He was to take this side of the road with a pistol and two grenades. He'd wait for Yardeni's shots to halt the Führer's car, then he'd go in close, shoot out the side window with the pistol, and toss in the grenades.

"Ten minutes to position." Shmulik shrugged his heavy shoulders. So stiff. The plan was good enough. It was what they had intended to do at the bridge over the Spree until the British bomb destroyed the von Bredow mansion. The bridge would have slowed Hitler's car, but this tight corner would bring it almost to a halt. It was a better location, but there had been little time to anticipate potential problems. He wasn't a spiritual man, but Shmulik's senses were disturbed by more than simple nerves. He felt like saying some kind of farewell to these two young boys in case it all went wrong. He opened his mouth to speak.

A shot sounded in the quiet night.

"Son of a whore," Yardeni said. "That came from the villa."

"Did it?" Richter opened the window.

Another shot, and then a loud volley, six or perhaps seven pistols all at once.

"I think you're right, Aryeh."

Shmulik got out of the car. In the darkness of the blackout, the lake and the channel under the bridge were like infinite pools of nothingness.

"Are we going ahead, Shmulik?" Now Richter was out of the car too.

Shmulik looked through the windscreen. Yardeni had his hand on the starter. He didn't think the operation was a go. He was ready to get out of there.

Shmulik knew he should give the order to abort. Gunshots in the villa where Hitler sat would at the very least put his bodyguards on high alert. Surviving an assassination attempt—if it was an attempted hit that they had just heard from the villa, and if he *had* survived—would make Hitler more cautious than ever. But the deportations had started. Jews were dying. He should have killed Hitler months ago and he might never get another chance.

Engines started up along Am Grossen Wannsee. Hitler's people were leaving the villa.

Shmulik beckoned for Yardeni to get out of the car. The two Mossad men huddled round him. He put his big hands on their shoulders. "I don't have to tell you *why* we do this, boys. I only have to tell you—I'm proud of you. Go." He turned away quickly so they wouldn't see his emotion.

The cars roared out of the villa's gates a half mile away.

Richter knelt beside the hedge on the near corner. Yardeni had reached the middle of the narrow road when he turned back. "Don't let them take me alive, Shmulik," he said.

"Do your job." Shmulik took his Schmeisser submachine gun from the rear of the car.

Hitler and his escort approached down the lane.

"Shmulik?" Yardeni called again.

"It's okay. They won't take you. Get in position."

Yardeni went to the rear of an empty milk truck across the street. He crouched behind it.

Hitler's convoy arrived. There was only one car. The other engines belonged to three motorcycles with ss riders, two in front and one in the rear. Shmulik saw them approach from his position behind the trunk of the Adler Trumpf. He touched the grenades in his pocket. He would use them if Richter didn't succeed. The cyanide capsule in his cheek seemed to vibrate, calling him.

The first two motorbikes slowed at the corner. Yardeni rose and sprayed them with machine-gun fire just as the Führer's car reached the hairpin. The bikers both went down, as planned. But one of them leaned back on his throttle, trying to speed up and escape even as he died. The bike slewed out from under him and spun across the narrow lane.

Yardeni was focused on the car. He didn't see the heavy bike in the darkness. It swept into him and crushed his leg as it pulled him to the ground. His head struck the rear fender of the milk truck.

Hitler's car threaded between the two fallen bikers. Richter ran from cover and leapt onto the running board. He raised his pistol to shoot out the glass.

The third outrider sped up to him. Richter hadn't seen him. Shmulik cursed himself. He should have given his boys a count when he saw the vehicles approaching. This was about to go wrong and it was because of him. His stomach felt like ice. He called to Richter. "Another bike."

Richter turned as the last biker brought up his pistol. The shot took the Mossad man in the neck. As he went down he pulled the pin from his grenade. The ss biker dropped on top of him and grappled for the grenade.

Another pair of engines sounded, coming down the lane from the villa. Shmulik went for Hitler's car, focused on the man who had to die. He had his grenade ready in his left hand. He raised the Schmeisser to shoot out the window.

Richter's grenade exploded. It smashed through the body of the ss outrider. Shmulik felt shrapnel cut into the muscles of his legs and he fell to the ground.

Hitler's car jerked away from the fallen motorbikes. Its rear wheels thumped over the bodies of Richter and the ss man. It sped onto the bridge and away.

Shmulik was on his back on the sidewalk. Yardeni whimpered in the darkness. "Shmulik, help me."

The other cars grew louder. There were more than two now. Perhaps four of them approaching.

Shmulik pushed himself to his feet with the machine gun. His left leg felt absent, as though it had been amputated. He limped past the corpses of Richter and the ss outrider. To Yardeni. The young man was trapped by the motorbike.

Bellowing with pain, Shmulik lifted the bike off him. He dropped it aside, took a look at Yardeni, then turned his head away. The boy's legs were crushed and flattened, bleeding hard. The arteries in his thighs must have been severed.

Yardeni saw the wounds and grabbed at Shmulik's trouser leg. "Go, Shmulik. Get out of here. I'm done."

"You're not finished until I say so." Shmulik put his machine gun over his shoulder. He lifted Yardeni and slung him over his shoulder. He resisted the urge to scream at the pain in his own leg. Yardeni's cries turned to sobs, as though he could no longer disguise his youth. Shmulik snarled and whimpered at once. It was as if his own son were dying in his arms. If only the boy would pass out, beyond the pain. But instead, Yardeni pounded his fists against Shmulik's back.

"Put me down. I'm going to die. Just let me shoot some of these bastards before I do. It'll give you time to get out of here."

"Shut up already."

The first of the approaching cars slowed through the gears before the corner. Shmulik made for the driveway behind the Adler Trumpf. He opened his mouth to whisper to Yardeni. Suddenly the young man jammed his fingers into Shmulik's mouth. He scrabbled inside a moment and came out with the cyanide capsule.

Shmulik coughed and choked.

Yardeni put the capsule in his mouth. "You thought I didn't know about the cyanide? I know you better than you think, Shmulik. I'm going to kill a few of these sons of whores and then I'm going to bite this pill. But *you're* leaving *now*."

Shmulik glanced at the lane. The car halted and doors opened. Voices—surprised, shocked, angry. German officers, come to examine the scene.

He laid Yardeni on the roof of the Adler Trumpf. He took the boy's hand and kissed it. He limped through the bushes behind the car.

As he reached the shore of the lake, he heard a rattle of gunfire from Yardeni's Schmeisser. A few screams, some more shots. Then silence.

Shmulik shivered. He waded into the freezing water of late fall. He felt as if the blood from his wounded leg would turn the entire lake red. He struck out slowly, as the voices of more Germans arriving at the failed ambush echoed through the night.

Forty minutes later, he crawled across the beach on the other side of the lake and disappeared among the trees of the Grunewald.

Chapter 43

Heydrich wiped his forehead with a handkerchief. Eichmann hovered around his boss in a state of near panic as the Wehrmacht staff and ss guards hauled the corpses of Gottfried and the Countess across the floor. Eichmann blanched and turned away from the wide smears of blood left by the bodies as they were dragged away. Dan heard Heydrich say something about "this concert" and "a mistake," and saw fear turn Eichmann's face still paler. It appeared the blame for the evening's events was being laid at the door of the lower-ranked man.

Eichmann was not about to let it remain with him. He spun around toward Dan. "Arrest this man," he called.

A big ss Scharführer grabbed Dan's arms and pulled them behind his back.

"Damn you, Lavi," Eichmann said.

"This is nothing to do with me." Dan was glad that the ss man was holding him. It covered the shaking that overcame him now. "In any case, you can't arrest me. I'm the ambassador of a neutral country. Diplomatic immunity—"

"Silence. You're lucky I don't just march you into the garden and shoot you right now. Take him to Prinz-Albrecht-Strasse."

The Gestapo headquarters. Dan's legs shook. He kept his mouth shut. He didn't want Eichmann to hear the fear that would be evident in any word he spoke.

Brückner groaned. He lifted himself from the floor, rubbing his bruised jaw. He stared at Dan and the ss man who restrained him. "You didn't know, did you?"

"Of course I didn't."

Eichmann slapped Dan across the face with his gloves. The ss guard shoved him through the hallway to the entrance.

The front drive could hardly have displayed greater signs of panic had Hitler actually been killed. Through the chaos of departing cars and jogging guard details, a Mercedes pulled up. Draxler jumped out. He ran up the steps, breathless, and stopped when he saw Dan under guard.

"That's my prisoner." He took Dan's sleeve.

"I'm to take him to the Gestapo," the ss man protested.

"I saved you the trouble." Draxler yanked Dan across the gravel to his car. He cuffed his hands behind his back and pushed him into the backseat. The Gestapo man's breath billowed in the cold night. "You're mine now, Jew boy."

Draxler's driver sped along Am Grossen Wannsee. He slowed for the hairpin before the bridge. Troopers from the *Leibstandarte ss* loomed around the car in their greatcoats. They glowered at Dan and the hostile features of Draxler beside him, and signaled for the Mercedes to continue.

They rolled by a pair of parked Gestapo cars and a staff car riddled with bullet holes. Three motorbikes with ss plates were leant against the hedge, their lights shattered and decals scratched. Round the corner, the Adler Trumpf was shot up too. Dan looked around anxiously for Shmulik and his boys. The Mossad attempt on Hitler's life had surely been made here. He felt a surge of hope that Shmulik might have been successful, and an immediate snap of guilt that he had ever tried to stop the plan.

Bodies lay under blankets in a rank by the bridge. The clouds cleared from over the moon and glinted on the jackboots of the dead men. They were ss, or perhaps Wehrmacht. Or Hitler himself? No, they would have taken their Führer to a hospital, even if he were dead.

A huddle of Gestapo officers were crouched over something at the side of the wrecked Adler Trumpf. One of them stood and lit a cigarette. The others poked at the remains of two men. White in the night, their faces bore the wasted expressions of saints in a medieval church. Dan felt a surge of nausea. He recognized the faces. The Gestapo man drew on his cigarette and kicked at Richter's devastated corpse. The dead agent's head twisted around to face Yardeni's body, as though he sought to pass on some final confidence.

Then Dan realized that the dead man's unspoken message was for him, and he felt a strength in his core that dissipated his fear of Draxler and the torture chambers. He would survive, because he had a mission to carry out.

The Gestapo car accelerated onto the main road that led to the center of Berlin.

Part III

I wasn't only issued orders. In that case I'd have been a moron. But I rather anticipated. I was an idealist.

Adolf Eichmann

Entrance to Auschwitz I, 1942

Chapter 44

Berlin, December 1941

The Gestapo made the arrests swiftly. Almost everyone who attended the Countess von Bredow's musical soirees found themselves in the basements along Prinz-Albrecht-Strasse. Some got word to powerful protectors. Schulze, the Luftwaffe officer, came out alive because of the intervention of Hermann Göring, who wanted to keep the security services away from his air force. Kritzinger, the deputy head of the Chancellery, turned to his boss, an honorary ss general, who vouched for him and secured his release. The others were strung up with nooses of thin wire, hung in a row on butcher's hooks. Their deaths were filmed to be played on the newsreels that ran before the Westerns at the cinema.

Dan Lavi waited in his cell under the Gestapo headquarters, expecting Draxler to arrive at any moment to torture him. He wondered if he was being sweated, to increase his panic. He worked hard to calm himself, to control the adrenaline that rushed through him almost as loud as the screams he heard from the other cells. He pictured Shmulik, imagined him alive, still struggling to survive, to continue his fight against the Nazis. He saw Anna, back at the embassy. Without him. He reached out in the dark and touched the hands of the Jews who came to his office for their salvation. He was ready for the torture. They wouldn't kill him. In fact, he felt something growing in him that could never be killed.

On the second day, the door swung open and Eichmann stepped inside. He sniffed at the foul smell of the toilet bucket. "The Führer has made no mention of the presence of the Israeli ambassador at the shooting. We can assume the—the excitement of the ensuing moments erased your face from his memory, Lavi. I managed to convince the Obergruppenführer Heydrich that you came to Wannsee because you suspected the Countess von Bredow intended to carry out her atrocity."

Perhaps I was there to help, Dan thought. *But not anymore.* He said nothing.

"In any case, you can leave now."

Dan stood, unsteadily. He stumbled forward. Eichmann maneuvered quickly out of his way. "It remains a matter of Reich policy to coordinate the emigration of Jews to Israel. You may be thankful for that. Otherwise I'd have let them string you up like the rest of the conspirators."

"I'm not a conspirator."

"The Obergruppenführer Heydrich agrees that you may be returned to your old duties on behalf of the Reich."

"On behalf of the State of Israel."

Eichmann shook his head with contempt. "Hold your tongue. Don't you realize I'm doing you a big favor? Your friend Hauptmann Brückner is the hero of the hour, of course. He stopped the old bitch just in time. Even though she was his aunt."

A cramp gripped Dan's stomach. He bent over sharply. The Nazis were releasing him because they needed him. For now. He retched, but there was nothing in his belly to come up. Eichmann flicked his hand and the Gestapo guard dragged Dan from the cell.

As Dan staggered down the long, white-walled corridor toward the exit, he heard Eichmann call after him: "Remember what I have done for you, Lavi."

Back at the embassy, Anna shut out the world for a day and tended to him. Bertha Polkes fed him soup to give him back the strength he had lost in the cell, expending so much nervous energy. But the next day he forced Anna to let him get on with his work. The embassy hadn't heard from Shmulik. He assumed the Mossad chief had been captured. He tried to prepare Devorah for the worst, but she shrugged off his attempts to talk about Shmulik's fate.

After a week passed, he concluded that Shmulik was dead. He found Devorah in the embassy kitchen and told her Shmulik must have died somewhere out near Wannsee after the assassination attempt. If he'd been captured, then surely he would have succumbed to Gestapo torture, and the secret police would have descended on the embassy. No one could hold out against them, not even Shmulik.

Devorah snorted at him derisively. "What do you know about holding out against them?"

"I realize you love him, Devorah. But you don't think he's immune to—to the terrible things they do?" Dan said. "That he can't be hurt?"

"On the contrary," she said. "I know exactly how much he suffers. That's why I know he's not dead. I can still feel his pain."

"Devorah, we have to be realistic."

"We're in love, Shmulik and I. Perhaps you find it hard to imagine that Shmulik can experience that emotion, but it's very much alive in him. When he dies, I'll know it."

Her intensity convinced him. He touched her shoulder to comfort her. As she turned away, he caught the trace of a smirk on her lips. The triumph of a successful lie. He realized that it wasn't a spiritual connection with her husband that made Devorah so certain he was alive. "You know where he is, don't you?"

She left the kitchen without a word. He followed her through the lobby. They passed the group of hopeful emigrants waiting at the door of Dan's office and descended to the basement.

"Devorah, you have to tell me where he is."

She sat down at her coding table. "When you need him, he'll be there."

"In the meantime, how am I supposed to explain his absence?"

"To Jerusalem?"

"To the Gestapo."

She gave a disgusted laugh and turned away.

For the next few hours Dan processed Jews seeking Israeli visas. As the afternoon went on, he collected the papers and went to Gottfried's old office. Anna dozed there, with her elbows on the desk. He touched the crown of her head gently. She jolted awake.

"Sorry, sweetheart," he said. "I'm going over to Eichmann. Can I have the papers you've done so far?"

"Sure." She pushed a pile of applications toward him and sighed. "Have fun."

He picked up the forms, but her voice halted him. It contained a resignation and bitterness he hadn't heard before. "What's eating you?"

She put her hand briefly over her eyes. When she took it away, he saw no love there, only frustration and grief. "How can you even be in that man's presence? He helped kill Wili and Hannah."

"The Countess tried to assassinate Hitler. If Eichmann and his people hadn't been there, someone else would've finished her off. Wili, too." He packed the papers into his briefcase.

She shook her head. "Maybe they tried to kill the wrong guy."

"They should've killed Eichmann? Is that what you mean? How would we get all these Jews out of Germany without him?" He brandished his briefcase impatiently and raised his voice. "Do you have an answer for that?"

She twisted her mouth and stared at her hands.

Her silence was a goad to his anger. "I have to make difficult compromises. I'm not proud of working with Eichmann. He's an anti-Semitic bastard. But I'm proud that we've saved so many Jews from the Nazis. How many Jews did Shmulik save? I had to listen to this hard-line shit from him all the time. Now he's gone, I won't tolerate it from you."

"I'm not asking for your toleration." The last word come slowly, loaded with sarcasm. "You're the boss here. You're the ambassador. But I'm not *working* for you. Or for Eichmann."

He knew he should apologize. He couldn't do it. For too long he had swallowed everything he had wanted to say to Eichmann and Draxler and the other Nazis he encountered in his work. Now his resentment exploded. At his wife. "Do you think I like doing any of this?" he yelled. "One day I'll pay a heavy price for this work."

"At least you won't be dead, like Wili." She shouted too. She wasn't backing down.

"Well, that could happen any fucking day, couldn't it?"

"I doubt it. You're too useful to them. Who would do their dirty work?"

"Is that what you really think of me?"

"I think the Israeli ambassador should be standing up to them, not stamping their papers."

"I did stand up to them. I told them Wili would *not* do the concert for Hitler."

"And then you backed down. Did you forget that?"

He slammed his briefcase onto the desk. "I didn't forget. I'll never forget." Again he saw Richter and Yardeni, dead on the ground. He had known since then that he must do more than process visa applications. But he still didn't know *what* and that fact enraged him.

She went still, shocked by the force of his anger.

He took a deep breath, made his voice quiet, looking for an example that would show his wife why he had to carry on as before. "What if there were thousands of sick children and someone said to you, 'Doctor, you can save *some* of them. But the only way to do it is to nurture the bacillus that's killing them all. You have to keep the germ alive, because that will help some of the children find health, and meanwhile others among them will die.' What would you do, as a doctor, Anna?"

There was love in her expression, but also defiance. "I would remember what happens when you come into close contact with a disease."

"No, Anna, don't say that."

"I would realize that it might infect me too."

"You think I'm like Eichmann?"

"You have power. I don't know if it's your job as ambassador, or that you're a citizen of a new state which suddenly has the apparatus of power. Have you been corrupted by it, Dan?"

"I have no power, Anna. No power at all. Neither does Israel."

"Then you'd better find a way for you and Israel to get some. Or all this is for nothing." She stood and touched her hand to her brow wearily. "Take the papers to Eichmann."

Chapter 45

After the attempt on Hitler's life, Eichmann's officiousness and disdain increased, just as Dan's ability to swallow it declined. He started carrying his papers over to the Central Office for Jewish Emigration late in the evenings, when he expected to find one of the SS deputies on duty. He preferred to avoid Eichmann's frosty put-downs and allusions as to how much Dan owed him. On his lonely walks back along the edge of the Tiergarten park to the embassy, he had to acknowledge that he was now truly scared of the man. One dreary, cold evening, however, he found Eichmann still at the office, and full of excitement. "Herr Ambassador, it is a historic day, is it not?" He clapped his hands and rolled his shoulders in his field-gray tunic.

Dan opened his briefcase and took out the papers. "I'm glad to see the Herr Sturmbannführer in such good spirits."

"No, no, you must congratulate the Herr *Ober*sturmbannführer."

So Eichmann had been promoted from Major to Lieutenant-Colonel. Jews were good business. Dan showed himself to be suitably impressed. "My hearty congratulations, Herr Obersturmbannführer."

"But that's just one source of my joy. There is still better news. For today, the war is truly global. Our eventual victory was never in doubt, but now it promises to be a triumph of truly millennial proportions."

Dan stacked the papers before Eichmann. The ss officer slapped his hand down on them. "Yes, yes, I'll get to these. But first, a drink."

He took a glass from the bottom drawer of his desk and poured himself a measure of schnapps from a silver flask. He didn't offer any to Dan. He raised the glass to his lips. "*L'chaim.*" To life.

Dan made a brief bow to acknowledge the German's Hebrew. "What is the great event?"

"It may have consequences for your dear wife."

Dan's eyes flared wide.

Eichmann wagged a finger at him. "I observe from your reaction that the good lady doctor is the way to get at you. Never mind, I expect she has an Israeli passport too. As well as an American one, no?"

"She does."

"Then perhaps it will all be fine."

"I don't understand."

"The Japanese have attacked Pearl Harbor."

"Pearl what?"

"The base of the American fleet in Hawaii. There was great destruction, apparently. The attack itself took place within the last few hours. America will surely retaliate by declaring war on Japan, and soon Germany shall join on the side of her ally in Tokyo. I have this from Obergruppenführer Heydrich, who has just returned from the Chancellery."

Dan swallowed hard. Even once war was declared, he couldn't imagine the Germans would be as vicious toward American civilians as he had heard they were toward Poles and Russians in the east. Surely they would want to live alongside America? They couldn't believe they would defeat it. Anyone who knew America's geographic enormity, and witnessed its industrial strength as Dan had during his time at Harvard, must know that Germany couldn't beat the us. Still, Anna was an American *and* a Jew. How much protection would her status as the wife of the Israeli ambassador bring her?

"Why must Germany declare war against the United States?" he said.

"We and Japan are signatories of the Anti-Comintern Pact." Eichmann spread his hands, as if the logic were immediately evident.

"But that treaty compels you to support Japan in the event that Japan is attacked."

"It does."

"Didn't you say that *Japan* attacked the American fleet? Germany has no obligation to support Japan in a war of aggression."

"The Americans are the aggressors. They have violated their neutrality repeatedly in the last couple of months. Their ships have fired on our U-Boats. They concluded a treaty with Canada, a *British* dependency. It is the Americans who are responsible for this war. But it is Germany that shall be the victor."

Dan touched his brow. He tried to calculate where this would leave Israel. Bitterly, he thought, perhaps the Americans would have an ultimatum for Ben-Gurion now, too.

"How do you say it in Hebrew?" Eichmann said. "Germany and Japan are *bashert*. Our relationship is meant to be."

Dan tried to avoid quibbling with the ss's "Jewish expert" in matters of culture, but he was off-balance, and allowed himself this one correction. "It's Yiddish, and it's usually applied to a soulmate in love, not an ally in war."

"Love and war are happy occasions. Shall we agree that it can be applied to all moments of celebration?"

Very quietly, Dan said, "As you wish."

"Though, as with all things, this happy event is not without its inconveniences." Eichmann lifted a file from his desk and waved it, an expression of modest vexation on his face. "I had sent out invitations on behalf of Obergruppenführer Heydrich to a conference at the villa in Wannsee. The scene of the recent treacherous assassination attempt against our Führer. Now I must change the date."

"What is the subject of the conference?"

Again the Nazi's finger wagged and his face took on a look of private amusement. "The conference must be delayed because of the diplomatic preparations for war with the United States. There is to be a speech before the Reichstag by the Führer, but our European allies must first be informed, as well as the Japanese ambassador and his staff, and there must be coordination on an administrative and leadership level of all aspects of propaganda and supply and transport. I must make my contribution to all this."

"No doubt."

"So I shall be sending out new invitations for a date in January. Can you imagine? A conference of only a few hours, but so much organization is required. There are ten government bodies whose representatives must attend, and six departments within the ss alone. Six, including mine. Such a lot to do."

A conference that involved Eichmann's department must concern the Jews. Dan ran his finger nervously along the top of his briefcase. He snapped the locks shut. "Who else must you call upon to attend?"

Eichmann blew out a weary breath. It was clear to Dan that the man wished to show the scope of his power, and the extent to which his office reached into the work of other parts of the Nazi system. "Besides the most important ministries, and the bodies responsible for Poland and the occupied east, there must be a representative from the Party's highest office. Then there's the Security Service, the Security Police, the Security Headquarters, and of course the Gestapo."

"You're going to be very busy."

"Not as busy as I'm going to be if all goes well."

"At the conference?"

Eichmann glanced at the empty glass. He seemed to regret his good spirits and the part the schnapps might have played in them. "I've already said more than is necessary for you to know."

As he walked toward the zoo to take the S-Bahn back to the embassy, Dan thought over what he had heard. Visa applications were no longer enough. He was the ambassador of Israel. Israel's role was to provide a haven for Jews, but it was also supposed to be a protector of Jews around the world. *You sound like Shmulik*, he told himself. Shmulik would have worked to find out more about this conference at the Wannsee villa. Then, if it was a threat to Jews, he would have taken action. But Shmulik was out of the picture. *So I must do it.*

Dan crossed the plaza in front of the Zoo Station and bent his head into the wind that gusted cold through the arches under the elevated tracks. Devorah didn't believe her husband was dead. Dan hoped she was right. But even if she was wrong, the tough Mossad man was now alive in him.

Chapter 46

Berlin, January 1942

Snow collected in the ruins of the Countess von Bredow's home. With Gottfried's violin case under his arm, Brückner clambered through the spray of debris in the garden, gathering photos and books, piecing together the life he might have had as the son of a Prussian aristocrat and the famous violinist, her Jewish lover. He stood the case upright against a chunk of masonry. He had brought the violin home. It was all the family he had left. At the Wannsee villa, sluggish as he had been after the blow to his head, Brückner had wrenched the Stradivarius away from Maestro Furtwängler in the confusion that followed the shooting. He blew on his fingers. The cold pierced him.

Here he was, a Wehrmacht captain, Hitler's adjutant, an aristocrat descended from the great Chancellor Bismarck, and the son of a Jew. But what kind of a man was he? It struck him that a man confronted the truth about himself only when he was torn apart like this house, his most private relics exposed, the walls that compartmentalized them smashed. If he were to walk the streets from his mother's bombed-out home to his desk at the Chancellery, he would pass thousands of Berliners, each with a demeanor as inscrutable as the facade of a bourgeois dwelling. None would act on what they knew about the world around them. If their inner truth contradicted the aims of the Nazi regime, almost every one would defy his true self rather than go against the Gestapo. Their minds had become like homes they never entered, whose rooms were unlit. Because the alternative was a devastating explosion that would collapse the ceilings and rip out the pipes. Maybe it was the shock of recent weeks, of learning his parentage and seeing his mother and father executed, but Brückner had uncovered a compulsion to rebuild himself with an entirely different architecture. He felt his jaw, the bruise where Gottfried knocked him out with the pistol butt so that it would look as though the younger man had been fighting to save Hitler, instead of trying to protect the assassin. The bruise would heal and fade, but the love that it embodied would remain. The Countess's son, Wili Gottfried's son, would salvage the soul they had created. He would act in the name of the love they had shared, the love that had brought him into being.

He tossed aside the mementoes he had gathered in the ruins and picked up the violin case once more, then vaulted the wall into the embassy garden. The snow covered the black char of Shmulik's secret bonfire. In the kitchen, a dark woman bent over a soup tureen, stirring and tasting, adding salt. He rapped on the window of the kitchen. The woman dropped her spoon and reeled away. He waved his hand and shook his head.

"Don't be afraid." He mouthed his words exaggeratedly so she would understand through the glass.

Bertha Polkes opened the door hesitantly. Her eyes were frightened and wet. The room smelled of boiled vegetables and broth.

The German shivered. The need for comfort overcame all other impulses. So did the sense that he wouldn't be denied here—that she recognized him for who he truly was. His mother was gone, but he found his desire for motherly comfort was not. His eyes teared up. "I'm very hungry," he said.

Bertha went to the tureen and spooned out a bowlful. He ate at the kitchen table.

Dan Lavi came from the hallway. "It's good, isn't it?"

"The soup? Wonderful." Brückner smiled. His hair was lank from the snow and lay over his forehead.

Dan gestured at the violin case by Brückner's feet. "Is that for me?"

Brückner put down his spoon. "It's for Israel."

Chapter 47

They went down to the firing range in the basement. Devorah stared at the uniformed Wehrmacht man and kicked shut the door to the closet where she kept her code books. She locked it, put on her coat, and headed up the stairs.

"She doesn't need to worry, does she?" Dan said.

"She does. But not about me." Brückner laid the violin case on the gun table. He took off his greatcoat and shook the snow from its shoulders. He took a long shuddering breath and smiled sadly. "I want to help you. With anything you need."

"Is that why you came in the back door?" Dan smiled.

"I won't be the only Wehrmacht officer to fear the Gestapo torture cells before this war is over. I don't know if I'm even the first to risk being caught by them. I do know that what happened to my... my mother and father has changed me. It's hard to explain. Maybe it's like what you felt on the day Israel became a country. You found a home. You knew who you were."

"I was happy that day. I expect you feel loss."

"I do. But in a strange way, I am happy too. Like a ruined city liberated from occupation."

"So what will you do for me? Gather information?"

"I'll do more than that, if you ask me to. Whatever you need."

"Will you kill Hitler?" Dan watched the German's reaction. He wondered if it was what he wanted now—to send a man to kill the German leader.

"It can't be done. That was a big risk in the first place, but now it's simply not possible."

Dan loaded a Luger. The pistol noise would cover their words if anyone was listening. The rooms of the embassy might be bugged by the Gestapo. Or by Shmulik and Devorah. "Why not?"

"The Führer's gone to his headquarters in East Prussia. The Wolf's Lair."

"When's he coming back?"

"He's not. He intends to stay there until…until victory."

"So he ran away?"

Brückner paused and frowned. "There is a reason I was convinced of him for so long, Herr Ambassador. His charisma, his devotion to our country seemed to justify all my pride in being a German, and perhaps also his luck. It has all deserted him."

"Because of Russia?"

"Mostly. It was madness to invade the Soviet Union when we thought the Russians had two-to-one numerical superiority. Now our field intelligence units inform us that our army is actually outnumbered ten-to-one, but the Führer continues to insist we must press our advance. Things are bad out there for us."

"You're here to help because now you see that Germany will lose the war?" Dan lifted the pistol and took aim along the gallery. Shmulik had pinned a photo of a man in a military cap to the target.

"I told you, I want to work for Israel to honor my mother and father. I'm just explaining *why* things are going wrong for Hitler. The dreadful massacres on the Russian front, the killing of Soviet prisoners and of Jews, it will all rebound on us Germans in the end."

"So if we're not going to kill Hitler, what have you to offer me?"

Brückner kneaded his hands. "There was a meeting recently. The Führer took Himmler and Heydrich into his office alone."

"To talk about what?"

"Sometimes the Führer prefers to leave the dirty work to someone else. To keep his hands clean. But the rumor at the Chancellery is that it was to do with the Jews. Now Heydrich is convening a conference. About the Jewish question."

Dan fired the Luger. A shred of photo paper flew off the target as his bullet struck. "Wannsee?"

"How did you know?" Brückner looked at him in shock.

"Eichmann is a little too boastful for his own good."

"These ss leaders have never seen action in the field. At heart they're queasy about the destruction they send other men to carry out."

"Which is to be what, exactly?"

Brückner shrugged. "In the summer, it was still thought that we could ship most of the Jews to Siberia, and the rest could go to your Israel. But then our advance broke down in Russia. So Siberia is out, and frankly I don't think even Israel would take the number of Jews we're talking about. You just wouldn't have the means for it. So Heydrich is working on another solution."

Shmulik's Zyklon B document, the letter from the Nazi chief in Poland to the ss in Berlin. "The final solution."

"The Führer ordered Heydrich to exterminate all the Jews. Physically. To kill them all."

Dan fired the pistol, but this time it was not to create a cover for their words. The shot expressed the shriek of anguish and rage that echoed within him. Again a bullet struck the photo. "Wannsee will be where they make the plans?"

"The conference will be attended by some of the most ruthless men in Germany. Heydrich, Gestapo Chief Müller, that scheming bastard Martin Luther from the foreign ministry."

"Could you get into the conference?"

"Not a chance. It's very high-level."

"Who's going from the Chancellery?"

"Kritzinger, the state secretary."

The man who had hovered at the fringes of the Countess's soirees. Pale and old-fashioned, an upright Prussian civil servant. Dan wondered whether Kritzinger's devotion to duty would override the humanity that connected him to Hannah von Bredow and her anti-Nazi circle. He fired. The Luger filled the gallery again with its short bellow. "Can you get information from Kritzinger?"

"I think he'd be against anything that Heydrich has in mind. He's not that kind of man. But I don't think he'd trust me with details. He'd be afraid it would get back to the Führer."

"You can try."

"I will. But you'd better try to gather the information elsewhere, too. Just in case."

Dan paced down the length of the firing range. The face Shmulik had pinned to the target belonged to Adolf Eichmann. Dan's bullet had pierced the Death's Head on the ss man's hat. He poked his finger into the hole and smiled.

"I know just the man."

Chapter 48

Devorah made her way to the apartment in Friedrichshain without being followed, as far as she could tell. She slipped through the courtyard of a tenement and under an arch in the rear of the block, then knocked at the low door of the coal hole. It swung open and she climbed in.

A single oil lamp lit the cellar. The flickering orange light lit the face of the old communist who bolted the hatch behind her. Devorah crossed the room and knelt beside the bed. She took the cold hand of the man who lay under the thin blanket.

Shmulik squeezed her fingers.

She kissed his forehead. He was feverish. She pulled a package from her handbag. "Sausages, and cheese," she said. She pushed them at him.

He moaned a little as he smiled. "Later. I'm not hungry now."

His skin was pale, his eyes ringed with black. A fetid smell surrounded him. The wounds were rotting. She would have to get him out of here for treatment.

"You're sick, my love." She stroked his sweaty hair. "You're not getting better."

"Kasia's taking good care of me."

The old communist nudged Devorah's shoulder. "He needs a doctor. It's a month since I cut the shrapnel out of his leg, but the wounds haven't healed."

The smell. Devorah asked, "Gangrene?"

"It needs cutting away, so the wounds can heal up."

Shmulik grabbed at his wife's elbow. "We'll talk about my stinking leg in a minute. First I want to know what's been happening."

"Dan brought a Wehrmacht officer into the basement. That Brückner asshole."

"Did he?" Shmulik gave a dreamy smile.

"You don't think that's a stupid risk? I thought you'd be angry."

He worked his tongue for some spit so he could speak. "Stupid or not, I think the Herr Ambassador has finally decided to take a risk."

"Do you want me to do something about it?"

"Not yet. I want you to bring Anna to me. Without Dan's knowledge."

"It won't be easy. Dan has been trying to get her to leave the country since the Germans declared war on America. She refuses to go, but she did agree to inform him whenever she leaves the embassy."

"You'll think of something. Tell her to come with a very sharp knife. It's time I got out of here."

Chapter 49

Eichmann's Kurfürstenstrasse offices were like a college dorm the night before finals when Dan entered. It was after 8 p.m., but the corridors were busy with preoccupied young men, moving fast, scanning documents as they went. Every room Dan passed emitted the scent of cigarettes and coffee, and at every desk a glistening head of hair framed an expression of concentration so deep it seemed painful.

Identical young officers surrounded Eichmann's desk, as though he could give them the answers to all the questions on the exam. They turned with blankly superior faces when Dan knocked at the door. Eichmann gave an irritated frown and ushered his men out.

"What do you want? I'm very busy. I can't process any of your papers this week." Eichmann sifted through a file of statistics on the desk.

"I know. How are preparations for your Wannsee conference progressing?"

"I already asked you, what do you want? Don't make me repeat myself, Lavi." Eichmann looked up, ready to lash out. But Dan's face was so placid before his anger that it made him pause.

"The conference is on January twentieth, the day after tomorrow? At the very villa where Gottfried gave his last concert." Dan came to the side of Eichmann's desk. He had only ever stood before it, like a naughty schoolboy called to the principal. Eichmann drew back in his chair warily, as though a potentially vicious dog approached him.

"My God, don't bring up that concert."

"Uncomfortable events for all of us," Dan said. "But perhaps we can turn them to our advantage."

Eichmann blew out his cheeks and dropped his pen, impatient.

"After Wili Gottfried met his end, you and the other members of the Führer's entourage were concerned for his well-being alone." Even as he spoke, Dan remembered the shots those men had fired into the bodies of the Countess and poor Gottfried. "Someone, on the other hand, remained mindful of an object of great value that was otherwise overlooked."

"Get to the point."

"I have that object at my embassy."

"What object?"

"Wili Gottfried's Stradivarius."

Eichmann perked up. "That must be worth—"

"Several million reichsmarks. The maker's label says it was made in 1719."

"My God, Stradivarius's Golden Period."

"I assume that you, as a connoisseur of the violin, would like to buy it. Either for your personal disposal or as a gift for the Obergruppenführer Heydrich. He's a devoted musician. I'm sure he'd be extremely grateful."

Eichmann was so stunned by the possibility of owning a Stradivarius worth millions that it was a few moments before the conspiratorial expression came over his face. "What do you want for it?"

Dan could have phrased his answer as a request. But it was time this Nazi got used to receiving orders from him. "Bring me Arvid Polkes."

Chapter 50

Dan's plans hinged on the Stradivarius. He was on his way upstairs to bed when he decided he couldn't let it out of his sight. He returned to his office and took the violin case from under his desk. He was slipping it beneath his bed as Anna came in from the dressing room.

"Wili's violin?" She pulled the last pins from her hair. "How did you get hold of that?"

"Brückner brought it." Dan was on his knees. He dropped the bedspread over the violin and stood. "I need to keep an eye on it."

"You're planning something." She brought her arms up around his neck. "What are you up to, Herr Ambassador?"

"Nothing." His lie was so transparent, he laughed. "Nothing you need to know about."

"Bertha said you took Brückner down to the basement earlier today."

"Shooting practice."

She started to ask him a question, but she changed her mind. "I can't get through to Boston. The phone lines are cut off."

After Pearl Harbor, it had taken Hitler four days to make his declaration of war against the United States. Ribbentrop called the US chargé d'affaires to the Foreign Ministry and read him a pack of self-justificatory lies. Then he sent the embassy staff into confinement in a spa town. Other American citizens either got out of Germany or were swiftly interned.

"Do you think they'll come for me?" Anna laid her head against Dan's chest.

"Not as long as they need this embassy working."

"That's all the protection I've got?"

"Welcome to my world." He lifted her chin. "Darling, in all seriousness, it might be best if you left after all. I'd hate to say good-bye, but I've already asked you to risk too much by being here in Berlin. It's time for you to get to safety."

She blinked, and her dark eyes were wide and wet. "I knew all too well that the Nazis were evil, but now that I'm potentially on the receiving end of their crimes…it's only now that I really understand what so many people have been experiencing."

He worried for her, but he was thankful that ignorance kept her empathy directed to Jews whose lives had been constrained, whose employment and civil freedoms were restricted. He was glad she didn't know about the murder squads and the Jews digging their own graves for the executioners out east, because then her fears would grow to all-encompassing terror. "Things are happening that we can't imagine. Really happening, to real people."

"I'm proud of the work you're doing, Danny."

He kissed her forehead.

She murmured into his chest as he held her. "Would you give your life to save other people?"

"What kind of question is that?" He smiled, brushing her off.

She lifted her eyes to his. They were serious and sincere. "The risks you take here might cost you your life, Danny. You have to know that it's worth it."

"I'm not going to lose my life."

"You might. So you must be sure that it's worth it. I love you above all things, but I'd understand if you decided to give your life to save many, many innocent people. I'd understand if you sacrificed me, too."

"That's crazy, sweetheart."

"Listen to me. If you ever face the choice, I want you to remember this. If you must choose between me and a thousand other lives, let me go."

"Darling, don't say that."

"I've treated the ailments of so many little children, Danny. Imagine how I would feel if they were all murdered just to save me."

"No one's talking about murder."

"Yes, they are." Her voice was loud, insisting that he take her seriously. "Draxler hinted at what's happening in the east. He told me to get out of here."

"On that, at least, I agree with Draxler."

"Just promise me that you'll do as I've asked."

He stared at his reflection in her dark eyes. It was more real to him than his own body. The intensity of her gaze forced him to concede. "I promise."

"Thank you, Danny."

"Now *you* promise something to *me*. I don't want to be without you, but, even so, maybe you should get away from here."

"To Israel?"

He considered what might happen to Israel if the "final solution" went ahead, or if Field Marshall Rommel's troops in North Africa succeeded in their push toward the Suez Canal and on into the Middle East oil fields. "I think it's best if you go to Boston. I'll join you when the embassy closes here."

"I can't be without you all that time."

"It won't be forever. It might be less time than you think. I'd say there's a distinct possibility things are going to get extreme here."

"What does that mean?"

She was deeply disturbed. But he couldn't tell her about the Wannsee conference. "I don't know. But I doubt we'll be able to carry on the emigrations much longer. At which point Ben-Gurion will probably send me over to the US to continue my diplomatic work.

I studied there. I have a lot of contacts. And if my wife is there, I'm going to tell him I insist."

"You'd choose me over Ben-Gurion?" She sniffed, smiling.

"He has pretty eyes, but you have nicer legs."

She slapped his shoulder.

"I'll make a reservation for you to fly to Sweden. From there you can get a boat to the States."

She held him tight. "I don't want to go. What will my patients do? What will you do?"

He shuddered with the force of her embrace. His plans for the next day ticked around his head and his adrenaline surged. The risks suddenly seemed greater now that he was holding in his arms the one thing he couldn't stand to lose.

"You'd better start packing," he said.

Chapter 51

Within the massive structure of the Reich Chancellery there were relatively few actual offices. Though guarded by intimidating men of the *Leibstandarte ss Adolf Hitler*, several of the entrances from the street were dummies, placed for architectural effect alone. The massive doors opened onto brick walls. At the center of the complex, Hitler had his office. Little work was ever done in it, little study or discussion. The Führer already knew what he thought and what needed to be done. He used the office to rant and ramble until the early hours of the morning, keeping others from their work or their beds. He was all words. One day, when people stopped listening, he would be nothing. But by then, he would have made millions of others into nothing.

One of the few men in the great architectural white elephant who treated the Chancellery as a genuine place of labor was Friedrich Kritzinger. After almost two decades in the Prussian civil service, he had joined the Nazi Party in 1938 and was transferred to Hitler's staff. He was now the deputy chief of the Chancellery and officials came and went from his office all day. Even so, the arrival of the Führer's adjutant, Brückner, gave him pause. The young man was a reminder of Kritzinger's uncomfortable friendship with the traitor, the Countess von Bredow. He was doubly irritated and anxious at Brückner's presence because he had only one more hour to prepare himself for the conference at the villa in Wannsee. The meeting would draw him into the presence of the Blond Beast, Heydrich, and the Gestapo's senior officers. Even had he not feared the possible policy conclusions of the conference, the attendees would have made his skin crawl. Now he was in the presence of a man who might recall enough of the Countess's soirees to reinforce the Gestapo's unpleasant interest in Kritzinger.

"Hauptmann Brückner, how may I help you?"

The adjutant shut the door behind him. Kritzinger stretched his neck in his old-fashioned round collar and turned his head to one side. His long service in the Nazi government had trained him in silence when another man prepared to speak.

"I represent a group of gentlemen who would be very interested in immediately learning the results of today's conference at Wannsee." Brückner leaned close to the state secretary, his hands on the man's desk.

"Which gentlemen?"

"It would be best not to say."

"The conference is organized by Obergruppenführer Heydrich." That name was enough to signal the extreme risk Brückner was asking him to take.

"I occupy a position very close to the Führer," Brückner said. "In a couple of days I shall be joining him at the Wolf's Lair. There are certain powerful persons in the leadership of the Wehrmacht—"

Kritzinger cut him off. "Plotters? I don't want to know about this."

Brückner hammered down his hand on the desk. "You *shall* know about it. You know enough of the conduct of the war in Russia to understand that we can no longer win, but the Führer will never sue for peace. A change is leadership is inevitable. Once Hitler is gone, questions will be asked about those who made criminal decisions on behalf of the Nazi regime. Do you want to be among those who stand trial when this war is lost?"

"What on earth are you talking about? What criminal decisions?"

"You know the subject of this Wannsee Conference. You understand what you're involving yourself in, Kritzinger."

So, it *was* the Jews Brückner wanted to know about. "My aim is to provide a moderating voice—"

"Moderation? When you're forced to answer for your participation in this venture, will you say, 'Heydrich wanted to exterminate a million Jews. I persuaded him to murder only a half million'? Kritzinger, you're a lawyer. Do you think that constitutes a convincing defense?"

"But I asked the Führer in person if there was any program of extermination against the Jews," Kritzinger said. "I told him that I couldn't believe he would allow such a thing. He reassured me entirely. His words were that he intended no mass murder of innocent civilians."

"Among the Jews or any other of our enemies, does Hitler consider anyone to be innocent? The man is toying with you, Kritzinger."

Kritzinger fingered the Nazi Party pin on his lapel. He had come late to membership, and it was not an ideological commitment. But it was there, like a tattoo on his body. He thought of all the apparently innocent decisions that had led him to this day, the moments of gradual surrender, the hints of freedom evident at the Countess's musical evenings. Yes, he was a lawyer, and he knew how his actions would be portrayed were he ever called before a tribunal. Following orders was no defense. Neither was fear of the consequences of doing what was right. Certainly, the desire to promote one's successful administrative career wouldn't impress any prosecutor.

"Eichmann is the official note taker for the conference," he murmured. "He will write the minutes."

"Bring them to me." Brückner laid his hand on Kritzinger's shoulder. "We are Prussians, you and I. We carry the legacy of centuries of honorable history, of military and governmental achievement. Are you going to let the Blond Beast tarnish that?"

Kritzinger vacillated. The fingers tightened on his shoulder.

"Are you going to let an Austrian corporal shit all over that legacy?"

The army, thought Kritzinger, was finally rejecting the excesses of the Nazi regime. Brückner wanted to show the minutes of the Wannsee conference to Wehrmacht men who perhaps remained on the fence. Surely it would bring them into action against Hitler. In any case, it would be best to play both sides of the game.

"The meeting is expected to last only a few hours," he said.

"I expect your report by—" Brückner checked his watch. "—fifteen hundred hours."

Kritzinger's stomach convulsed. But here was an order and in obeying it he gave himself a way out, some protection if the plotters— the army, or whoever they were—took over in Berlin. "You shall have it, Herr Hauptmann."

Chapter 52

Anna sliced carefully with her scalpel, but Shmulik's leg still shuddered at her touch. The anesthetic wasn't strong enough. She was cutting away dead, rotten flesh, but he must have felt as though an entire limb were coming off. "Almost done," she murmured. She laid the last strip of gangrenous flesh in the metal tray at her side.

Devorah wrung out the cloth with which she was cooling her husband's brow and dipped it into the water bowl on the side table.

"You shouldn't have waited so long to call me here, Shmulik," Anna whispered. She dabbed alcohol around the bullet holes to clean the wounds. "You almost missed me."

Shmulik and Devorah grew suddenly alert. Anna wondered if they were alarmed to think that they had been so close to finding themselves without a doctor. She focused on the raw, tender skin.

Shmulik grunted in pain. "Are you going somewhere?"

"I'm leaving for Sweden. Straight from here to the airport." Anna reached into her bag. "This one needs stitches."

"Why are you going to Sweden?"

"They're interning Americans. I have to go before they get around to me."

"But you're not in Berlin as an American. You're an Israeli. The ambassador's wife. Israel is neutral."

She threaded the surgical needle and pressed the lips of the wound together. "Israeli neutrality is how *you* got yourself shot."

"This was an accident."

"Which is why you're hiding in a cellar." She drove the needle through his skin and looped the thread around.

Shmulik winced and cleared his throat. "Won't Dan miss you in Sweden?"

"I'm not staying in Sweden. I'm going on to the States. Dan will probably join me soon enough."

"Will he? Really?"

She cut the thread and tied it off. "He seems to think the emigrations are going to be shut down before long. That'll be the end of the embassy here in Berlin."

Devorah rolled a bandage around Shmulik's wounds to dress them.

Anna packed up her bag. "I have to get going. Nearly time for my flight." She hugged Devorah. "I'll miss you."

"Safe trip," Devorah said.

Shmulik grabbed Anna's arm and squeezed. "Don't tell the Herr Ambassador where I am."

"Why not?"

"It's better he doesn't know. I might have to stay underground to continue my work here in Germany. Even after Dan closes the embassy. Promise me you won't tell him."

Anna stared, unnerved. She knew that Shmulik trusted no one other than his wife, but she was troubled to be part of this secret, just as she had been surprised to discover that he hadn't contacted Dan. "I won't."

She tried to move away, but Shmulik held onto her arm. "If the Gestapo take him—"

"Why would the Gestapo take Dan?"

"—he mustn't know more than he needs to know."

She climbed out of the hatch into the covered arch at the rear of the courtyard. Did Shmulik warn her because, underneath his hostility, he cared for Dan? Or was it that he didn't trust him to withstand Gestapo torture? Perhaps both were true. She whispered another farewell to Devorah and turned away.

The sky was a uniform white-gray. She imagined her plane climbing through that blank cloud to Sweden, to a world where everything wasn't oppressive and violent. Her heels clipped across the cobbles. She pictured the airplane faltering, failing to make cruising height because of the blanket of white. She closed her eyes and took a long breath. She was too stressed. Soon she would be away from here and Berlin would be just a memory.

When she opened her eyes again, a man in a long leather coat stood before her. His fedora was angled steeply because of the bandage on his wounded forehead. Anna felt a sudden pounding all through her body, her blood surging, her heart crushed by shock and fear.

Draxler motioned his Gestapo detail across the courtyard to the coal hole where Shmulik and Devorah were hiding. His black Mercedes pulled up at the curb in front of the gates at the courtyard exit. "Come with me, *Frau Doktor*," he said.

He took Anna's elbow. She wrenched it away and tried to run for the cellar. Draxler must have followed her here. She had led the Gestapo to Shmulik's hideout. She had to warn them. "Shmulik," she yelled. "Devorah, look out."

But where could they go? They were trapped in a basement, and Shmulik could barely move. Her cry was futile.

Draxler got her around the waist and, lifting her feet from the floor, hauled her to the street. The rear door of his car opened.

Struggling against Draxler's hold, Anna glimpsed the Gestapo men at the coal hole. They blew open the hatch with a grenade and knelt before the opening. Gunshots sounded down in the hideout, and one of the Gestapo men took a bullet. Another pulled the pin on a grenade and tossed it inside.

"No, no," she screamed.

Draxler wrestled her into the Mercedes.

The grenade boomed and smoke billowed from the cellar.

She bit Draxler's hand through his leather glove. He pulled away. She clawed at his face, wrenched the bandage from his wound down over his eyes.

"You're lucky I like you," he growled. He gave her a single sharp jab with the heel of his hand on the side of her neck. It was the practiced strike of a violent policeman who knows how to subdue a suspect with a knock-out blow.

The Mercedes door slammed and the engine roared. But Anna heard nothing. She faded away. She was in the sky, flying through the blank clouds. The world was far below. She was on her way to safety. The air up there was so very thin, so hard to breathe. She passed out.

Chapter 53

Down the leafy, peaceful drive and through the elegant portico of the Wannsee villa, Kritzinger found the bureaucrats relaxing with tulip glasses of cognac. He took a drink and held it in both hands so that it wouldn't shake. When Heydrich offered a toast to the work they would do at their conference that day, the State Secretary of the Chancellery brought the brandy to his mouth quickly. He drank too fast, but his choking cough was lost in the general merriment. They had great tasks ahead of them at the Führer's behest. They chatted about history, and how the Reich would remember them. Each man, thought Kritzinger, carried a spark of avarice in his eyes, as though the power that would accrue to him as a result of the day's proceedings was money in the bank. No doubt for some of them it truly was. For all of them, dominance was the aphrodisiac that excited.

Eichmann clinked his glass against Kritzinger's cognac. The contact was too strong, as though Eichmann were a little drunk, or nervous. *Perhaps it's both*, Kritzinger thought. Their business that day would have been enough to drive anyone to drink, to calm the nerves or to court oblivion.

"*Prost*, Herr State Secretary," Eichmann said. "A proud day for us all."

Kritzinger lowered his eyes. Brückner had seemed so sure of himself, and he argued so convincingly that the war had turned against Germany. But now that he was in the presence of the Blond Beast Heydrich and his entourage, Kritzinger wondered if a decent man like Brückner could ever have a chance against such ruthless figures. "A proud day, yes, indeed," he murmured. "Thank you for organizing this conference, Herr Obersturmbannführer."

Eichmann clicked his heels. "The honor is mine." He turned to the group. "Herr Obergruppenführer Heydrich, all is prepared."

"Then let's begin. Gentlemen," Heydrich said in his reedy falsetto, "let us step into the conference room, and into the future of the German people."

Fifteen men settled around the long table, with Heydrich at the head and Eichmann keeping the official record of the discussion. Kritzinger found himself seated across from Heinrich Müller. The Gestapo chief stared at him, his brow angled downward, eyes disapproving, mouth sullen. Kritzinger's neck twitched and he looked away, focusing on his papers.

Heydrich tapped his knuckles on the tabletop. "The Reichsführer-ss has appointed me delegate for the preparations of a final solution for the Jewish question in Europe. The Reichsführer wishes to have a draft sent to him concerning the organizational, factual, and material interests in relation to this final solution. Therefore, we have brought together in your persons the central offices immediately concerned. I shall begin with a brief report on the effort so far, inasmuch as it concerns the expulsion of Jews from every sphere of life, and from the living space of the German people."

Kritzinger listened to Heydrich's summary of the Jewish emigrations, the founding of Eichmann's Central Office for Jewish Emigration and the extortion, bullying, and fear—Heydrich called them "procedures"—used to speed the expulsion of the Jews. "All this was carried out in a legal manner," Heydrich said.

Legal within a system of illegality, Kritzinger thought. He clapped his hand over his mouth as though he had spoken aloud and his eyes flickered around the table. He shivered. What would he have done had Brückner not offered him a channel for his sense of disgust? Would he still have sat here silently?

"In spite of the difficulties with encouraging emigration," Heydrich went on, "such as the demand by various foreign governments for increasing sums of money to be presented by Jews at the time of their immigration, the lack of shipping space, increasing restrictions on entry permits, or the cancelling of such, five hundred and thirty-seven thousand Jews were sent out of the Reich between the assumption of power by the Party and October 31, 1941."

Several of the men at the table turned briefly toward Eichmann. This was the work of his office. Though Kritzinger read jealousy and dislike on their faces, rather than congratulation, Eichmann gave a businesslike smile and bowed his head in acknowledgement.

"Another possible solution of the problem has now taken the place of emigration," Heydrich said. "That is, the evacuation of the Jews to the East, provided that the Führer gives the appropriate approval in advance."

Gestapo Chief Müller made a whispering hiss, like escaping gas, and grinned at Stuckart, the interior ministry's expert on race law. Stuckart shrank his shoulders down into his double-breasted jacket.

Heydrich watched Müller. As always, he registered no emotion, but he let the silence linger long enough for even Müller to appear a little cowed. "Practical experience is already being collected—" Heydrich gestured toward Eichmann, who again bowed slightly "—which is of the greatest importance in relation to the future final solution of the Jewish question."

At a nod from the chairman, Eichmann produced a sheet of paper. "You have in your dossiers a copy of the statistics compiled by my office. Approximately eleven million Jews will be involved in the final solution of the European Jewish question."

Kritzinger scanned the list of countries and the numbers of Jews. List A for Jews already under Nazi control in Germany, Poland, Norway, Belgium, France, and so on. List B for those in countries soon to be conquered, or coerced as allies into a role in the final solution—England, Ireland, Slovakia, the USSR.

"I'm glad you didn't leave Sardinia out of your calculation of Italian Jews, Obersturmbannführer Eichmann." Müller leered sarcastically, waving Eichmann's precise tables of figures. The Gestapo chief was given to blunter methods. "Or the two hundred Jews of Albania."

Heydrich licked his lips, the nearest he ever got to an outward display of displeasure. "The statistics are of necessity comprehensive. That is the task of the Obersturmbannführer Eichmann's office."

"Fine." Müller waved his hand in the air. "We find a Jew. We send him east. He dies."

Eichmann broke in. "The statistics must be maintained throughout the execution of the final solution, Gruppenführer Müller. If our forces were to, say, execute a considerable number of Jews in the field, but were subsequently to fail to document and report it, how would we know if *all* the Jews of Europe had been removed to the east or killed? The statistics compiled by my office will ensure that we know exactly how much work has been done and enable us to give the Führer a definitive report when the final Jew is removed from Europe."

A brittle, tense voice spoke up. It took Kritzinger a moment to realize it came from him. "It cannot be that the final solution should mean the actual extermination of the Jews of Europe. I ask you, Herr Obergruppenführer Heydrich, to confirm for me, now, that the insinuations of Herr Gruppenführer Müller are not the policy of the Reich."

The men about the table grumbled under their breath, as though an overenthusiastic student had asked a pointless question of the teacher when everyone else was ready to pack up their books and head for recess. Heydrich's gaze swept from Kritzinger's hands to his face. "The ss has commenced the construction of extermination camps for the Jews in the *Generalgouvernement* of Poland."

"But the Führer—" Kritzinger said.

"In Poland? You haven't cleared that with us," bellowed Bühler, the representative of the Nazi governor of Poland.

"The Führer promised me in person that extermination was not being considered." Kritzinger recalled Hitler's voice as he had

spoken those words to him, and wondered what other lies the Führer had told him.

Heydrich merely pursed his lips and ignored him.

Stuckart started protesting that the interior ministry ought
to have been consulted about extermination camps and the process
for killing the Jews. Kritzinger settled back into his chair. His objec-
tions were over, for this meeting at least. He would give Brückner
the report on the conference he wanted.

Within a few minutes, the representatives of the ministries
and the other Reich bodies fell silent. They brooded, knowing now,
as Kritzinger did, that the conference was not about formulating a
solution to the Jewish question, as Heydrich had said. That job was
already done. The extermination camps were built. The Wannsee
conference was a forum for Heydrich to instruct the ministries and
offices of the entire regime that it was the ss which would be solely
responsible for the Jews. For the murder of millions. Of an entire
people.

"It falls to me now," Heydrich said, "to ask for the support of
every man around the table."

He went from one functionary to the next, watching them
keenly, daring them to look him in the eye. None of them did. Some
offered caveats about the need for Jews to be kept alive as slave labor
for the sake of the war economy, but all acceded to the demands of
the ss.

When his turn came, Kritzinger gave a curt nod and said, "I
am with you." His nervousness abated. His struggle was over.

Heydrich brought them all into the salon for a cognac while
Eichmann dictated the minutes of the meeting to a group of secretaries upstairs. The functionaries lingered over their drinks as Heydrich
grew drunk. When the representative from the Ministry of Justice
got up from his chair, Heydrich ordered him to sit. "I want you all
to approve the minutes before you leave," he slurred.

Eichmann came down the stairs and distributed a thin sheaf
of papers to each man.

Kritzinger took his copy and glanced through it. "These are
not verbatim."

"A summary is enough," Heydrich said. "Sign for them and you may go."

Kritzinger initialed Eichmann's register and put the minutes in his briefcase. Before he closed the case he saw his name on the first page in the list of participants. It may as well have been branded on his forehead. He was marked forever. He bade good day to Heydrich. The chief of the state security services ignored him and took another sip of brandy.

Chapter 54

Water was dripping from Arvid Polkes's head when the Gestapo man brought him up into the airy, vaulted hallway at 8 Prinz-Albrecht-Strasse. His massive shoulders shook. He held his hands before his groin as though they were still cuffed. He seemed near death. Dan put his arm around him, then stumbled under the man's considerable weight. He felt a chill through his jacket. Polkes was soaking wet.

"Bertha is waiting for you, Arvid," Dan whispered.

The staring, terrified eyes flickered.

The Gestapo man strolled over to them, rolling breezily on his heels. "Get that sack of shit out of here before I decide to give you a bit of what he got."

"He's being released by Obersturmbannführer Eichmann, who will hear about the treatment to which his prisoner was subjected."

The officer took a pack of cigarettes from his pocket and lit one. "I'll be glad to draw the Obersturmbannführer a diagram of what we did to the big Yid." He shoved Polkes playfully on the shoulder. "Want another ice bath, Jew boy?"

Dan bit his tongue. The Gestapo man's eyes dared him to speak, to curse, but he refused to give him the satisfaction. Dan hurried Polkes out into the street and into the embassy car. He wrapped him in a blanket and headed up Wilhelmstrasse.

They turned onto Unter den Linden in a silence broken only by the chattering of Polkes's teeth. As they passed under the air-raid camouflage, Dan felt a cold touch on his hand. He pulled away reflexively.

Polkes smiled at him. A few of his teeth were missing. "Thank you, Dan. How did you get me out?"

Dan reached for the cold hand and clasped it. It was like a big steak just out of the freezer. Eventually he felt it warm, blood moving through the poor man's beaten body again. "I made someone an irresistible offer."

"How can I repay you?"

"You can help me close the deal. How badly hurt are you?"

Polkes shrugged his big shoulders. "I doubt that I'll father any more children. But no bones are broken."

He was six inches taller than Dan, and twice as wide. Once he warmed up and stood straight, he'd be intimidating enough. Dan figured Polkes might enjoy the task he wanted him to perform.

"How would you like to beat up a Nazi?" he said.

Chapter 55

Brückner took the papers from Kritzinger's shaking hand. The state secretary let out a sigh, as though he had held his breath all the way from Wannsee to the Chancellery.

The first page was stamped in red: *Top Secret*. Brückner scanned the page.

Minutes of Discussion

The following persons took part in the discussion about the final solution of the Jewish question which took place in Berlin, Am Grossen Wannsee No. 56/58 on January 20, 1942...

He flipped through all fifteen pages, reading one paragraph several times, the awful meaning too much to take in at first. *"Another possible solution of the problem has now taken the place of emigration, i.e. the evacuation of the Jews to the East, provided that the Führer gives the appropriate approval in advance."* No more emigration. Now it was evacuation. Forcible deportation. To who knew where.

He glanced at the end. The conclusion was anodyne enough. *"The meeting was closed with the request of the Chief of the Security Police and the* SD *to the participants that they afford him appropriate support during the carrying out of the tasks involved in the solution."* He looked up at Kritzinger. "What happened?"

"The Jews belong to the SS," Kritzinger whispered. "Heydrich has frozen out all other governmental bodies."

"And what will the SS do with the Jews?" Brückner put the minutes of the Wannsee conference into his attaché case. "Where will they send them?"

Kritzinger put his hand to his chest. It covered the Nazi Party pin on his lapel, and also his heart. Both items were presently assaulting his guilty conscience, Brückner thought.

"They will exterminate them," Kritzinger said. "In Poland. I intend to tender my resignation today. To the Führer himself."

"Are you going to tell him why? I'm sure he'll be touched by your concern for the Jews while he's off in East Prussia planning his next suicidal assault against the Russians."

"I believe that the Führer would never approve of this—"

"Heydrich will exterminate the Jews only with the Führer's approval. He even says so in your damned minutes. The Blond Beast is doing this at the Führer's behest, and he knows that the approval is a mere formality. If Jews are being gassed en masse then this document proves that Hitler wants it done." Brückner took his greatcoat from the hat stand. "I'm going out. When I get back, I want to know exactly where these camps are."

"I told you, it's an SS matter. They won't give that information to me."

"Tell them the Führer wants to have a better idea of the numbers of rolling stock needed to transport the Jews, so he can figure out how many troops the railways will be able to move to Russia while these Jews are being shipped to Poland. It's just the kind of detail he likes to meddle in. Get a breakdown by camp. Make it something bureaucratic and statistical like that. That way the SS won't even notice that you're asking for a list of death camps and their locations. Tell them it's an immediate necessity."

Kritzinger stiffened his back and nodded his head curtly. Perhaps he had already managed to forget that this wasn't a real order. He had converted his subterfuge into a command received, and so the obligation to carry it out overcame his fear.

The captain exited to the corridor and made the long, echoing walk down the center of the Chancellery's massive hallway toward the exit. Kritzinger sidled along the red marble wall to his office.

Chapter 56

Eichmann stopped his driver at the Hackescher Market and told him to go get a beer and wait for him. He walked under the elevated rail lines and hurried into the Monbijou Park. His mouth was dry and his pulse fast with anticipation. What a day. He had earned the respect of the Obergruppenführer Heydrich for his precise delineation of the statistical scope of the Jewish question that morning at the Wannsee conference. Now he would secure wealth and comfort for the remainder of his life by taking possession of the Stradivarius. All at the cost of one Jew freed from the Gestapo cellars. Freed for the time being. His lips trembled as he suppressed a smile.

Eichmann walked briskly past the empty yellow benches for Jews in the park to reach Monbijoustrasse. The wind off the Spree was icy. He pulled his collar up around his neck. Two, perhaps three million reichsmarks, the violin was worth. A glance at his watch. Twelve fifty-nine. Right on time. He crossed the road and scuttled toward the ruins of Countess von Bredow's home. As he did so, a woman emerged from the door of the Israeli embassy. A Jew of the Polish sort, Eichmann thought, with a touch of Romania in the gypsy olive skin and the big almond eyes. The Polkes woman. She carried a tray of large cups down the steps. The soup in the cups steamed around her. She smiled nervously and invited the Gestapo guards to take some. They clapped their cold hands and joined her on the stone bench beside the steps. Out of sight of the road and the sidewalk. It was shocking that they should fraternize with a Jew that way. Still, the ambassador was keeping to the deal. He had sent out this woman, who was supposed to be in hiding, to signal to Eichmann that he was ready for him.

Eichmann slipped into the rubble of the bombed-out mansion, scrambling over the debris. He stumbled and jammed his knee painfully against a broken chair. A spray of splinters stuck through his breeches. He limped over the first mound and fell again. This time his shoulder took the impact.

He rested briefly, panting. He was out of sight of the Gestapo detail, even if they did decide to abandon the shelter of the stairway and the presence of an attractive woman to drink their soup in the windy street. But they wouldn't. The Gestapo was the laziest organ of the Nazi regime. Without its energetic informants, its agents would never arrest a soul. Eichmann picked himself up and climbed more carefully now across the stone and shattered furnishings and scattered clothing to the garden at the rear. He lifted his leg onto the garden wall and hauled himself over.

As he landed, his ankle twisted. He cursed and rolled onto his back. He flexed his foot inside his jackboot. The dampness of the grass seeped into his clothing. He forced himself to his feet.

The rear door of the embassy opened. Eichmann went gingerly toward it.

Chapter 57

Dan shut the kitchen door. Eichmann leaned against the table, shaking his injured leg. He turned to the ambassador and grinned. "Lucky I have a comfortable desk job," he said.

Dan didn't return the smile. He gestured toward the hall. "This way."

They went across the lobby, toward the office where Wili Gottfried had worked. Eichmann stared about him. He processed thousands of Jews who made their applications through this embassy. Dan figured it had never occurred to the man that it was a real place of bricks and stairs and wall-mounted radiators, just as the lists of Jews he compiled couldn't really have been made up of actual people who hurt themselves when they fell. He saw Eichmann as he truly was, now that he had him on his own territory. The ss man was fairly stupid, deeply egotistical, and capable of profound hatred. But most of all, he was weak. A day in the front lines of battle would have finished him. Dan would break him easily.

"Gottfried worked in that room," he said. "Sometimes he would practice his pieces there, too."

"I can hear the traces of music." Eichmann went over the rug to the door of Gottfried's office. "I really can."

He went inside. Polkes spun out from behind the door and smashed Eichmann in the face with his big fist. He wore a long leather coat similar to those favored by Gestapo agents.

Eichmann tumbled to the ground, and Polkes dropped onto him. The Nazi fumbled for his pistol, but the weight on him was too much. His face turned purple as Polkes cut off his windpipe.

Eichmann swiveled his eyes toward Dan and tried to croak out a plea for mercy.

The snarl on Polkes's lips was almost enough to make Dan forget his plans. He wished he could just let the poor tortured fellow finish Eichmann right now. He shook his head. "Arvid, that's enough."

Polkes relaxed his grip on Eichmann's neck. He slapped him hard across the face, then back again with his knuckles.

Eichmann cried out.

"Get undressed," Dan ordered. "Arvid. Help him."

Eichmann struggled against Polkes as the big man unbuttoned him and pulled off his clothing. Dan took a damp, ragged suit and a collarless shirt from the wing chair by the door. "Put these on," he said.

Polkes grinned. "They're mine, see? They may be a bit big on you, little man. But the ice bath at Prinz-Albrecht-Strasse might've shrunk them. You could be in luck."

Eichmann stepped into the freezing pants and shivered. "What about the violin?"

"You can give up on that. It's not going to be yours."

"What do you want from me? I'll cooperate. If I do what you want, you'll give me the Stradivarius? I'm prepared to help. Talk to me, for God's sake. I'm fucking freezing."

"We're going somewhere."

"You won't get me past the Gestapo out on the sidewalk." Eichmann pushed his arms through the sodden sleeves of Polkes's discarded jacket. "Give me the violin and we'll forget all about this."

Dan almost admired Eichmann's avarice. It was stronger than self-preservation. For now.

When Dan took off his own clothes and put on Eichmann's uniform, the Nazi's face grew cunning. "So that's your idea? You look about as much like an ss man as that nigger, Jesse Owens. No one's going to swallow it. You'll be questioned right away."

"Unfortunately for you, no one asks questions of the ss."

The door opened. Brückner came through. He glanced at Eichmann with disgust. He opened his attaché case and handed a sheaf of papers to Dan.

Eichmann wrestled against Polkes's hold. "That document is a top state secret. You traitor, Brückner."

"A man can't betray that which doesn't exist." Brückner shut his case. "Nazism is a fake ideal, an unreal world. If anything is betrayed in these documents, it's humanity. Germany, too. Which makes *you* guilty, not me."

Dan slipped the papers inside his ss tunic and buttoned it up. "How do I look?"

"Like a mass murderer," Brückner said. "The car's outside."

"This is madness," Eichmann shouted. "Don't do it. Listen, I won't talk. Let's forget this happened."

"Shut him up," Dan said.

Polkes brought his arm around Eichmann's throat to cut off his blood. In a few seconds he'd be out.

"Wait, wait," Eichmann said. "There's something you need to know. Let me go and I'll free her."

"Free whom?" Dan tugged Eichmann's leather gloves onto his hands.

"You don't know?" Eichmann stood upright. He smiled. "You don't, do you? Your wife is at Prinz-Albrecht-Strasse. When you went to collect your friend Polkes, she was probably in the basement with electrodes on her tits." Dan's breath grew shallow. Anna, in the Gestapo cells.

"She went to treat the wounds of your secret service man on her way to the airport. We picked her up this morning." Eichmann was laughing with relief. "Herr and Frau Shmulik Shoham didn't go so easily. They were killed resisting arrest."

Dan glanced down the staircase to the Mossad office in the basement. The door was open. Devorah's desk was unoccupied.

"So you'd better forget your little plan." Eichmann wriggled out of Polkes's grasp. "Get out of my uniform, you shitty Yid bastard, and hand over the violin if you ever want to see your wife alive again."

Polkes watched for a sign, waiting to see what he should do.

Dan heard Anna's voice, sensed her touch on the back of his neck. She was alive, he knew it. He would go to her, wherever she was. He would save her. He took off the ss cap and unfastened the top few buttons on the tunic. His fingers brushed the minutes of the Wannsee conference hidden against his chest. He paused, remembering Anna's gaze as she forced a promise from him. *If you must choose between me and a thousand other lives, let me go.*

What if he rescued Anna now? She would learn what he had given up for her. He was working to save hundreds of thousands of Jews, perhaps even millions. What would she think of him if, instead, he gave in to Eichmann's threats? Because of her. *Let me go.*

"Get out of my uniform." Eichmann started to take off his jacket. "Give me the violin, and I will arrange for your wife to be freed."

"This isn't about my wife." Dan spoke quietly.

"Don't be ridiculous. Do you know what's going to happen to your little *Frau* if you try anything stupid with me? This traitor Brückner just gave you the outline of the conference, but I know the details. Everything starts right away. If you play this wrong, the final solution starts with your wife. Tomorrow she goes east. On a train, in a cattle car, packed in with a load of other Yids from the Gestapo cellars."

"East? To the ghettoes?"

"To Auschwitz, you sack of shit. To the death camp. She'll be exterminated, just as the rest of you will soon be." Eichmann dropped the wet jacket on the floor and shook his head, smiling. "I really thought this was all about her."

Dan took a pace toward him. "It's not about her at all. It's about an entire people. Anna knows that. Which is why you're coming with us now, whatever happens to my wife."

Polkes shook his head. "Dan, you can't."

Dan slipped Eichmann's holster over his shoulder and cinched the belt. He took the Luger out. "It's not about saving one person, Arvid. No matter how much she means to me."

"You're crazy." Eichmann's assurance seeped away. "What are you going to do?"

"The last time you went to Palestine, in 1936, the British deported you." Dan held the Luger by the barrel and rested the grip against Eichmann's jaw. "Fortunately for you, there's a new regime there. Israel will have a much more eager welcome for you."

"You're kidnapping me? Me, the Obersturmbannführer?"

Dan swung the pistol sharply against Eichmann's face. It struck in front of his ear, where the jaw met the skull. The Nazi slumped, unconscious, into Polkes's arms.

"That'll keep him under for a while," Dan said. "Let's go."

Bertha was beside the steps with the Gestapo watchers when Dan came out. She looked up at the doorway. Polkes carried the unconscious Nazi roughly, as a Gestapo agent would be expected to handle a Jew. Brückner slammed the door behind them.

Bertha dropped the tray of empty soup cups. The Gestapo men, who were now enjoying contraband American cigarettes she had brought them, wheeled toward the door.

"My husband," she bawled. "Arvid. Where are you taking my husband?"

She rushed to the foot of the steps. Dan pushed her away, but she grabbed at Eichmann's limp body. "Arvid, no. Don't take my Arvid."

Dan backhanded Bertha on her nose. He barked at the Gestapo men. "Do your job, for God's sake. Hold this bitch until she calms down."

The two guards needed no more urging than the command in his voice and the Death's Head on his cap. They hauled Bertha away from the steps. One of them gave her a sharp jab in the solar plexus and she doubled over, gasping and breathless.

Arvid Polkes squeezed his eyes shut. He thrust Eichmann's body into the back of the Mercedes staff car at the curb. Brückner went to the driver's seat.

Dan called to the two Gestapo men. "Stick her in the car too. Her husband may talk faster if he sees her hanging upside down in the cells."

The two men leered. Dan waited for them to shove Bertha into the backseat, then closed the door and climbed into the front.

Brückner took the car fast, to the south, toward the airfield. Dan stared ahead as they crossed the Spree and skirted the government district.

"Polkes can take Eichmann to Palestine on his own," Brückner said. "You can tell him who to contact. But you should stay here. I'll help you get Anna out before she's sent east."

"Polkes won't be able to convince Ben-Gurion. I'm close to the prime minister. He'll listen to me. God knows, if someone told me the Nazis intended to exterminate every last Jew in Europe, I'd find it hard enough to believe. I have to be there to drive this home. I mustn't deviate from the plan."

Dan wondered if he could have been so decisive, so ruthless, had he not been wearing an ss uniform.

Chapter 58

Schulze laughed harder than any man about to risk his life had a right to. He grabbed for the lapels of Dan's ss uniform and shook him. The Luftwaffe pilot was as filled with good humor as he had been when Dan first met him at the Countess's soiree. He helped Polkes and Bertha pull Eichmann out of the car and cram him behind the backseat of his Messerschmitt Bf 108 personnel transport.

Dan shook Brückner's hand in farewell and the young adjutant pulled his Mercedes across the outer field at Tempelhof, heading back to the Chancellery. He took the copilot's seat in the Messerschmitt. Schulze started the V8 engine and got the propeller moving.

"Here, hold this." Schulze shoved a folded map into Dan's lap and pulled his radio mask over his face.

"Tempelhof tower, this is Parrot three. Requesting confirmation, takeoff south lane." He gave a thumbs up and grinned.

Through the flickering blades of the propeller, Dan watched the runway stretch before them as the small, long-range transport plane came around. Schulze let out the throttle and they rumbled along the tarmac, picking up speed. Then the wheels left the ground and there was only the humming of the engine and the quiet sobbing of Bertha Polkes against her husband's chest. Inside his tunic, Dan carried the minutes of the Wannsee meeting. They felt cold on his belly. Then he realized it was the chill of the unheated aircraft as they passed into the winter cloud above Berlin.

The world was below him. Between the clouds, he caught glimpses of the Prussian plain. Down there, on the surface of the earth, the lives of millions of Jews depended upon him and on how he played his hand. Anna waited there, too. He had to get Eichmann and the Wannsee notes to Ben-Gurion. Then he had to persuade the Old Man to take a step which he hoped would change the course of the war. Certainly it was the only hope for the millions listed in Eichmann's Wannsee protocols.

Schulze banked to the southwest. "Next stop Bucharest, for a refuel."

"We can get that far in this plane?"

"The Typhoon has a range of one thousand kilometers. That's why I picked her. I have an old flying school pal in Romania who's going to make sure we get tanked up, no questions asked. Then it's straight on to our final destination."

Eichmann groaned and raised his head. He looked about the cockpit, seeming unsurprised to be stuffed into the small space behind the two rear seats. He scrabbled to make himself more comfortable, wriggling against the bonds Polkes had tied on his wrists. Recognizing the Luftwaffe pilot from the soiree at the Countess's mansion, he shouted, "Oberleutnant Schulze, you will be executed for this. I insist you free me now and return to Tempelhof field."

With a broad smile, Schulze called back over the din of the engine. "Obersturmbannführer Eichmann, thanks to Nazis like you, Germany is doomed. So it makes no difference to me if I live or die. On the other hand, I am quite determined that *you* shall not live."

"You're a traitor."

"Filthy pig." Bertha Polkes hammered her fist into Eichmann's jaw. She sniffled and shook her hand. The blow had hurt her knuckles. "That was from Anna," she said. Arvid touched her face gently. She leaned over the seat and spat at the bound Nazi.

No, Dan thought. *I'm the one who will strike the blows for Anna.*
He opened up the map. With a red pencil, Schulze had plotted their
route across the Carpathians to Bucharest. He unfolded the next section, which covered the Black Sea and Turkey, then went all the way
down into the Levant. The red line ended with a point over a country
that wasn't even marked on the Luftwaffe chart. They were going to
Israel. Carrying with them the ss plan for the extermination of the
Jews. Taking Eichmann to Jerusalem.

Chapter 59

The pages of the Wannsee minutes turned slowly. Ben-Gurion shut his eyes. He seemed to be imagining these unconscionable deliberations, as if they unfolded before him. He read on, shaking his head when he reached page six. The table of statistics, the Jewish populations that were to be eradicated. He looked up at Dan. The ambassador to Berlin had removed the SS tunic and cap, but still wore Eichmann's riding breeches and jackboots. "How will I find him?" Ben-Gurion said.

"Unashamed." Dan thought of other words he could use to describe Eichmann. But he left it at that.

"When people do terrible things, they usually try to tell you they were just a cog in a machine."

"Eichmann got his orders from above. He would never have conceived of the killing of millions of people. But once they ordered him to do it, he was no cog. He made this machine. Proudly."

Ben-Gurion shrugged and beckoned. "Bring him in."

Dan opened the door. Polkes shoved Eichmann into the prime minister's office. The Obersturmbannführer drew himself up straight, defiant and yet aquiver. For a moment, Dan thought of the times he had stood before Eichmann's desk. He wondered if his own conflicting emotions had showed so clearly on his face and in his trembling muscles. Eichmann was surely calculating how long it would be before he died. He must know his life was forfeit. But Dan had another role in mind for him before that end came. He watched Ben-Gurion examine the exaggerated insolence on the Nazi's face. The Old Man had yet to pass judgment on Dan's plan. He wanted to assess Eichmann, to see if he would be a convincing witness when they took him before…. *You're getting ahead of yourself,* Dan thought. *Let Ben-Gurion judge him now. Then move to the next step.*

"How many Jews are already dead, Eichmann?" Ben-Gurion gestured with the minutes of the Wannsee conference.

The German's chin quivered. To be addressed without his title, and by a Jew. The double shock rattled him. To see the conference minutes already on the desk of the Israeli prime minister, within a day of his dictating them to his secretaries. His Führer was right. The Jews truly did possess mysterious powers.

"Answer me."

"One point two million—" Eichmann cut himself off, as if he felt unable to complete his statement without bestowing an honorific on the man who ordered him to speak. He wouldn't say Herr Prime Minister. But without appending a title to his comments, his very words seemed weak, floating and directionless, like dust in the light.

He had aged immensely during the flight over Central Europe. His hair looked thinner, almost as though he had started down the road to baldness overnight. He squinted over baggy sacks of loose skin that hung in crescents below his eyes. His mouth contorted, drawn to the side by the muscular effort of suppressing the nervous tremors of his fear. He tried to be defiant, but his voice quivered. "You may execute me, you Jews," he said. "I will leap laughing into the grave. The feeling that I have been responsible for the death of so many enemies of the Reich will be a source of extraordinary satisfaction to me."

Ben-Gurion rubbed his bald scalp. The Old Man was accustomed to engaging with angry men—Zionists from other streams of the movement, underlings who rejected the deferential behavior of the European bureaucrats who used to persecute them. Dan saw it as a measure of his chief's strength of character that he simply brushed off Eichmann's vitriol and continued with his calculations.

The Old Man nodded his head, a decision made. He twitched his hand at Polkes, who yanked Eichmann out of the room.

"Anna?" Ben-Gurion said.

"In the hands of the Gestapo. She was arrested when she went to treat Shmulik's wounds."

Ben-Gurion lowered his head and murmured a regretful syllable.

"Shmulik and Devorah are, I believe, dead," Dan said. "Eichmann assures me Anna will be sent to the new death camp at Auschwitz."

"Yet you still came."

"We have to stop it—this project being planned by the Nazis."

Ben-Gurion went to the window. He looked out over the quiet Rehavia street. A heavy rain watered the newly planted maples on the sidewalks. "It never drizzles here in Jerusalem. It's all or nothing. Bright desert sunshine, or a downpour." He touched the cold glass. "Shmulik gave you a hard time because you were dealing with the Nazis? Even though you were following my orders?"

"Maybe he was right all along."

The Old Man turned. "You're a Jew, Dan. That means you have inherited five thousand years of second-guessing and lamenting the mistakes of our people. But you're also an Israeli. So let's talk about the future."

It was true. The world seemed about to end. Not only for the millions of Jews on Eichmann's list, or the six million in the territories currently under Nazi control. It teetered on the brink of a disaster that would stain humanity for generations. "There's only one way to stop it," Dan said.

"Your plan."

"We have the conference minutes. We have Eichmann. We know where the camps are. We can convince the Allies to bomb them, to destroy the Nazi infrastructure of extermination before it can do its job. They will do it now, because we can offer them military assistance in North Africa. The British army there is on the run. Israeli troops can make the difference."

Ben-Gurion rocked back and forth on his heels. He had taken momentous decisions before. But Dan sensed that the deeply philosophical prime minister was considering implications far beyond the question at hand.

"You accomplished a great feat of Jewish defiance in kidnapping this Nazi," Ben-Gurion said.

"Thank you, Prime Minister."

Ben-Gurion smiled gently. He looked out the window again as if he were staring into the future. Then his voice was firm again. "They're holding a conference now in Cairo."

"The Allied military commanders?"

"Better. Roosevelt and Churchill."

Dan breathed deeply. "Then we must take Eichmann to them."

"The Nazi is not all we take," Ben-Gurion said. "The fate of Europe's Jews travels with us."

Chapter 60

Cairo

Dan awaited Boustead by the tall glass doors facing onto the veranda of Shepheard's Hotel. The Englishman entered the bar wearing the uniform of a major in military intelligence. As Dan took his hand, he sensed considerable tension. It didn't surprise him. Adding to the pressure of the summit meeting between Boustead's prime minister and the American president was the fact that the British army had been swept steadily back into Egypt. The Germans were only a day's drive from Alexandria, in the Nile delta, ready to cut off Cairo and push toward the Suez Canal. He let go of the major's sweating palm and called a waiter. "Drink?"

"Christ, I'll have a gin, I suppose," Boustead said. "A bit rattled to tell you the truth, old chap."

"I thought you were made of sterner stuff."

"Don't try talking English-English to me. It doesn't sound right from you. Your accent has gone rather *German*, in fact. Aren't you keeping up your American language practice with your lovely wife?"

The reminder of Anna chilled Dan. He said nothing.

"I *had* been looking forward to coming back out here. Been on desk operations since I left Berlin," Boustead said. "An office in

Whitehall the size of a hatbox, that was the extent of my roving. London's a bloody dour place at the best of times, once you've felt the Middle Eastern sun on your neck. Anyway, I haven't had a day in the field in all that time until now, and I must say as soon as I arrived in Cairo I felt rather exposed, so near the front line."

"I'm glad you have time to meet me at such short notice."

"Ah, rather lucky for you that I was here. I don't usually travel with the PM, but his intelligence staff was expanded for the big chinwag with FDR. With my background in the Middle East, Winston insisted I come along."

Winston. Did first-name terms mean the British leader would listen to Boustead? Dan hoped so.

The waiter returned. Boustead gulped hard at his gin and put the glass on the table. He glanced down at the jackboots and gray riding breeches Dan wore. "I say, that's definitely not Israeli army gear."

"It's the bottom half of Obersturmbannführer Adolf Eichmann's uniform."

Boustead drank the rest of the gin. His face took on its old cunning.

"That's better," Dan said.

"You've got him, have you? You bloody devil, Lavi. By God, where is he?"

"Here in Cairo. I'm hoping to introduce him to your boss."

Boustead licked the tip of his mustache. He gave a knowing smile. "Only too happy to help, my dear chap."

Chapter 61

For Roosevelt, the war was less than two months old. He had been drawn steadily and not unwillingly closer to involvement by Churchill's persuasions over the previous year. Still, it was Pearl Harbor and Hitler's foolhardy desire to take on every world power at once that had brought the American president to this conference with the British prime minister, a short walk from the east bank of the Nile. Through the open French doors of the balcony, Dan watched the lowering sun purple the surface of the ancient river. Beyond the water and across the Libyan Desert, the Eighth Army continued its fight against Field Marshall Rommel's Afrika Korps. The British came in second best in every measure, but it was in leadership and battle experience that they were most badly outmatched. That, Dan knew, was Ben-Gurion's opportunity.

Churchill sat in a deep armchair, across from FDR. The Israelis had few worries about securing the agreement of the British leader. He had been an early backer of a Jewish state. The British needed support in North Africa, and Churchill was particularly given to outrageous schemes that might change the strategic situation dramatically. Boustead had arranged this meeting swiftly because he knew Dan's plan was tailor-made to appeal to the British prime minister's renegade streak. But for the plan to succeed, it needed Roosevelt's support.

Churchill growled, "Shall we begin, Franklin?"

Roosevelt rolled his hand back on his right wheel and brought his chair toward them with a sigh. He smiled wanly at Ben-Gurion, who was swallowed by the hotel's deep couch, his high-waisted pants riding up almost to his chest. "Mister Prime Minister, we've had only a few moments to look over the translation of the document presented to us by your colleague, Ambassador Lavi. The minutes of a conference at—" He glanced at the papers in his lap.

"Wannsee. A suburb of Berlin." Dan tried to subdue his nervousness at meeting these two powerful leaders. *Calm down. You were face to face with Hitler,* he told himself. *These are men you can handle, if only because they aren't insane. Focus on the issue.*

"Well, we shall have to check on its validity, of course. Before we can decide on a course of action."

Ben-Gurion waved his hand and shifted his tubby body forward. "No need, Mister President."

"To check its validity? Or do you mean there's no need to deliberate over what to do?" Roosevelt's smile was thin.

"We have an excellent method by which you may assess the truth of what is contained in this document. We also know what you must do."

"Do you?"

"Mister President, if you'll allow me." Dan rose and went into the anteroom. Boustead waited among the British and American military adjutants and the soberly suited diplomats, clad in his olive green dress uniform. Dan nodded to him, and the major swiftly turned to open a door and ushered out Polkes and Eichmann. Polkes was still feeling the effects of his Gestapo ice baths, sneezing and coughing. Eichmann sulked, one of his cold, matinee-idol eyes swollen from Bertha's punch. His shackles rattled as he shuffled across the room. He looked about at the stern faces of the Allied officers and halted.

Boustead beckoned for Eichmann to keep moving. "Come on, old boy. *Jedem das Seine.*" Dan remembered Shmulik quoting those words, the phrase inscribed over the gate at Buchenwald concentration camp. Everyone gets what he deserves.

Polkes dragged the German into the main suite. He stood him beside Ben-Gurion's sofa, facing the two Allied leaders.

Roosevelt regarded the bedraggled man coolly.

"Introduce yourself," Ben-Gurion said.

Eichmann snapped his heels. His shoes were soft and made no sound, but the chains on his ankles clicked. "Obersturmbannführer Adolf Eichmann. Commander, Central Office for Jewish Emigration, Gestapo Office IV-B4, Reich Main Security Office, Berlin."

Churchill lit a cigar. He seemed to be enjoying himself.

Roosevelt twitched his eyes toward Dan. "How do you come to be here?" Searching for the correct manner of address, he settled on, "Herr Eichmann."

"I am a prisoner of war. I must protest against my treatment—"

"You're a criminal, not a prisoner of war. Israel is not at war with Germany." Ben-Gurion pulled at a bushy eyebrow and directed his comment at the American leader. "Or not yet."

"What evidence is there as to this man's identity?" Roosevelt asked.

Dan took a booklet of folded tan cardstock from his pocket. It was printed with Gothic script. *ss-Ausweis.* ss identity card. He opened it. A circular stamp containing the spread wings of the eagle and the swastika crawled over the edge of the holder's photo. Dan passed it to Roosevelt. The president took the card hesitantly, as though it might carry some infection. The card displayed Eichmann's smug features.

Then Dan walked over to Eichmann and grabbed his shirt, wrenching it open and yanking it to the left. He lifted Eichmann's arm. A small blue tattoo stood out on the pale skin a few inches below the armpit. "The ss have their blood group tattooed here on their bodies. Wehrmacht soldiers do not."

Roosevelt laid the identity card on the coffee table. He displayed the front page of the Wannsee document to Eichmann. "You recognize this?"

Dan held his breath. Would he deny it? He felt sure Eichmann was proud of his work. He wouldn't see the criminality of the plan, its violation of every human law.

Eichmann gave one curt nod of his head. "I prepared this document."

"You don't deny the content?" Roosevelt said.

"I do not. This project is at the heart of the historic mission of National Socialism. It is the Führer's order and it will be carried out, whatever my fate. If my part in the final solution of the Jewish question has been played, then I am content to have done my duty."

Disgust clouded Roosevelt's face. It seemed to Dan that it was more powerful than his skepticism. He gestured toward the Israelis. "These gentlemen suggest that there is a network of death camps in Poland."

"I have nothing more to say." Eichmann lifted his chin. "I am a prisoner of war and I am under no obligation to discuss the final solution of the Jewish question with men such as you, whose politics are controlled by the Jewish cabals on Wall Street and in the City of London."

"It seems to me," Churchill said, "that Jews have far more influence over German policy than they do over British or American matters of state."

Eichmann looked confused. Ben-Gurion jerked his thumb at Polkes and the big man dragged Eichmann out of the room. Boustead shut the door behind them and perched against the sideboard, close to Churchill. Dan sat down next to Ben-Gurion.

Roosevelt rubbed his brow. "You're going to ask us to bomb the camps again, Mister Prime Minister?"

"Do not call them camps, Mister President. Camps are places where soldiers bivouac or children gather for fun. These are extermination factories. They are bloody abattoirs for an entire people." Ben-Gurion made a fist and shook it. "This is no longer a matter of Jewish survival. It is a question of the moral compass of the Allied nations. We present you here with documentary and human testimony about the enormous crime the Nazis are in the process of committing. To do nothing is to engage alongside them in the annihilation of millions of people."

"These camps in Poland are not military targets," Churchill said.

Dan recognized the comment for what it was—a prompt, an opportunity to counter FDR's most likely objection to the Israeli demand. Churchill was already on board.

He took his cue. "Mister Prime Minister, if I may. The Jews being transported to the ghettoes and the death camps are to be worked to death in munitions factories located within the perimeters of these camps. One of my colleagues at our Berlin embassy obtained construction plans for the camp at Auschwitz, in southeastern Poland. The purpose of the camp is to exterminate Jews, but also to create a synthetic rubber and to utilize the Jews as workers in this project. Such projects could undoubtedly be categorized as vital to the German war effort."

Dan watched Roosevelt as he considered the situation. He realized that his fingers were clenched tight around his knees. He wanted to shout at the American to make up his mind. Every second that passed took them a moment closer to the extinction of his people. It was a second in which his wife remained at risk. Perhaps even the one during which she drew her final breath. Ben-Gurion reached for him and laid a steadying hand on his own.

The Old Man's signal was understood. Dan had to be the ambassador, the diplomat, the man who convinced others through reference to paragraphs and clauses, not through shouting and emotional appeals. He spoke once more.

"I refer you to page fourteen. The third paragraph from the bottom of the page." He read off the English translation he had made on the plane to Cairo. It was in Roosevelt's lap, and on the coffee table before Churchill, but he wanted them to hear it read aloud. "'With regard to the issue of the effect of the evacuation of Jews on the economy, State Secretary Neumann'—he's from the office of the Four-Year Plan—'stated that Jews working in industries vital to the war effort, provided that no replacements are available, cannot be evacuated.'"

Churchill murmured and shook his head.

"Please turn to the final page," Dan said. "The end of the paragraph third from bottom, and the penultimate paragraph. This is from Bühler, of the Nazi office in control of Poland, discussing the Jews presently in his sphere. 'Of the approximately two and a half million Jews concerned, the majority are unfit for work.' He goes on to say that he has 'only one request, to solve the Jewish question as quickly as possible.' He also wishes that to be done 'without alarming the populace.'"

"Jesus Christ, who the hell are we fighting?" Roosevelt said.

"The bloody devil himself." Churchill sucked on his cigar.

"Not the devil, sir. You are fighting men like Eichmann." Dan pointed toward the door through which the ss man had been taken. "I have been in daily contact with them since 1938, when Prime Minister Ben-Gurion sent me to Berlin as Israel's ambassador. I know them to be capable of barbarities beyond description, of cruelty beyond credence for two humane men such as you. It's almost as though you must be inhuman yourself to even accept that such inhumanity could be carried out by man. Perhaps I can accomplish this more easily than you. You see, they classify me as subhuman. Because I'm a Jew."

Roosevelt looked sickened. "My God."

"I don't expect you to help us out of concern for Jews," Dan said. "Unlike the Nazis, I know that Jews don't dictate your every move. You're fighting a war. You must act according to strategy and, no doubt, you will entertain inhuman ideas yourselves before victory is won. That is in the nature of war. However, my prime minister has a strategic incentive for you to intervene."

"Before I get to that." Ben-Gurion laid his hand on Dan's shoulder. "My colleague's wife, Anna Lavi, is an American citizen, born in Boston, and a Jew. She is presently on her way to the death camp at Auschwitz."

Roosevelt snapped his attention back toward Dan. Churchill lowered his cigar and stared with a guarded astonishment.

"Yet Dan is here," Ben-Gurion said. "To my mind, his actions provide you with a physical symbol of the resilience of our new country. He has been my ambassador in Hell. He has been in the place where the slain lie, and he carries their plea to you. Now I will lay out for you his plan for the exorcism of Satan."

Churchill rumbled a low, appreciative murmur.

"At the foundation of our state, in 1938, our army, the Israel Defense Force, faced immediate attack from all sides. The armies of the Arab nations descended upon us. But we fought them off." Ben-Gurion's reedy voice rose. To the Allied leaders it no doubt seemed that he had slipped into the mode of political address, as if there were a large gathering in the room. Dan recognized that Ben-Gurion was, in fact, reliving some of the desperation of those days, when all Zionism's achievements were threatened.

"In those days, our army was a ragtag band. It was more a set of militias than a national military. But the War of Independence was a true proving ground for our officers and our troops. They are now better equipped, more experienced, and more ready for war than any unit in the British army, I'd say. Certainly more so than the US army."

Roosevelt tapped his thumb against his wheelchair. He was irritated, perhaps because he had no counter to the argument. The US wouldn't be ready to put troops in the field with any real expectation of success for almost a year.

"Here is what we propose." Ben-Gurion slapped his palms on his thighs. Time for the deal. "Israel will join the war against Nazi Germany. Until now we have been pressured by Berlin to remain neutral and we complied because to go against Hitler was to abandon the Jews of Europe to that madman's depredations. Now we have proof that he intends to exterminate all Jews, and that his policy of sending them to Israel or elsewhere has been abandoned. So we shall join with you, the Allies."

"Very good." Roosevelt's tone demonstrated that he was waiting for the caveat.

Ben-Gurion wasn't done selling yet. "The British army in North Africa is under threat. The battle with the Afrika Korps is finely balanced. You recently had a bad defeat at Tobruk and other reverses all across the Western Desert."

Churchill grumbled and loosened some phlegm.

"With the Israel Defense Forces at your side, you will have the numbers and the desert experience to defeat Rommel swiftly. You will have an extra layer of protection for the Suez Canal, the lifeline of Britain's Asian colonies. Think how disastrous it will be if Rommel succeeds in his plan to drive on beyond Egypt to the Persian Gulf. It would end Germany's dependence on the Romanian oilfields, currently threatened by the Russian advance, and would revive Germany's flagging Panzer armies."

The British prime minister grew excited at these new strategic possibilities. Boustead had assured Dan he would. "By God, we'd be finished with Rommel in a month," Churchill enthused. "Franklin, we could move ahead with a strike against Italy. Once North Africa is won and the Suez Canal is secured, we can invade Hitler's soft underbelly, as we've discussed."

Roosevelt slipped a cigarette into his long black plastic holder. "And much earlier than we had planned."

"Our forces will take Italy by the end of this year. From there we could strike through France to open up the Channel ports for a landing."

"It would certainly get Uncle Joe Stalin off our backs with his bitching for us to open up a second front in Europe."

Churchill stabbed his cigar toward FDR. "Not to mention that *we* would be the ones to control Europe, not Red Russia."

"Now Winston, I can handle Uncle Joe."

"Certainly you can." Churchill licked his lips. A nervous tell that Roosevelt appeared to miss. The Briton was less than convinced of Roosevelt's ability to deal with the Soviet dictator. "Nonetheless, we'd be negotiating with Stalin from a position of power. He will still be pushing the Germans back through the Ukraine and Belorussia while we'll be crossing the Rhine. Berlin will be ours and the Reds will be kept out of Western and Central Europe."

Churchill's assessment was even more enthusiastic than Dan had hoped. It was also accurate. He could see that Roosevelt wanted to go for it, but something held him back. Dan cut in. "Ending the war in Europe will give Stalin the incentive to declare war in the east, against Japan. That would relieve the United States of its solo burden in the Pacific theater."

A little color rose in the president's cheeks. He smiled. "I gather you're a Harvard man, Mister Lavi, as am I."

"That's correct, Mister President."

"They never taught me anything worth a damn there. How did you get so smart?"

"I have learned the necessity of survival from watching some of my friends fail in that task."

FDR pulled on his cigarette thoughtfully. "What exactly would you expect of us? To destroy the rail connections to these camps?"

"Rail tracks can be replaced easily. Moreover, I doubt that a bomber can hit a track that measures five feet across from half a mile up. No, we have the locations of the camps. We can identify the purposes of the buildings inside the camps. We are able to pinpoint these buildings with an accuracy that's within the capability of your bombers to hit."

"This is on the basis of your consultations with Israeli Air Force people?"

Dan smiled. "No. With the Luftwaffe."

FDR took the cigarette holder from his mouth and cocked his head.

"The pilot who brought me and Eichmann to the Middle East is a Luftwaffe officer committed to the fight against Hitler."

"So let's say we *can* hit these locations within the camps. What exactly are the targets?"

"The main targets, from our point of view, must be the gas chambers and the crematoria where the Nazis plan to incinerate the bodies of their victims."

Churchill rasped a disdainful cough. "Those bloody Huns."

"The extermination plan is to gas the Jews and then to incinerate their bodies. Those are the facilities your bombers must attack, because they are relatively complicated industrial facilities which can't be replaced as easily as rail tracks. Once they are destroyed, it's likely that you will have won the war before the Germans are able to rebuild them and put them back into operation."

"How many locations?"

"Six camps in Poland."

"It's a major operation to launch raids there. It's not a short hop. What do you think, Winston?" FDR said.

"We have bombers with sufficient range. I expect that if these camps are under construction or only recently completed, as I gather from Mister Lavi's report, there will be little air defense to threaten our planes. The introduction of Israel to the war, with the consequent securing of Suez, victory in North Africa, and a swifter invasion of Europe, is well-worth the immediate effort on the parts of our air forces. I am enthusiastically in favor, Franklin." Churchill watched Roosevelt like a man who has bet all he has, and now senses the roulette wheel begin to slow.

Dan felt the cushions of the sofa tip forward. Ben-Gurion was almost toppling to the floor in anticipation. FDR laid his cigarette holder in the ashtray at his side and addressed the two Israelis.

"War is a contagion, gentlemen," he said. "If Israel enters into this one, perhaps you will find yourself more afflicted than you think."

"We have already built up a resistance to the ill effects of war," Ben-Gurion replied.

"I wonder if there is such a thing." FDR touched his forehead softly. He pulled his shoulders back. "Well, when you see a rattlesnake poised to strike, you do not wait until he has struck to crush him."

Churchill clapped his hands and his eyes glittered with joy. Cigar between his teeth, he reached out a hand to Ben-Gurion. "Bravo, Franklin, dear chap."

Ben-Gurion hadn't grasped FDR's figure of speech. He looked confused.

"The rattlesnake is Nazism," Churchill said. "We shall crush the blighters."

"The rattlesnake is the wickedness of these death camps," FDR corrected. "Let us hope that America's destiny is to crush it, before it destroys all that is left of goodness in our world."

Ben-Gurion gripped Dan's knee, his hand shaking, his emotions seeming to funnel through him into his ambassador. But the Old Man was a dealmaker, a man who had prevailed at contentious

Zionist conferences and in whispered dialogues, always squeezing everything he could from his interlocutor. He cleared his throat. "One more thing," he said.

FDR murmured, a questioning sound.

Ben-Gurion smiled. "I also want a dozen Flying Fortress bombers."

Chapter 62

Exhausted, Schulze draped himself over a wicker chair, a cold beer in his hand. Having concluded that his blue Luftwaffe uniform might cause too much of a stir on the veranda of Shepheard's Hotel, the center of British Cairo's social life, he wore the untidy olive green shirt and pants of the Israeli army. Among the other patrons—the starchy Sandhurst graduates and the Eton boys of Churchill's staff—he looked like a flight mechanic on a brief break. He was in the midst of a protracted yawn when Dan threaded through the tables and sat down beside him.

"How did it go?" He ruffled his blond hair.

"They will bomb Auschwitz in three days," Dan whispered.

Schulze gripped Dan's shoulder and shook him. "You did it. Thank God. Germany will thank you."

"The day after that, they will bomb the other camps."

"All of them. Dan, by Christ." Schulze touched his knuckles to his bleary, tired eyes. It all burst from him now, the tension of their escape from Berlin and of all the months in which he had watched his Luftwaffe comrades shot from the skies in aid of a hopeless war, a criminal war. He wept, his hands over his face.

The British officers at nearby tables looked away. Their ladies made small talk to cover the embarrassment.

Schulze wiped his face on the rolled-up sleeve of his Israeli shirt. "I'm so tired. I'm a bit of an emotional mess. I need to go to my room and sleep for a week. God bless you, Dan, for what you've accomplished."

Dan was not crying yet. He stared out at the elaborate Victorian facades of the Azbakeya district. The ponies and traps and the dust must have changed little since the hotel was built a century before. A military jeep pulled up, and it brought with it all the horror and bloodletting that characterized the present. Anna, Anna was so distant, so much in jeopardy. And it was his fault. He should never have taken her to Berlin, into the clutches of those maniacs. He should have stayed in Jerusalem, or Boston. Cut off from the fate of his people in Europe. But, no, she would never have allowed that.

"I must go back," he said.

"To find Anna?"

"I've done what I came here to do for the Jewish people. Now I must do something for love."

Schulze sipped his beer. "Then so must I."

Dan stared. "You can't come with me. You took your plane out of Reich airspace. You won't be able to explain that away."

"How else will you get there in time?"

"My dear Ansgar, no, I won't let you do this."

"Here we are, in Egypt, so I will quote to you from the Book of Exodus. 'Let us take a three-day journey into the wilderness that we may offer sacrifices to the Lord, our God.' If I'm to be the sacrifice, I'm ready for it. In gratitude for what you've done on behalf of my country. I believe you've saved us from eternal shame. Or at the least, you've diminished the horror, let's put it that way."

The German was right. Without Schulze to fly him, Dan wouldn't get back to Germany before the bombs fell on the death camps. By then, Anna might already have been transferred to Auschwitz. He had persuaded the British and Americans to launch the raids that might kill her.

Schulze put down his beer and reached out his hand. "So you accept?"

Dan shook the pilot's hand. "We can get back to Israel tonight. Tomorrow we'll fly your Messerschmitt to Berlin. Then, the next day, I'll go to Poland. The timing will be tight, but you're right that I can do it. If you help."

"Why not fly straight to Poland?"

"I need to see someone in Berlin first."

Schulze stretched his back. He reached into his pocket for a tube of Benzedrine. "So much for sleep. It's a good job I didn't throw away my Luftwaffe uniform."

Chapter 63

Berlin

Brückner saw Kritzinger coming down the long Chancellery corridor. The State Secretary seemed determined not to notice him, burying his attention in a file of papers. Brückner understood. He had made this upright civil servant an accomplice in something—and he hadn't even fully explained what. The poor man no doubt presumed he wouldn't find out until either Hitler was assassinated or the Gestapo interrogators strung him up by his thumbs and told him all about the plot. Brückner was at least grateful that the man had enough decency to have gone along with his plan, even if he had done so in a cowardly fashion, just as he implemented the laws of the Third Reich with a twinge of misgiving.

Kritzinger was almost beside him when he looked up. He halted and spoke in a low voice. In the grandiose corridor it was like a whisper echoing through a cathedral. "It is probable that the Führer merely wishes your presence to assist him as his adjutant. But, nonetheless, I beg of you to be prepared for the worst."

"The Führer—what?" Brückner glanced each way. The massive space was empty except for the ss guards at the end, two hundred paces away.

"Take a cyanide capsule. In case."

Brückner tasted the civil servant's stale breath, as though the last air were being squeezed from the very bottom of his lungs. Kritzinger saw his confusion. His eyes opened wide.

"You don't know? The order didn't come to you? Then it must be true." Kritzinger backed away.

Brückner shuddered. "What order, Herr State Secretary?"

"The Führer wants you at the Wolf's Lair. The personnel memo came across my desk an hour ago. From Günsche."

Günsche, Hitler's ss adjutant. Brückner swallowed hard. If the order hadn't reached him directly, it meant Günsche didn't want to give him a chance to flee before others found out about it. Perhaps it was simply a mistake. He went over his incomplete memory of what had happened at the Wannsee concert. Had he said anything to his mother as she died? To his father? It wouldn't take much to give him away. He had been with Hitler long enough that the Führer might call him to East Prussia to give him a chance to explain himself.

Or to see him die.

"You are to depart immediately on a plane from the Führer's squadron," Kritzinger said. "Please remember what I said."

Brückner made himself focus. He laid his hand on Kritzinger's arm. "Don't worry yourself. I know what to do. I thank you for the courage you showed in assisting me. It will not be forgotten."

"It is my hope that *everything* will be forgotten." Kritzinger hustled away, his heels echoing like gunshots.

Brückner rushed to his office. He had no choice but to go to Hitler. To the Wolf's Lair. He picked up the small overnight bag he always kept under his desk and set it before him. The gloomy forest around Hitler's East Prussian headquarters seemed to close in around him. He opened a drawer of his desk and took out a small tin of cyanide capsules. He put it in the pocket of his bag. In which grim bunker would they kill him? They would torture him first. The Führer would rave about his betrayal.

But Brückner would act before he was arrested. He would shoot the leader of the nation. It came clear to him with astonishing clarity. The solution to a puzzle that had always been there.

He carried the bag to his door, threw his greatcoat over his shoulders and headed for the garage. As he descended the stairs, he caught the sound of steps behind him. He halted and waited. Nothing. *You can't go all the way to the Wolf's Lair in this condition,* he told himself. *Calm down, or you'll be too nervous to raise your pistol and kill the swine once you get there.*

He entered the dark garage. An ss Rottenführer came out of the dispatcher's cubicle and bellowed a Heil Hitler.

"I need a car and driver for Tempelhof airfield," Brückner said.

The Rottenführer snapped his heels and beckoned to one of the ss men lounging by his cubicle. The driver was a private with a finger in his nose and a cigarette in the corner of his mouth. He pulled himself out of his chair and jogged to a bmw. He opened the back door, but Brückner climbed into the front seat. The private shrugged, threw the cigarette away, and ran round to the driver's side. He started the engine. The car rolled forward toward the gate onto Wilhelmstrasse.

A voice behind them called out. "Halt, wait."

Brückner stared ahead. They had come for him already. He smiled grimly, because rather than fear, he felt offense that the Führer might have thought he would refuse to present himself at the Wolf's Lair. That he would try to save himself.

The Rottenführer rushed to the side of the car, puffing. He leaned in through the front passenger-side window beside Brückner. "Hang on, will you?"

"What is it? I have a plane to catch," Brückner snapped.

"The Obersturmbannführer's order. He wishes to accompany you." The Rottenführer stepped back and gave the Nazi salute.

An ss lieutenant-colonel reached for the rear door of the car. He kept his head down. Brückner saw only the four pips on his collar and the silver shoulder braid. He understood. This man would kill him with a bullet to the back of the head on the way to the airfield. The officer climbed in and sat behind him. They probably weren't even going to Tempelhof. How long would it be before he knew where they were taking him? He slipped his fingers into the pocket of the case by his legs and brought the cyanide capsules out. He kept the tin hidden in his palm.

"Go," the officer said.

The BMW roared into the gray afternoon light. They turned south and went through the government district toward Kreuzberg. Brückner listened for a word from the SS officer behind him. He eased open the tin as they crossed the bridge over the Landwehr Canal.

"Pull into that side street," the SS officer ordered.

"Aren't we going to the airport?" the driver said.

"Do as you're told."

The driver glided the big car to the curb beside the cemetery of the Jerusalem Church. The street was empty of worshippers or visitors to the cemetery. So it was to happen here, Brückner thought, looking down the quiet road. Even if someone came along, who would question two SS men engaged in the execution of an army officer? No one would do anything for him.

"Kindly offer the private one of the candies from your tin," the SS officer said from the backseat.

Brückner closed his hand over the tin of cyanide capsules in confusion.

The driver glanced back at the officer in the rear of the car. "Candies?"

The SS officer pounded his fist into the driver's face. The man grunted in surprise and pain.

Brückner dropped the capsules. Dan Lavi slipped between the two front seats and slammed his weight into the struggling driver. "Give him one of those, Brückner," he yelled.

The last time Brückner saw Dan he had been wearing an Obersturmbannführer's uniform. But it still gave him a moment's start to see his friend in Eichmann's field-gray SS tunic.

Dan pressed down on the driver's nose. He shoved the gloved fingers of his hand between the man's teeth and wrenched his mouth open. "Give him a capsule. Quickly."

The driver snarled and bit down on Dan's finger. Dan pulled hard and jerked his hand from side to side until the driver's jaw dislocated. "Damn it, the cyanide. Hurry."

Brückner picked up the tin from the floor of the car with shaking hands and pulled out a capsule. He shoved it into the man's mouth. The driver struggled, pushing the capsule away with his tongue. Dan jammed his mouth shut.

Within thirty seconds, the driver went limp. He was dead. Dan jumped from the car. He scanned the street. Finding it still empty, he tugged the driver's body out onto the sidewalk and lifted him over the wall into the cemetery.

Brückner got out of the car and followed Dan over the wall. He watched the Israeli pull the dead man through the gravestones to a big tomb guarded by a bronze angel. Dan hid the ss driver behind the angel and ran back to the car.

He dragged Brückner behind the wheel. "You must drive." His voice quavered. He had killed a man. Brückner felt the weight of death in Dan's words.

He raced the BMW onto Belle Alliance and headed south.

"Slower. We can't afford a crash."

Brückner nodded. Or perhaps he only shivered a little more. "Dan, where are we going?"

With Dan's answer, the shock of the driver's killing was erased. But death remained, lurking in every syllable. "To Auschwitz."

Chapter 64

Draxler dozed on the sofa as darkness fell. His children raced through the apartment. His wife had a vegetable soup on the stove. It was a bad time for the Reich when even the Gestapo couldn't get meat, he thought. He wondered what their life would have been like if he had stayed in Palestine. Well, he couldn't have stayed in Palestine, could he? It wasn't there anymore. It was the land of the Jews now. The rest of the German Templers had been expelled from their Jerusalem enclave, deported. They ought to have seen that coming when they flew the Swastika flag. Maybe he had sensed the looming cataclysm and thus brought his family to Berlin. He laughed at himself. If he had been able to foresee that little tragedy, how had he managed to miss the global conflagration at whose center he now found himself? It was all crap. Everything they said, the leaders. When you were inside the machine, you saw how filthy it all was. The men at the top looked after themselves. Everyone else ate shit, while they feasted on steak. He sniffed the aroma of vegetables in the air. Time he did the same. He'd put a scare into one of the butchers on Schönhauser Allee tomorrow and bring home a side of beef.

His six-year-old daughter kissed him, her face chubby and soft. Draxler smiled and proffered his cheek for another. Traudl touched her lips to his stubble and said, "Mmmmwa." Then she rubbed her face and made a comical frown. "Papa, you need to shave."

"I'm sorry, my little love. But Papa has been working very hard."

She put her hands on her hips and grinned. "I can see that."

She cartwheeled through the door and walked on her hands across the landing to play with her friend in the next apartment. "Shut the door behind you," he shouted.

She poked out her tongue playfully and swung the door shut.

She might make the national team as a gymnast if she carried on like that. A six-year-old, and yet so strong. He wouldn't have thought she'd ever become that strong three years ago. He closed his eyes. The panic he had felt on Kristallnacht came over him once more. He interlaced his fingers and gripped them tight. While the rest of the Party had been torching synagogues and roughing up Jews, he had been fretting over his little girl, feverish, her eyes rolling up into her head, her body spasming. Instead of joining his Gestapo colleagues in the roundup of Jewish intellectuals and community leaders and supposed Commies, he had rushed to the Israeli embassy and begged the ambassador's wife to come and treat his dying daughter. *You didn't know where that would lead, did you?* he told himself. So now he loved a Jew, and a married one, at that. Even better, a Jew he had found himself compelled to arrest. Well, she'd be safer in the cells, where he could look after her. The round-ups were to start in earnest now. Gruppenführer Müller had given the word to all his Gestapo agents that Jewish emigration was over and evacuation was underway.

His shirt was wrapped too tightly around him, gripping him in its sweaty cotton. His youngest boy was three now, as Traudl had been when Anna saved her. Little Martin rolled on his back in front of the fire, pretending to wrestle an invisible enemy, calling out incomprehensible words of defiance. *Is that what I've been doing too?* Draxler thought.

If only that was all I'd done.

He wondered what the boy would've looked like if Anna had been his mother, instead of the shrew in his kitchen. He could go to her cell and tell her the things he dreamed of. He shook his head. How would that look? Turning up at the torture chamber to talk about love? She'd think he meant to rape her. But no, she wouldn't. She'd understand that he just needed to talk, to tell her who he really was.

He took his suit jacket, leather trench coat, and fedora from the back of the sofa. As he went to the door, his wife looked out from the kitchen nook. "Sepp, where are you going?"

"Out."

"The soup's ready."

"I'm not hungry."

She cursed at him. His rage flared, then dissipated. Why was he angry at *her*? He stepped back into the room. She looked up resentfully from the stove.

"I'm sorry," he said.

She blew out her cheeks and turned away. He shrugged. She wouldn't be the only one who'd never forgive him.

He ran down the stairs and climbed into his Mercedes. He sped onto Schönhauser Allee and headed toward the government quarter. He cut across behind the Sophienkirche and went down Monbijoustrasse. The Israeli embassy was silent and dark. Two of his men lingered in their car outside, but Draxler knew there was no point to the stakeout. He had heard about the business with the soup, the distraction created by the hysterical Polkes woman, and he had figured it out. The Israelis were gone.

All but one of them.

He wove through the streets behind the Brandenburg Gate to Prinz-Albrecht-Strasse. He left his car at the curb and quickly entered the Gestapo headquarters. Wall lamps lit the high-vaulted corridors sparsely. It was like a monastery, except that the people who lived here liked to flagellate other people, rather than themselves.

He went down to the cells. The Kriminalsekretär at the top of the corridor gave him a puzzled look. Draxler wondered if his concern for Anna showed on his face. Certainly it wouldn't be an expression this man would expect to see there.

Pull yourself together, he told himself. *You'll give yourself away.*

He removed his fedora and swiped his sweating forehead with the cuff of his trench coat. "I need to see a prisoner. Anna Lavi. I was the one who brought her in."

The guard went to his desk. "The American woman?"

"That's her. Has she been interrogated since I left her?"

"Of course not. You instructed that this was not to happen." He ran his finger down a register. "She's in forty-six."

Draxler walked down the steps and along the corridor. The light was low. The only sound was a quiet chorus of whimpering. No one was getting the treatments just now. His chest throbbed. Despite the Kriminalsekretär's assurance, he feared that someone might have come on shift overnight and decided that the American Jew needed to spend some time with her head under water, or hanging upside down, naked. He had done it himself often enough. It worked quicker on men. Women were there to be savored. *Jesus, Draxler, you bastard.*

He found the door to cell forty-six open. The wooden bench that was all prisoners had for a bed was empty. The floor was mopped clean. Anna Lavi was gone. A pulse of desperation blasted through him.

"Herr Kriminalinspektor?" The Kriminalsekretär's voice came down the corridor.

Draxler rushed toward him. "Where the fuck is she? What've you done with her?"

The officer waved a thin sheet of paper. "This was put through while I was on a break."

"What the hell is it?" Draxler grabbed the flimsy page.

"It's an order from the Reich Main Security Office. A transit paper."

Draxler scanned the sheet. Transit to where? He couldn't make sense of the handwriting. Panic distorted his vision. *Generalgouvernement*, he read. Poland, Anna had been shipped to Poland. "Where has she gone? To one of the ghettoes?"

"All the Jews were cleared out of here. She was sent too."

Draxler stuffed the paper into his pocket so that the guard wouldn't see his hand shake.

"Please, Herr Kriminalinspektor, I need to keep that copy for the file. We started a new file recently for all deportations to Auschwitz."

Draxler ignored the man. He ran along the corridor.

Chapter 65

Southern Poland

Fourteen hours after Dan had touched down in the Messerschmitt at Tempelhof, the BMW crossed the snow-covered Silesian plain, Brückner at the wheel. Dan fingered Eichmann's SS identity card. He was cold in the SS man's uniform. The car was draughty. He felt, over and over, the desperation of the driver as he killed him, as if his own body would always be in a death struggle with the soul of the slain private. Of course it would be. If it were otherwise, he would be no better than the Death's Head guards he set himself now to outwit.

They skirted along the northern border of Heydrich's fiefdom, the Protectorate of Bohemia and Moravia, and around Breslau. Three hundred and fifty miles into their journey, they turned south at Kattowitz for the final hour's drive to Auschwitz.

Dan looked up at the night sky. It was almost midnight. The bombers would come soon.

"I should be the one to go in," Brückner said. "It's too dangerous for you. If they find out who you are—"

"They won't."

"How can you be sure?"

"They'll do as they're told." He smiled. "You seem to forget that you aren't talking to the Israeli ambassador anymore. I'm an Obersturmbannführer of the ss."

"But what if one of them met Eichmann on his reconnaissance visit? They'll know you're not him."

"I'll scream in his face until he backs down."

Brückner laughed with resignation. "Yes, well, I have to admit that will probably work."

"I've had a couple of years to observe how Nazis behave. I'm *sure* it'll work."

They were quiet as the road pushed through silent villages, sand dunes, mists, and wetlands. They sensed the approach of something darker than the night around them. They crossed the rail tracks that Eichmann had designated as the necessary infrastructure along which he could activate Auschwitz's murder machine. Dan read off the plans Shmulik had received from the resistance. "Go right."

The rail lines headed south to Prague and Vienna. The road stopped at Birkenau.

Brückner gazed at the perimeter wire, twelve feet high, and the ss watch towers. Hunched low in the darkness, the camp huts stood, rank after rank. "You're sure this is the one we want?"

"Straight on through the village, we'd get to the workshops. North of that, IG Farben has its factory for the slave laborers."

"But this one?"

"The extermination camp."

Brückner slowed as they came within sight of the gate. "Imagine a place that no one comes out of. It's awful."

Dan clapped his hand on the captain's epaulette. "I'm coming out. So's my wife."

They pulled up at the main gate. The ss guard stamped a salute. "Heil Hitler," he bellowed.

The Wehrmacht didn't respond to that salute. It was one of the few ways in which the army manifested some independence. Instead, Brückner raised his hand to his brow in the traditional military salute.

"Heil Hitler." Dan called so loudly that Brückner's fingers jumped against the brim of his cap and almost knocked it off.

"I need to locate a prisoner," Dan barked.

"Yes, Herr Obersturmbannführer."

Dan handed his identity papers through the window. The guard read them. When he saw that the man was from the Reich Security Head Office in Berlin, he looked almost as sick as the Death's Head on his cap. He dashed to the guard hut. Thirty seconds later he was back, handing the card to Dan.

"The Untersturmführer will be here soon to assist the Herr Obersturmbannführer. Please go through the gate and wait for him on the left. That's the women's camp."

Brückner brought the staff car to a halt beside a pile of luggage. The names of the owners were chalked on each case. Irene, Karin, Margarete. As if they were coming back to pick them up later. The contents of the cases spilled out onto the frozen dirt. A group of women, skeletal, shaven-headed, dressed in thin smocks, were combing through the linens and the shoes and the toiletries, sorting them and depositing them in piles. The women shivered, moving in silence. A bored ss guard rubbed his face and watched them as though they were vermin scampering for scraps of garbage in an alley.

Brückner groaned and covered his mouth. Dan clenched his fists in Eichmann's leather gloves. The scent of the perfume on the clothing drifted into the car. It bore an undertone of decay and filth. That, Dan thought, must be those poor women themselves.

Ahead of the car, the road followed a single rail line through the camp. There were a dozen rows of huts on each side. Beyond the group of women sorting clothing, the camp was dark and silent, as though the inmates were practicing for the death that would soon claim them.

The sound of footsteps called Dan back to his mission. An NCO and a young ss officer with a big ledger under his arm marched out from between the rows of huts in the men's camp. Dan got out of the car with Brückner. Again, he bellowed the salute to Hitler, wondering how it sounded to the quivering women as they emptied the suitcases.

It scared him to hear the growl in his throat, his voice made somehow animal in pronouncing these three syllables.

"You have an American woman here. Anna Lavi. She must have arrived within the last few days," he said.

"We can check, Herr Obersturmbannführer." The officer swallowed. The arrival of a senior Berlin man intimidated him, too.

"Do so. Find her and bring her to me."

The younger man hesitated. Dan saw him considering whether to ask why the woman was wanted.

"Do it now. I must take her directly to Obergruppenführer Heydrich."

The two ss men almost crapped themselves at that name. The officer flipped through the ledger with a trembling hand. He pointed out an entry to the other man. Together they jogged into the darkness.

"We must hope she doesn't run toward you," Brückner whispered.

"I'd scare my own mother in this uniform. Anna will be confused and that will give her pause. It'll be long enough for me to take control of the situation."

They waited. A guard shouted at the women around the suitcases and marched them off to their hut. A low hum sounded through the night sky. The ss guard dogs started barking.

"The bombers are coming," Dan said. "How close are they?"

Brückner tuned in to the noise. "Five minutes away. Maybe a little more."

There were shouts from one of the huts. A woman shrieked. Along the row of shacks he saw the young officer. A woman tumbled out of the hut and fell at his feet. The other ss man emerged behind her.

The officer looked down at the woman and pulled his leg back, ready to kick. He glanced toward Dan and set his foot on the ground, deciding against any punishment. He helped the fallen woman to her feet stiffly, as though he were picking up a soiled rag. He shoved her at the junior soldier and marched to the main track. The soldier and the woman came behind.

"This is the American woman, Herr Obersturmbannführer," the officer bellowed.

Anna stumbled across the cold dirt in bare feet. She wore a long, striped smock and covered her head with a thin blanket, like a shawl. Her eyes were wide with terror.

Dan put a single fist on his hip. He stepped forward and barked an order at the ss man. "In the car with her, right away."

She gaped at the man in the ss uniform who bore the face of her husband. The guard pulled her forward. She dropped to her knees. He hauled her along the ground.

The young officer frowned at the sky. "What's that noise?"

Dan snapped his heels. "Heil Hitler."

Brückner was already starting up the car. Dan climbed into the passenger seat. Anna cowered on the backseat.

"Where are you taking me?" she whimpered.

Brückner spun the car around, jolting over the rail tracks at the apex of his turn.

"Is that you, Herr Hauptmann Brückner?" she said.

The two men stared ahead, ignoring the woman on the backseat.

The ss guards pulled the gate open and the car rolled through. The sound of the bombers overhead was very loud now. Brückner turned onto the road and accelerated.

"We have to get away from here," he said.

Dan twisted in his seat. He took off the Death's Head cap. "Anna, it's me. Sweetheart, it's going to be okay."

Anna's jaw trembled. She sprang forward, toward him, and wept as he held her. The movement drew the shawl back from her head. It was shaved. He pressed his cheek to the stubble of her beautiful hair.

"It's going to be okay, my love." He held her close again as the detonations of the first bombs sounded.

Brückner drove south quickly. The flashes of the explosions came from a half mile away to the east. "That's not right," he murmured.

Dan broke the embrace with Anna. "What's wrong?" He looked up at the bombers, dark wide silhouettes against the night sky. "That's the IG Farben plant. They're bombing the wrong place."

"Maybe your friends Churchill and Roosevelt decided the factory was a military target after all. But this place—" Brückner jerked his thumb over his shoulder toward the extermination camp. "This place isn't."

Dan glared at the explosions and the gathering flames. "Turn around."

"Are you crazy?"

"Go back."

Brückner swung into a three-point turn. "What're you going to do?"

"Pull over here." Dan put his cap back on. He jumped from the car and wrenched open the trunk. He unsnapped the clasps on the box of emergency equipment welded to the chassis and opened it. He took out a pair of signal flares and stuffed them into his tunic.

He leapt back in the car, shouting for Brückner to speed up. They were back at the gate of the death camp within two minutes. "Stop here, across the road from the entrance. I don't want them to see Anna."

As Brückner pulled to a halt, a big Mercedes reached the gate. The guards opened the barricade and let it through. It drove slowly into the dark.

Dan got out. He slammed the door shut and leaned in through the open window. "Take her to Budapest, Brückner."

"Without you? What're you going to do?"

"I won't leave you," Anna cried. "Danny, please. I can't go without you."

"Anna, you have to be quiet." Dan glanced at the frightened guards across the road. The bombs drowned out the sound of his wife's grief. "I will see you again, my love." He touched her face and jogged toward the gate.

Brückner put the car into gear and took off fast.

Dan waved for the guards to open the gate. "Move, damn it. Move."

The ss men shoved the gate back once more. "What's happening, Herr Obersturmbannführer?"

"The Allies are bombing. They'll try for the gas chambers. Where are they?"

"On the far perimeter."

"I'm going to check on them now. There may be saboteurs preparing to guide the bombers in. Remain at your posts. Allow no one into the camp. No one, you hear me? Call the watch towers. I want all spotlights switched off immediately. That's how the bombers know where to target us."

Dan sprinted along the side of the rail tracks. The Mercedes was pulled up by the huts where Anna had been housed. The young ss officer he had dealt with was halfway along the row. His head was bowed. He stood before a man in a leather trench coat and a fedora who gesticulated broadly and impatiently.

The man slapped the ss officer in the face and marched back toward his car. He looked up at the sound of Dan's feet. Dan drew his pistol as he met his gaze.

"What the hell?" Draxler said. "Where is she?"

"She's safe from all of this." He lifted the gun and fired.

The young ss officer ducked. Draxler moved forward, toward Dan.

Dan stumbled away to the dark at the edge of the men's camp, cutting along the rail track toward the gas chambers. The Gestapo man had come for his wife. He had rescued her just in time. His breath came hard. Someone was running behind him. He didn't turn. It couldn't be Draxler, the tread was too light.

The ss officer. He was young, fit, coming to stop him.

"Halt," the officer bellowed. "Halt now."

The footsteps slowed. Dan looked over his shoulder. The officer had the pistol out of his holster.

The spotlights on the guard towers cut out just as a new fusillade rumbled over the IG Farben plant and a wall of flame rose beyond the main road. The synthetic rubbers and chemicals of the factory burned bright, silhouetting the officer as he took aim.

Dan kept running, weaving to make a tougher target. But he was tired, from the flying, the driving, the tension of his mission to Cairo. Tired after three years of accumulated Nazi horrors.

A shot, and another shot. He heard them, but his legs continued to move and he felt no pain.

He turned. The ss officer was on his knees, wounded. The flames of the Allied bombing licked at the sky. Draxler stepped up quickly to the injured man. He put his pistol to the officer's head and pulled the trigger.

The fire that rose behind Draxler was like a Satanic halo. The Gestapo man's face registered a profound loss, like a dying man with no more will to fight. He turned and walked away.

Dan ran the last thirty yards to the building that housed the gas chamber and the crematorium. It was so small he could hardly credit the capacity for death Eichmann ascribed to it in his report at Wannsee. It was about forty paces long, a single story, with windows only at the ends and two tall chimneys rising from the shallow pitched roof.

Behind him, the ss gate guards rushed down the tracks. Draxler opened fire on them.

Dan bounded onto the hood of a truck parked beside the gas chamber. He remembered what Eichmann had said. The destruction of the bodies was the problem. Killing Jews was simple enough, but to dispose of their remains without forcing them to dig a pit and having German troops execute them was difficult. The purpose of Auschwitz was to separate the killers from the victims, so that they could persist in killing for longer, and thus kill more.

He climbed onto the top of the truck and from there onto the roof of the gas chamber. The Jews entered from this end. They died, panicking and scrambling for safety. Then they were shoveled into the ovens at the other end of the building and rose to whatever heaven awaited them as smoke from the chimneys.

The ss guards cried out as Draxler's bullets brought them down.

Dan pulled the cap off a flare and turned it to bring the rough striking surface to the ignition button on the end. He scraped the cap over the flare as if he were lighting a match.

A dense orange smoke and a bright red light fired up in his hand. He lifted the flare above his head. With the searchlights extinguished, the light in the flare illuminated the smoke so that it was a pillar of fire above him. In the blackout, it would be pinpoint clear to the bombers above.

He pulled the cap from the second flare with his teeth and lit it on the end of the other one. The two beacons climbed above him. He waved them and stumbled to the center of the gas chamber's roof.

"Come on, come on," he shouted. "Over here."

Another bomber dropped its load on the IG Farben plant. The explosions were like a distant breath over Dan's face.

"Over here, damn it. Please."

He detected a slight change in the pitch of the droning engines as some of the planes peeled away. He stared into the sky directly above him. The fire from the IG plant illuminated the wings of a Flying Fortress. On the underside, in white paint, the bold angular shape of the Star of David. It was the squadron Ben-Gurion had finagled out of Roosevelt in Cairo, the symbol the Old Man wanted, to show that with the founding of Israel, Jews were now responsible for their own security. The belly of the bomber opened and Dan heard a whistling sound descend toward him. His face melted into a smile as though it were his wife's arms coming to enfold him.

The gas chamber exploded around him. He tumbled to his knees. The flares—he held them up again. He had to mark the target.

The bombs carved a line down the west of the camp. Then another stock of high explosives roared through the night and Dan felt himself ascending on its power.

He came down on the trembling earth, battered by the rubble of the gas chamber. The flare lay in the mud in front of him. He tried to reach it, but his arm was gone. His vision blurred and the cold reached up out of the ground and shivered through to his core. He squinted to focus his eyes. He looked about him. Auschwitz was on fire.

Epilogue

Jerusalem, 1948

The Germans bought two apartments in Talbiyeh, the upmarket neighborhood where the Dutch, Chileans, and Venezuelans already had their diplomatic missions. One was to be for the embassy, the second the ambassador's residence. The other occupants of the building, most of whom happened to have fled Germany or lost relatives to the Nazis in Poland and Russia, were initially outraged to find that they were to share an entrance with the first post-war representative of their former oppressor. But the ambassador went door to door on the very day of his arrival to introduce himself, and his fine High German won over the *yekkes*, who were astonished to discover that, only five years after Hitler put a gun to his head in his besieged bunker in Berlin, Germany had sent as its representative a man whose father had been a Jew.

The ambassador left his residence on the third floor shortly after 9 a.m. on a bright April day. He wore white tie and a tailcoat. He opened the second-floor door to the embassy and called to his consular officer. "Come on, Michael. My penguin costume makes me enough of a spectacle on these streets without my having to run because you've made me late."

The young man scuttled into the stairway, pulling on his suit jacket. He pointed at the battered violin case the ambassador carried. "I hope no one thinks there's a machine gun in there."

The ambassador caught him by the elbow and they set off together through the stumpy apartment buildings toward the home of the Israeli president. The streets were decked with hundreds of blue and white Israeli flags. The Jewish State would be marking its tenth anniversary the following day. There would be a celebratory concert in the presence of the president. The ambassador had hurried along his appointment to his new post specifically so that he might arrive in time to attend.

As they walked, the sun was most effective in reminding the two Germans that, despite the trees planted by the European Jews who had settled this neighborhood in the Thirties, their posting was in a desert.

"Can you imagine?" the ambassador mused.

The young man strode swiftly to keep up. "Imagine what, Herr Ambassador?"

"All these people in all these houses. All Jews. And our country was ready to murder them. Every one of them. It's as if we were to come through this city and simply slaughter everybody we found, and then destroy another city, and another and another."

A boy and girl little older than toddlers ran laughing from the garden of an apartment house, waving tiny cloth flags of blue and white. They halted at the strange sight of the ambassador's formal wear. Most Israelis wore short-sleeved shirts, open at the neck. Many sported short pants, too.

The ambassador tipped his top hat. "*Boker tov, yeladim.*" Good morning, children. The kids stared after him in silence.

"They're lucky," the young diplomat said. "To have survived here, rather than—"

The ambassador interrupted. "They'd have been luckier if they were members of a people that was never persecuted."

"Of course, I meant only that they weren't among the ones we...we..."

"If you're going to work as a German diplomat here, Michael, you'd better get used to saying it."

"The ones we exterminated."

They marched up Lovers of Zion Street, toward the ridge where the president's mansion was nearing completion.

"I suppose it would've been a lot worse if the extermination camps hadn't been destroyed by the Allied bombers," the young man said.

"And the Israeli Air Force squadron," the ambassador said. "If it hadn't been for Israel's involvement in the North Africa campaign, the war would've most likely lasted until the middle of forty-five."

"Who would've won *that* war?" The young man laughed.

The ambassador shook his head, smiling. Then he was stern. "We lost the war the moment we murdered the first Jew."

They walked on, pondering the memory of horrors that seemed so out of place under the sunshine of the Levant.

"So many millions," the ambassador said. "Indeed, it would have been millions *more*, had it not been for the man we're about to meet." He gestured toward the low dome and the plain walls of the presidential residence.

The country's first figurehead, Chaim Weizmann, had lived in his own home, in the city of Rehovot, without an official residence. The man who recently took over from him had moved into the residential wing of the new structure while the reception rooms were still under construction. At the curb, a truck was delivering sacks of cement for the building's completion. It was parked alongside another vehicle loaded with folding chairs for the following day's ceremony.

A small detachment of security, sheltered by a canvas awning, guarded the entrance of the president's residence. They checked the ambassador and his assistant, and then directed them across the muddy yard.

The two Germans passed a marquee that was being assembled for the anniversary concert the next day. A dozen tanned young men labored, shirtless, on the structure, laying boards over the dirt, hammering the scaffold for the stage.

At the door of the residence, a woman of about forty with clear olive skin and prematurely white hair waited. She noticed the ambassador's surprise and touched her simple haircut. "It grew back this color." She laughed. "Doesn't it make me look stately?"

"It is fitting for the president's wife," the ambassador said.

She hugged him and drew him down the hall. A half dozen secretaries and aides bustled around the desks lining the walls.

"We live in these rooms to the left," she said. "The offices aren't finished yet, so the staff beavers away out here. As does His Honor the President."

At the far end of the hall, a man lifted himself from his chair. The short sleeve on the left of his shirt dangled, empty, and he crossed the floor with a stiff leg, the knee damaged permanently and clearly still painful. A boy of about four came with him.

"Let's do the formalities," the president said. "I don't care for them, but you're a German, so we probably should."

The ambassador held out a thin envelope. "Allow me to present the letters of credence by which Chancellor Konrad Adenauer has appointed me to be Ambassador Extraordinary and Plenipotentiary of the Federal Republic of Germany to the State of Israel."

The Israeli president took the envelope. He embraced the ambassador. "My dear Brückner. My dear, dear fellow."

"Dan, it's good to see you," Brückner said. "This must be your boy?"

Dan Lavi gripped the four-year-old's shoulder. "Shmulik, say hello to our old friend, Herr Brückner."

The boy blushed and struggled away behind his father's legs. "Don't want to."

"He has his own mind." Brückner laughed. "Just like his namesake."

Anna Lavi picked up her son. The boy brushed his mother's white hair back from her eyes. "Mommy, why are you crying?" he asked.

Anna kissed the child and touched her husband's scarred cheek. "Danny, did you see what our friend brought?"

Dan noticed the violin case. He looked at Brückner, questioning. "Can that be—?"

"Wili's Stradivarius. For the anniversary concert tomorrow." Brückner handed over the violin. Dan took it as if it were a new baby.

"Arvid," he called out. "Come and see."

The big form of Arvid Polkes filled the doorway of the president's suite of private rooms. He rushed over to Brückner and shook his hand. Bertha and the Polkes children came through the same door, the girls almost adults now, wearing the army's rough olive drab. Polkes took the violin case and opened its clasp. With his smile still showing the gaps in his teeth where the Gestapo had beaten him, he turned to show the Stradivarius to his wife and children.

It seemed to Brückner that the souls of his parents—the Jew who had once played this violin and the Prussian Countess who had loved him—emerged together from the battered old case. Dan and Anna smiled at him. He knew they felt the same presence.

"You told me once how Wili—how my father played "*Hatikva*" in Israel," Brückner said.

"Our national anthem. 'The Hope.' At our Declaration of Independence."

"Arvid, would you oblige me?"

"I can play. But I'm a stage manager, not a soloist." Polkes smiled.

"It won't *be* a solo." Brückner gestured toward his assistant.

Polkes brought the violin to his shoulder. He scraped the bow over the strings, tuning it from the A on the third string, then closed his eyes to play the opening notes of the anthem.

Brückner's assistant spread his chest and, in a pure tenor that brought the shirtless workmen in from the garden marquee, the young German sang out the Hebrew words of hope and freedom and life.

The End

Historical Note

Our fictional story ends at the historical moment of Israel's real foundation. Even if Israel—and Dan Lavi—had existed before World War II, it wouldn't have stopped the Holocaust in its entirety, such was the scope of the madness and the murder. In this book, we've served the memory of that time in two ways. First, by adhering as closely as possible to real people, to real places and events. Second, we've honored the true purpose of history, which is to learn from past times so that the future might be better.

The idea underlying the book—that decisive actions in international affairs can make a difference—is an important one with great resonance for a world still engaged in dreadful conflicts and with the potential for even greater ones. Dan's actions alter the course of history. Fictional history is easier to modify than real history. But both are susceptible to change, nonetheless.

Sometimes we think of the Holocaust as playing out over the entire period of World War II. In fact, Eichmann and other top Nazis favored expelling the Jews to the island of Madagascar in the Indian Ocean until that plan was deemed unworkable in 1940. Later, the wastes of Siberia were to be the dumping ground for the Jews, but that idea was abandoned when the German advance into the Soviet Union foundered in late 1941. Only then did the plan for extermination truly come to the fore. In January 1942, the conference at Wannsee plotted the Final Solution—our chapters on that event are closely based on the actual minutes of the meeting, which were noted down by Eichmann. Could immediate, decisive action at that time, of the kind taken by our fictional Israel and our fictional Dan Lavi, have changed the reality of the mass murder that soon unfolded? We leave the conclusion to you, but we will bring one statistic to your attention: When Heydrich convened the Wannsee conference, eighty percent of the Jews who would eventually be murdered in the Holocaust were still alive; only sixteen months later, eighty percent of them were already dead.

Up to the time of the Wannsee Conference, our narrative adheres quite closely to genuine historical timing. We sped up key events in the North African campaign and moved the Cairo Conference forward by a year to give *our* Ben-Gurion the opportunity to meet Roosevelt and Churchill there.

Though our premise rests on history taking a different turn, we used a great many actual historical sources to build our narrative, our characters, and their dialogue. The speech of some of our "real" characters includes actual quotes. For example, much of what our Hitler says constitutes the exact words he used in his speeches or in private conversations later recorded by memoirists. The moment when Heydrich tells Eichmann that Hitler has ordered the extermination of the Jews is drawn directly from Eichmann's interrogation after his kidnapping to Israel, as are some of Eichmann's other comments. The conversation between Eichmann and Auschwitz commandant Höss was compiled from Eichmann's own recollections and from comments Höss made during his war crimes trial.

Even where we deviated from quoted speech, it remained important to us that every historical character should respond in accordance with their real actions. Eichmann's staff did indeed refer to him as "Maestro" because of his passion for the violin. Heydrich was a classically trained musician, the son of an opera composer who also ran a music conservatory in his hometown of Halle. Historical veracity was important to us not just in building the Nazi characters, but also in providing a true representation of the disputes in the Zionist movement over Ben-Gurion's dealings with Berlin and his agreement to the partition of Palestine. After all, one of the authors actually worked under Ben-Gurion; this book aims to be true to what the man stood for, as well as to create a genuine portrayal of the horrors that he stood against.

As to the fates of our main non-fictional characters:

Reinhard Heydrich became Deputy Protector of Bohemia and Moravia. Four months after Wannsee, Czech and Slovak agents were dropped into Czechoslovakia by the British to assassinate him. He died of his wounds soon after the attack. In the reprisals that followed at Hitler's order, 1,300 Czechs were murdered, while 13,000 were arrested, deported, and imprisoned.

The real **Countess Hannah von Bredow** was a member of the Solf Circle, a group of anti-Nazi intellectuals, most of whom were killed by the Gestapo or died in concentration camps. The Countess escaped and died in Hamburg in 1971.

Friedrich Kritzinger tried to resign from his post at the Chancellery in protest of the conclusions of the Wannsee conference. As a witness at the Nuremburg Tribunals, he declared himself ashamed of the Nazi atrocities. He died at the age of fifty-seven, two years after the end of the war.

Sir Arthur Grenfell Wauchope was replaced as British high commissioner to Palestine in 1938 because of London's dissatisfaction with his handling of the Arab Revolt. He served as colonel of his regiment during World War II and spent his last years in India, where he died in 1947 at the age of seventy-three.

Transferred away from Auschwitz in 1943, **Rudolf Höss** returned to the camp in 1944 to supervise an operation named after him, in which 430,000 Hungarian Jews were exterminated in fifty-six days. A year after the war, his wife gave him up to British troops. He was tried in Poland and executed in 1947 by slow strangulation on a short-drop gallows.

Adolf Eichmann fled Germany for Argentina, where he and his family lived under cover until his kidnapping by Israeli agents in 1960.

His trial in Jerusalem was a seminal event in assessments of how the Nazis came to perpetrate the Holocaust. He was executed in 1962 at a prison in Ramla and his ashes were scattered in the Mediterranean.

David Ben-Gurion was twice prime minister of Israel. It was on his order that the Mossad captured Eichmann. Sirens sounded across Israel to mark his death in 1973 at the age of eighty-seven.

Yehuda Avner & Matt Rees

The fonts used in this book are from the Garamond family

The Toby Press publishes fine writing
on subjects of Israel and Jewish interest.
For more information, visit www.tobypress.com.